THE SECRET
OF
ROSALITA FLATS
A BLACKTIP ISLAND NOVEL

TIM W. JACKSON

Devonshire
House

Devonshire
House

Devonshire House Press
P.O. Box 195682
Dallas, TX 75209

Copyright © by Tim W. Jackson 2020

ISBN: 978-1-7351136-1-6

Library of Congress Control Number: 2020910064

Book formatting and cover design by www.ebooklaunch.com

ACKNOWLEDGEMENTS

Thanks to the many people who helped with this one along the way:

To beta readers extraordinaire:

Debi Belasco
Carol Borland
Joe Goellner
Cindy Sullivan

To *The Blacktip Times'* faithful readers for all their enthusiasm.

To Kay Russo, as ever, for her great editing. The Oxford commas are at her insistence.

To Dane Lowe, again, for the phenomenal cover art.

To Sandy Marak for somehow making me look less-than-awkward in the author photo.

And, of course, special thanks to my wife, Jana, for her support and for always believing.

"Because of the variety of species of sharks and their unpredictable behavior, no hard and fast rules for handling an encounter can be laid down to apply in every case."
    - *The New Science of Skin and Scuba Diving*, Revised Third Edition, Association Press, 1968

1

The house was named Batten's Down, and Cal Batten had no idea what to do with the damn thing. It was shaped like a football, with rounded outer walls, fake laces painted along the roofline, and vertical white stripes on either end where it narrowed to almost-pointed blobs. It sat apart from the other Mahogany Row homes on a headland separating Spider Bight from Rosalita Flats and the open sea. Fading pink paint flaked off in the afternoon sun. Cal's grandfather had built a solid house to weather any storm, and then his father had built the wooden football frame around it. Now it was all Cal's. And more than anything he wanted to get rid of the monstrosity and be quit of this grubby little island.

"Settle a bet?" Rafe Marquette, the island's police constable, loomed behind him, dark sunglasses reflecting the afternoon sun. Rafe had driven Cal down from Blacktip Island's airstrip.

"A bet?"

"Why'd your daddy shape it like that?"

"Oh. Mom said Rhodes didn't want her to get the house if they divorced. They did. It worked."

Cal stepped to the open doorway and froze. Skylights in both pointed ends lit the main room. Inside, a riot of junk covered every surface. Piles of papers and file folders. Old, leather-bound books that could have been from a museum. Yellowed nautical maps. A star chart stapled to the exposed-beam ceiling. Under it, antique brass scales, oil lamps, ropes, and rusty bicycle wheels dangled from the rafters. A ragged velour couch sat in the room's center. It was very orange.

Cal shuddered at the chaos, ran his thin fingers over his close-cropped black hair. He put one foot inside. Coughed at the reek of stale liquor, spilled chemicals, and something earthier he couldn't quite place. He flipped the nearest wall switch. It crackled, sparked behind its wall plate. An overhead light flickered twice, then went out. Cal's eye twitched. Even the lights were chaotic. And a fire hazard.

He picked up a dusty brass plate with marks engraved evenly around its edge and a rotating needle mounted to its center.

"What the hell is all this stuff?" Cal hadn't meant to say it aloud.

"That's an astrolabe," Rafe said. "You got his looks and light eyes, right enough, but not his temperament."

"Of course."

Cal had no idea what an astrolabe was. And didn't care. He stepped to the room's center, where a five-pointed star had been chalked inside a circle on the wooden floor, an oversized lizard skull beside it.

"Your daddy was a sorcerer."

"He was crazy." There was a twinge in his chest at that. His father was a name and some hazy memories. "I'm starting to see what drove Mom away. And made her warn me away from him and this place."

Rafe laughed, a rumbling sound like a rock slide. He glanced down at Cal's still-pressed polo shirt.

"Need help sorting through things? I get you a leaf blower. Or maybe a back hoe."

Cal closed his eyes. He could still see the disorder. He opened them, stepped farther in, scanning for anything familiar. Rafe followed him, running his fingers over the labels on the nearest stack of bulging file folders. What looked to be an iguana skin tacked to a weathered plank leaned against the wall by the door to his old bedroom. Now the room contained a low table crowded with test tubes, a Bunsen burner, and jars of bright-colored powders and gravel-sized crystals. A knee-high, bullet-shaped plastic something with handles on either side stood on end behind the door. Vanes that could have been stubby wings near its tip and a small propeller at the other end. An underwater scooter. By the window, a brass telescope perched on a tripod beside what looked like a modern GPS unit.

In the kitchen, a child's laminated Crayon drawing hung on a towel hook behind the stove: three turkeys made from tracing three kids' spread-out hands, with feathers and feet drawn in. Under the turkeys was printed, in his mom's precise handwriting, 'Cal,' 'Rafe,' and 'Marina.'

"Why in the world would Rhodes save that, much less preserve it and tack it on the wall?" Cal said.

"I remember that day. Kinda." Rafe leaned down, peered closer, muscles stretching against his uniform shirt. Cal kept himself fit, but nothing like Rafe. "That was twenty, twenty-five years ago."

Something that could have been remorse swept through Cal. He should have contacted Rhodes over the years, made some sort of effort. They might have gotten along, despite what Cal's mom always said. He should have stayed in touch with Rafe, to, despite their opposite personalities.

"When's the last time you saw your daddy?" Rafe's voice pulled Cal out of his thoughts.

"When Mom and I left. I lost touch with everyone, including you. My memories from back then are really hazy."

"And the last time you and he spoke?" Rafe picked up a stack of papers, leafed through them.

"The same time." Cal straightened the corners of the nearest pile of folders, shifted the pile so the edges were square with the table's edge.

Rafe watched Cal, face stern. No longer the cheery kid Cal had grown up with. Or the helpful policeman at the airport.

"You get any letters from him? Any . . . packages? Parcels? Papers?"

"We had zero contact since I was twelve. Why?"

"You never talked to your daddy all those years?" Rafe looked part suspicious, part shocked.

"Mom swore he was the devil, and Rhodes never reached out. First I heard of him in years was when you called." Cal straightened another stack of folders, squared them with the table. Why all the questions? "Was Rhodes' death suspicious?"

"Not suspicious. Not exactly." Rafe put down the papers, picked up a folder, thumbed through it. "You call your daddy by his first name?"

Reproach dripped from Rafe's voice.

"Only thing I knew him by."

Rafe looked down at Cal, said nothing.

"So where'd he die?" Cal said to break the silence.

"No one told you?"

"All I know is it was a heart attack. What's the big secret?"

"He passed in the bedroom . . . Oh! Here's Rosie. Your daddy's housekeeper." Rafe dropped the folder as if it had burned him. "She's the one . . . called 911. Rosalita Bottoms, this's Cal, Mister Rhodes' son."

A short, dark-haired woman, eyes level with Cal's chest, stood in the bedroom doorway, yellow feather duster in hand, face expressionless. Cal had a vague memory of Dermott Bottoms' goody-two-shoes, tattletale little niece Rosie, and the age was about right, but Cal couldn't be sure. Her black eyes went from Marquette, to Cal, then back to Marquette. Rafe eyed her, wary.

"I'll leave you with Rosie." Rafe backed out the door. The police truck started up and drove away.

"You found him?" Cal focused back on Rosie.

Rosie nodded once, eyes guarded, as if facing a travelling salesman.

"What happened?"

"Heart give out." Rosie shrugged. "One minute he was fine and happy, next he just went limp."

"You . . . were with him when he died?"

Rosie nodded again.

"You remember his last words?"

"I'm fixing to come." Rosie's face stayed expressionless.

"I . . . oh . . . I didn't realize." Cal searched for words, hoped he didn't look as blindsided as he felt. "You and he were . . . close, then."

"Nope." Rosie crossed her arms. "Randy old goat, Mister Rhodes. No telling what he'd want cleaned. Or when."

"Well, the place won't need cleaning anymore." Cal nearly choked as he said it. The place needed to be knocked down and rebuilt. "I'm selling it quick as I can. I'll pay you for the next two weeks and . . ."

"Can't sell Mister Rhodes' place just like that!" Rosie cut him off. "Got history. Years of memories to go through."

"And the new owner can go through all of it. Or burn it. Either way, I won't need you anymore."

"No." Rosie's eyes blazed. "Mister Rhodes, he paid me in advance. For the rest of the year. I been paid. I'm gonna clean."

"But you don't need to. I'm here now. Consider his advance pay a gift."

"Can't take money and not do the work!" Rosie shook the yellow feather duster in Cal's face. "Your daddy passed, but he's still here. *I'm* not gonna let him down."

"He'd understand."

Cal swatted the outermost ball on a mechanical solar system, sent all the planets spinning around a lemon-sized Sun.

Rosie scowled, made a show of straightening a knee-high pile of *National Geographics* beside an overstuffed armchair.

Cal stared, hands on his hips, not sure what to do. He had fired Rosie, but she wouldn't leave. He could pick her up and drop her outside. No, that wouldn't do. He could have Rafe Marquette talk to her. Or drag her away. They didn't seem to like each other anyway. Cal pulled out his phone. Cursed under his breath. No cell signal. Great. He was so far off the map his phone wouldn't work. Okay, then. He would let Rosie finish today, then change the locks.

Cal circled the room, resisting the urge to sort all the junk, the papers, catalogue it all . . . but where to start? And it would take months.

The far wall was covered with tacked-up maps and nautical charts. Some looked to be made of leather or some sort of animal skin. Clear glass globes, from watermelon- to softball-size, hung from the ceiling, each in its own rope fishnet. A small Tesla coil sat beside an armchair. The bookcase was overflowing, with books stacked sideways on top of the filed books. Some modern, others looking a hundred years old. Titles about astronomy, navigation, gardening, banking, sharks. Cal shuddered again, thankful he hadn't inherited Rhodes' lack of tidiness.

He needed to find Rhodes' will, the property deed. His computer, bank books, and wallet. Where was a likely place? Over-stuffed manila folders towered high on the dining table. Magazines covered the kitchen counters. Stray papers, hand-drawn charts, and calculations were strewn across the coffee table. Cal went to the spare bedroom-turned-chemistry lab, scanned the room for a filing cabinet, a safe. Nothing. No computer or cell phone, either. The will and deed had to be here somewhere. And information about Rhodes' attorney or estate agent or whoever else Cal would need to get the place sold.

A quick shuffle through the folders on the table in the main room showed no apparent order—electric bills for the last twenty years were filed between tree identification guides and automobile engine schematics in German. He didn't have time to plow through every paper in the house looking for the will. Cal would have to talk to Rafe, or someone, to find out who handled Rhodes' affairs.

Across the room, Rosie had stopped dusting, was watching him.

"Rosie, you have any idea where Rhodes kept important papers?"

"Dunno." She stared at him, as if daring him to ask more.

"How about his banking information? His checkbook?"

"Didn't hold with banks."

"Who doesn't use a bank?"

"Paid cash for everything."

Cal scanned the room. If Rhodes worked solely in cash, where was his money stashed?

"His wallet?"

Rosie shrugged.

"How about his cell phone or his computer?"

"Didn't have none," she said.

"Well, how did Rhodes keep records?"

"*Mister* Rhodes kept things in his head." Rosie tapped her temple, then flicked her feather duster over the books piled on the end table. "Lived by his wits."

Cal ground his teeth to keep from yelling at her. He needed air, a break from the house's chaos. And Rosie's belligerence. As if the place were hers.

He stepped outside, squinted in the sunlight. Waves crashed into the headland behind the house, set the ground vibrating. Yes, Cal remembered that. And the low moan of wind in the crevices in the island's central bluff towering 100-feet high across the road.

He remembered the rough sand-and-gravel grounds around the house, too. The house's walls were more weathered now. That was to be expected. The doors and windows, wide open, were laid out to catch any breeze. Rhodes hadn't believed in air conditioning. Cal would find out if the house was still breeze-cooled later when he tried to sleep.

"Yooo-hooo!"

A wavering voice came from behind him, from Mahogany Row. A tall woman with graying hair was picking her way toward him, amber bracelets rattling as she waved. Behind her came a man about the same age, in a wide straw hat. They looked vaguely familiar, but Cal couldn't place them.

"You must be young Cal," the woman said in a thick English accent. "Still thin as a rail. We're the Maples. Helen and Frank. We're *voisins* again!"

"We're sorry for your loss," Frank Maples said in a near monotone with the same accent.

"We are simply delighted to see you!" Helen cut in. "And all grown up. Last time we saw you, you were tussling with Rafe and Marina, right about where we're standing now. Have you three reconnected yet?"

"Rafe drove me from the airfield," Cal said. "He didn't seem impressed. Or happy to see me."

"Hmm, well, you should definitely find Marina, too. She's divemastering at Eagle Ray Cove these days." Helen's lips pursed. Her voice lowered, "*And* driving a boat."

Cal smiled, said nothing. He had no idea whether Marina driving a boat was good, bad, or just a shock for Helen. He hadn't thought about gangly Marina DeLow since he left Blacktip Island. The way things were going, she would probably be as happy to see him as Rafe or Rosie.

"Happy memories flooding back, though?" Helen said.

"No . . . I mostly blocked this place . . . those days out of my head."

"Ahh . . . Well, we're about to pop into town, if you need anything." Frank said.

"I . . ." Cal had no idea how much food was in the house, and he needed to find a lawyer, if there was one on the island, but he didn't dare leave the house with Rosie poking around. "No. I'm still settling in here. Thanks, though."

"Well, if you do, we're just there." Helen waved at the nearest house, a two-story affair nestled under coconut palms 100 yards away. "Think of us as your long-lost aunt and uncle."

Cal watched their Range Rover disappear up the dirt road, dust cloud swirling behind it. Cal had forgotten how dirty and gritty the island was. He stepped back inside the house. He had left Rosie alone too long. Sure enough, she was thumbing through one of the folders he had straightened on the table.

"You looking for something in particular?"

Rosie didn't budge, as if she had expected him to come in and find her there.

"Visiting old memories," she said. "Mister Rhodes, he was a character."

"Well, you have no business going through his papers." Cal snatched the folder from her, set it on the far side of the table. "Aren't you about finished cleaning for today?"

Rosie glared at him, then gathered her things and walked out to a rusty bicycle leaning against the house. She gave Cal one last, long nasty look before pedaling away.

Cal sat on the sunny front step, relaxed. Behind the house the waves breaking on the headland sounded like the house was grumbling. Cal cursed under his breath. He had forgotten to call Kat, let her know he had made it okay, tell her what was going on. She wouldn't care, but it was the ex-husbandly thing to do, and she *was* watching his shop. He dug his phone from his pocket out of habit, stared at the screen. No cell signal.

"Typical," he said aloud. "Just typical."

He could still call her on an old-school landline, cost be damned. Cal went inside, scanned the kitchen, the living room for a corded phone. Nothing. Not even a wall jack for a phone. The only communication gadget he saw was a VHF radio by the kitchen sink. Cal went back outside, walked to the Maples place.

They would have wireless service, but when he reached their house there was still no signal. He made a quick tour among the other Mahogany Row homes, boarded up now for the season. Still no signal. How did people communicate here?

He and Rafe had passed several resorts on the drive out. There would be a cell signal there. He would run back to one of them. And with Rosie gone, he was comfortable leaving the house unattended. He would grab Rhodes' car and drive in before it got too late.

Cal walked to the northern end of the house, where a one-sided corrugated tin lean-to was cobbled together beside the house as a makeshift storage shed. He looked inside and laughed. Sitting under the rusting tin, beside a mound of empty rum bottles, was a once-bright-orange Volkswagen Thing, its soft top in shreds across the car's rear and swathes of gray primer slathered across a host of dents. Three black-and-yellow feral chickens eyed him from the hood. Two more clucked at him from the rear seat. He hadn't seen a Thing in decades, yet here one was, battle-scarred, but still in one piece. Cal started for the house to find the keys. Stopped. This was Blacktip Island. One of the few hazy memories he had from childhood was people leaving their car keys in the ignition.

Sure enough, keys dangled from the steering column on the right side of the car. Right-hand drive. Okay. And a stick shift. Great. He knew how to drive a stick, in theory, but he had never actually done it. Challenging, but he could figure it out. Cal shooed the chickens from the car in a flurry of feathers. He climbed in, stepped on the brake pedal, cursed at himself, moved his foot to the clutch. He pumped the gas a few times and turned the key. The car coughed blue smoke but didn't start. He pumped the gas, tried again. More smoke billowed out, filling the lean-to with oily fumes. Cal coughed, staggered from the shelter, queasy from the exhaust. He retreated to the front steps, gulped fresh air.

Walking back the six, seven miles of dirt road to the nearest resort wasn't going to work. There had to be some alternate transportation. A bike or something. If Rosie could bike in, so could he. A quick search turned up no bicycle, though. Well then, he would flag down the first passing car, get a ride from whoever. Cal grabbed a bottle of water and sat under the palms by the road to make sure he didn't miss any passing vehicles. The island's central bluff towered across the road, its top fringed with hardwoods of some sort, with red, papery bark peeling from the trunks. An occasional cactus. The afternoon sun backlit the bark like stained glass.

After what seemed like forever, Cal looked at his watch. Forty-seven minutes had passed. Great. He was on a peach of an island, all right. No cell signal, no internet, and no traffic. He walked back to the house, worked the wall switch up and down until lights stayed on. Ceiling fans spun. At least he had electricity. He would put in a new wall switch tomorrow.

Cal explored the kitchen cabinets. Microwave popcorn. Canned chili. Smoked sardines. Saltines. A bottle proclaiming 'Blacktip Island's own Bottoms Up Rum!' Rosie was gone, but he still couldn't be rid of the Bottoms.

In the fridge was a pack of hotdogs and a dozen bottles of beer. Not ideal, but he could make do. He would catch a ride to the resort strip the next morning, maybe find a mechanic while he was hunting down a cell signal.

Cal opened a beer and went back outside. The sun was dropping. He walked to the house's seaward side, stopped. A grasshopper-looking contraption with a single swing-arm and a massive counterweight stood on the ironshore's edge, arm rising twenty-five, thirty feet in the air, a pouch like an oversized slingshot's dangling from the top of the lever arm. A catapult? Another of Rhodes' experiments, though why he had experimented with a medieval gizmo was a mystery. Probably the same reason he had an astrolabe. Or he expected seaborne invaders. Beside the catapult was a weathered lawn chair and a pile of scuba diving weights. Cal sat, watched the sea breaking on the headland. The ground vibrated with the waves slamming into the ironshore's hollows. He remembered lying in bed, feeling the nearly imperceptible sway of his mattress in time with the waves booming outside.

The wind gusted, set off a low moaning inland. Cal smiled, remembering wind in the caves high on the bluff, sounding like voices. Local legend said the moaning came from duppies, island spirits, tempting unwary people into the bush. When he was little, Cal had imagined the duppies were talking to him, trying to share their secrets.

A deeper boom pulled Cal out of his reverie. The ground pulsed from a big wave. Cal shuddered, too. He needed to sell the place before the ironshore headland eroded and took the house with it.

At dusk the mosquitos chased Cal back inside, half-soaked in sweat despite the breeze. He didn't remember the island being so humid. He turned on the kitchen faucet to splash water on his face. A stream of orangey-yellow water poured out, smelling like decayed vegetation. Great. Another island quirk. Cal wiped his face with a dish towel and waited for the tap water to run clear. And waited. And waited. All the water in the cistern must be yellow. He gave up, gritted his teeth, and washed his face as best he could, trying not to get any of the liquid in his mouth.

Cal broiled some hot dogs, poured canned chili over them, and wandered to the living room, floorboards creaking with each step. He settled into an overstuffed armchair by the bookcase, the only place clear of debris he could sit. He scanned the books closest to him. Great. The shark section.

Cal shuddered again, then laughed at himself for being so jumpy. They were just books. And he wasn't going in the water. Or on it. He tried to relax, but couldn't. Sure, his welcome hadn't been very welcoming, from an old friend, the new housekeeper, or the neighbors. But that wasn't it. Being in the house again had him on edge, and not entirely because Rhodes had died here. The sheer disorder of the place was overwhelming. A combination of everything, maybe. Being on Blacktip Island. In the house where his father had died. Surrounded by water. Water filled with sharks. And maybe sharks on land, too, if Rosie was any indication.

More incentive to sell. If he got enough for the place, he could pay off his shop debts and maybe throw some money Kat's way. Tomorrow he would find the will and find out what the place was worth. For now, though, he was exhausted, despite the early hour.

Cal lifted stacks of folders, magazines off the couch, stacked them neatly by the bookcase. One of the folders was marked 'CAL.' He flipped open the folder. Oddly-spaced writing on the top page made Cal pause. Rhodes had written . . . haiku? For him? Cal would never have guessed. He carried the folder back to the armchair, read the first poem:

> *In times of seeking*
> *Like a soft rain on sea swells*
> *Gold en la boca*

It made no sense, but poetry rarely did to Cal. And from what little his mother had told him, Cal had never imagined Rhodes going for this sort of thing. Hard drinking and hell raising was more like it. Cal scanned the next one:

> *Hidden in darkness*
> *Below the teeth, the belly*
> *And sea cave thunder*

And another, just as squirrelly:

To see clearly now
A thorny bluff-top sunset
And Euler angles

It was obvious the surroundings had inspired the poems. Rum and too much time alone, too. Cal closed the folder, put it on top of the others by the bookcase. He didn't have the mental energy to sort through poems. Maybe if he had known Rhodes, they would have made sense. Or made Cal feel some connection to him. As it was, they just made Cal's head hurt.

A scuffling sound came from outside, like shuffling feet. A faint snuffling. A person? An animal?

"Hello?" Cal said.

The shuffling stopped. Restarted.

Cal grabbed a truncheon-sized chrome flashlight from the kitchen counter, swung the front door open, and stepped outside. He held the light high, playing the beam across the grounds. Nothing. He shined the light back the other way. Still nothing. His imagination? He was wiped out from the 2 a.m. get up and multiple flights that day.

Cal went inside, started to lock the door. There was no lock button or mechanism of any kind other than a sliding bolt. He opened the door, looked at the outside knob. Sure enough, no keyhole. How had he not noticed that before? Out so far, on such a small island, maybe Rhodes hadn't felt the need to lock the place unless he was inside. No more. Tomorrow Cal would get a locking door knob. He could swap that out in a few minutes. The place would be secure. It would keep Rosie out, too.

Cal cleaned off the couch. There was no way he could sleep in the bed Rhodes died in while . . . screwing the cleaning woman. Cal piled the throw pillows at one end, lay down, and turned off the light. There was enough of a cross breeze the heat didn't seem so bad.

A buzzing near his ear. Then more. Cal swatted the mosquitos away. More buzzing. Then pinpricks in his arm as others bit him. He had forgotten how horrific Blacktip's mosquitos were. And half the mosquitos on the island must have swarmed in when he opened the door. Cal turned on the light, grabbed a blanket off the back of the chair, and curled up in a fetal position on the couch, completely covered. It was stuffy under the blanket, but the mosquitos left him alone. Soon, he fell into a fitful sleep, dreaming of jewels and sharks and kids playing.

2

A rooster's crow jolted Cal awake in charcoal blackness. Another crow, more eruption than bird sound, from outside the screened window. All was dark, but sunrise was close. Another eruption outside the window. There was no sleeping through it. Cal rose, back aching from the sagging couch, and went to the kitchen to start coffee.

The coffeemaker clock read 2:38. That couldn't be right. Cal rubbed his eyes, checked his watch. Sure enough, 2:38. The rooster went off again. Cal snatched Rosie's broom and stormed outside, yelling and swinging the broom blindly to scare the chickens away. Wings erupted in the blackness. Squawks all around him. Feathers slapped across his bare arms. Then angry clucking from farther away, scolding him from the safety of the sea grapes.

Cal scuttled back inside, swatting mosquitoes, and retreated under the sweaty blanket. Waves rumbled, a barely-heard, animal-like sound from all around, as if the house was struggling to breathe. Cal closed his eyes. The rooster kept crowing, though from a distance now. Cal tossed under the blanket, half suffocating. But when he poked his head out, the mosquitos swarmed him. He jammed a pillow over his ears and slept as best he could.

At first light he gave up, put on jeans and a long-sleeved shirt, and fogged the room with what little mosquito spray Rhodes had left. Then, coffee brewing, Cal stepped outside so he wouldn't breathe the spray. The sun glowed orange across the sharp-toothed waves to the east, beyond the catapult. In the open air, the moaning from the caves wasn't so loud, as if the house was an echo chamber, intensifying the sounds. Cal checked the dirt outside for shoe prints or animal tracks, but saw only his own bare footprints and random chicken scratches.

During a breakfast of microwave popcorn, Cal watched the Maples' place. He needed a ride to the store, to a working phone. Sure enough, their Land Rover backed onto the road. Cal dropped the popcorn and bolted out the door, waving his arms to get their attention.

"We'd *love* to drop you in town," Helen said.

"Town?" Cal hadn't seen anything on Blacktip to call a town.

'Well, so to speak." Helen smiled, eyes crinkling. "The store, the post office, the airfield. They're all right together. And it's an easy walk from there to Sandy Bottoms."

"Excuse me?"

"Sandy Bottoms Beach Resort," Frank Maples said. "I suppose it *is* new since you were here. Poshest place on the island."

"They have internet?"

"Most likely. They draw that sort of guest."

Cal stared at the back of Frank's head in disbelief. The sort of guest who liked to be connected to the outside world? What did the Maples think of Cal and his need for connectivity?

"Say, what do you do for phone service?" Cal said.

"Oh, we have a satellite phone for emergencies," Frank said. "Don't use it much. Any important off-island conversations we need to have, we go to Sandy's."

"And for on-island conversations?"

"We usually just go find the person. And there's always the VHF if you don't mind everyone on Blacktip listening in."

Cal sat back, digesting that. There was the two-way radio on the kitchen counter, but he would never have thought of using it in place of a telephone.

"By the by, we're having a little soiree tonight." Helen turned to face Cal, bracelets clattering. "We'd love for you to stop by. You'll be able to meet the island. Everyone certainly wants to meet you!"

"Sure," Cal said. "By 'everyone' you mean . . .?"

"Oh, you're the talk of Blacktip: who you are, why you're here, whether you're staying, what you'll be doing with the house." Helen gave him a wink. "All the female dive staff will be chatting you up, too, as soon as you set foot in town."

"What if I'm married?" A small lie—the divorce had just come through—but if people thought he was married it would make life on the island simpler.

"That doesn't always matter," Frank said. "What *will* you be doing with the house?"

"Selling it. Quick as I can."

"No sentiment there, eh?"

"I need to get back." Another sort-of lie, but Cal couldn't tell them he hated this grimy little rock.

"Back to the grindstone, eh? What is it you do?"

"I repair clocks." It sounded ridiculous as he said it. "And watches. Armature mechanisms. That sort of thing. It's pretty specialized work."

"Is there much call for a clock repairman?" Helen's brows knotted, puzzled.

"No. But I make jewelry, too. That pays the bills. Mostly."

"So. Looks from your father, but tick-tock mind from your mother," Helen said.

"I should send my grandfather's pocket watch back with you," Frank said. "Hasn't worked in years, but no one in the Tiperons works on the things."

"I'd love to take a look at it," Cal said. "There's a heart and soul to those old stem-set watches. I don't have any tools here, but it may just need a simple cleaning."

"I'd be grateful." Frank half smiled.

"You should stay a while, enjoy the place." Helen said.

"My wife would disagree." Cal paused at the blatant lie. "Ex-wife. She's minding the shop while I'm here."

Helen turned to face him, eyebrows raised.

"The shop's about the only thing she didn't get in the divorce," he said.

"She's attached to it?"

"She hates clocks. Calls it 'the millstone.' I guilted her into watching it for a few days. I need a quick sale here."

"Well, waterfront property that nice is pricey. It won't sell overnight. Unless you really drop the price."

"You're not interested, then?"

"Oh, we don't have that kind of money to throw around," Frank said. "Unless you *really* drop the price . . ."

Great. The place was worth more than enough to get him out of debt, but no one could afford it. He needed to hold out however long it took to sell. But he needed cash for that.

"There an attorney or estate agent on Blacktip?"

"Attorney-wise, there's Skerritt and Skulkin, but Bob Skulkin has a reputation for skinning off-islanders," Frank said. "And Ferris Skerritt's worse. Your best bet may be Jack Cobia. De facto island mayor, but a land agent, too. A bit of a Jack of all trades, if you take my drift. Ha-ha!"

Cal didn't get the drift, but Cobia sounded like a better bet than the skinners.

"Is that who Rho . . . my dad used? I couldn't find any paperwork on the property."

"Rhodes? He used himself." Frank shook his head, steered the Range Rover through a tight left turn. "Trusted no one with anything. Especially money. Crusty old devil."

"Frank!" Helen cut in.

"Well, he was," Frank said. "Odd man. And odd goings on, what with the racket and the boat engines and odd noises."

"Speaking of, are there any large animals on the island?" Cal tried to sound nonchalant.

"Just people," Frank said. "Why?"

"No reason. Just wondering." Someone had been messing with him the night before, then.

The Maples looked at each other, but said nothing. The car barreled up the east coast road to where the island's central bluff came to an abrupt end, as if a giant axe had chopped it off. They turned left there, following the gravel road crossing to the island's west side. The bluff loomed above them, hints of bungalow rooftops peeking through the trees. To the right a broad pond spread, rimmed with dead trees. Ducks, herons waded in the shallows. Seabirds circled above.

"That's Blacktip Haven up on the bluff top. Eco-friendly resort," Helen said. "Beautiful views out over the booby pond." She waved a hand at the marsh.

"*Booby* pond?" The locals were pulling the newbie's leg.

"Red-footed boobies." Helen pointed to the circling seabirds. "One of the largest rookeries in the Caribbean. Lack of development does that."

The stench from the pond hit him then, a reek of rotted vegetation and bird poop made his eyes water. He remembered that now, too. The wind had been blowing the opposite direction the day before, on the ride out with Rafe.

"Is the smell always so strong?" Cal said.

"This time of year, I'm afraid so," Helen said. "One of the reasons we like living so far south."

At the west coast Frank turned right, and they passed a spread of low cement buildings strewn across the beach, with a sign proclaiming them 'Club Scuba Doo.' A few minutes later they passed a three-story, bright pink resort that blocked any view of the sea.

"There's Sandy Bottoms," Frank said.

Two hundred yards farther they stopped at the gravel airstrip. To one side stood the shack that served as the terminal, with a kiosk labeled 'Post Office' cobbled onto it. Beyond that was a squat building of weathered wood with 'Peachy Bottoms' stenciled over the door, and 'Groceries and Sundries' hand painted across its plate-glass window. Cal checked his phone. Sure enough, there was a signal here. He could call Kat after he was sure he had everything he needed from the store.

Inside, the pond stench was eased by air conditioning. Four low mismatched rows of metal shelves held an assortment of canned and dried goods. A two-door, glass-front cooler stood in the back, mostly empty, but holding a few packs of frozen food. Along the far wall were shelves of hardware supplies.

Cal scanned the wall for a door knob, eyes skimming over nails, screws, spray paint, and caulk. The closest he could find was a set of brass hinges.

"I help you find something?" A woman with graying hair peered up at him through thick glasses.

"I'm looking for a locking door knob," Cal said.

The woman looked at him as if he had spoken Mandarin.

"Don't have any," she said after a long pause.

"In the back room, maybe? It's a pretty basic hardware item."

"Don't get much call for them," the woman said. "Whaddya need it for?"

"For locking my door," Cal said.

The woman stared, uncomprehending.

"So no one can get in," Cal snapped. "You know, what people use door locks for."

"That's a good one!" The woman laughed. "I can get you a hasp and a bike lock, if you want. What house you in, anyway?"

"The Batten place. On the east side."

"Oh! You must be Cal!" The woman's face lit up. "I'm Peachy. Heard Mister Rhodes' family was on island." She leaned close, like a conspirator "Securing the family treasure, eh?"

"There's no treasure. I mean . . . it's very nice to meet you . . . I'm trying to keep people out while I sort through all the junk."

"Rhodes did hoard all kinds of things. Shall we just leave it at that?" She gave him a knowing wink.

"I just need to secure the place 'til I can sell it." A thought struck him. "Peachy, are you related to Rosie?"

"First cousins." She smiled. "For property concerns, you'll be checking with Jack Cobia. Has his hands in a bit of everything."

"Great. In the meantime, you mentioned a lock?"

Peachy gave Cal an amused look, pulled a galvanized hasp off the rack, then rummaged in a box in the corner and came up with a child's bicycle chain, sheathed in bright pink vinyl tubing, with a four-tumbler lock built into it. Cal stared in disbelief. He didn't have the patience or strength to argue further. He thanked Peachy and moved on down the aisle. He grabbed a wall switch, two cans of bug spray, and a box of mosquito coils before moving to the food aisles. Locals shuffled in. Some glanced at Cal. Most ignored the pale stranger.

"Little Calvin Batten! I know that face anywhere!"

A semi-shaved man with graying hair ambled toward him, belly bulging.

"Hey, Antonio!" The man was grayer and fatter, but it was the same Antonio who had fixed things around Batten's Down, telling Cal and his friends island tales about duppies and sea serpents and pirate wrecks.

Antonio put his arms around Cal, lifted him off the ground in a sweaty bear hug.

"Good to have you back, even in trying times." Antonio grinned, gray stubble on his cheeks standing out in the dusty window light. "Come back to battle some monsters, hey?"

"Only monsters I'm fighting are mosquitoes. And a loudmouth rooster."

"Monsters'll find you soon enough. If they haven't already. Got to go down in the dark. Where they live. All tangled up down there, you know."

"Good advice." Cal wasn't sure how to respond.

"That old mersquatch's down your way, too. Got to watch out for him."

"The what?"

"Mersquatch. Bigfoot, but from the sea." Antonio lowered his voice, stepped closer. "Likes those flats down there. Tear your place up, you're not careful."

"Thanks for the warning, 'Tonio." Cal grinned. He had forgotten how wild Antonio's spook tales could be. "The big worry right now's getting the house in order, though."

"We get that place straightened out in no time."

"I just need it straightened enough to sell."

"Oh, no." Antonio wagged a finger at Cal. "You'll be staying." He tapped his temple with a forefinger.

"The Sight's steering you wrong on this one Antonio. I have a life to get back to."

"Know how to make the duppies laugh?" Antonio chuckled. "Make plans. Welcome back."

Cal waved him away, went back to shopping. The shelves looked to have been stocked at random. Bottles of hot sauce sat between boxes of tea bags and rolls of paper towels. He fought back the urge to rearrange like items together, or even put food with the food and supplies with supplies, preferably on different shelves. Instead, he inched down the aisle alert for anything he might need. Cans of black beans, a bag of rice, dried pasta, and jarred sauce. In the cooler in the back he found butter, eggs, and the last loaf of bread, which looked like it had been used as a soccer ball. Price tags on everything were mismarked, with prices all far too high.

From the end of the aisle, a woman studied him. Brown eyes and dark skin. A blue 'Dive Staff' t-shirt, bright orange sunglasses hooked in the shirt's neck. Green board shorts. A broad-brimmed straw hat perched on the back of her head. Black hair falling over her shoulders. And tall. Taller than Cal. She smiled at him, approached, hips moving as if she were swimming. One of the 'female dive staff' Helen Maples had warned him about?

"Hey." Her voice was high and throaty all at once, with a faint island lilt. "You just get in?"

She stepped close, closer than any stranger should. Smiling, brown eyes with flecks of green searching his.

"Sure." Cal stepped back a pace, made a show of digging through cans of stewed tomatoes.

"I was hoping I'd run into you." She stepped close again.

"Look, lady, I'm married." Cal rounded on her. "And not interested in some one-night hookup, either, so go chat up some other mark."

"I'm Marina, you ass." Her dark eyes blazed. "And I have *zero* interest in anything romantic with *you.*"

"Oh, crap." Cal's gut tightened as if she had punched him. "I'm sorry . . . Helen Maples warned me about . . . I'm here to sort out Rhodes' . . . my dad's stuff."

"Rafe said. Sorry about your dad." Her mouth tightened. Then her voiced hardened again. "Selling to the highest bidder, or the first lowball offer you get?"

"Either. I have no need for the creepy old place." Cal said it half-jokingly, glad to be on firmer ground.

"Wasn't creepy when we were little."

The firm ground turned to quicksand. Cal needed out.

"Times change. Say, I'm rushed right now—I'm bumming a ride from the Maples—but could we get together later, have a do-over?" Drinks couldn't hurt.

"I'm busy," she said. "And you'll have your hands full ditching your dad's house."

Marina walked back to the cooler, still moving as if she were gliding through water.

At the register, Cal watched Peachy, eager to see what the actual prices were when she rang up each item. The first was the wall switch.

"Whoa! You're charging ten dollars for a light switch?" he said.

"It *is* a heavy-duty switch," Peachy said.

"It's a two-pole switch. It should be sixty-five, seventy cents, tops!"

"It's expensive to ship things here."

"Expensive? It's robbery!"

"You want your lights to work or not?"

Peachy rang up the rest of his items. Cal clenched his teeth to keep from complaining about each one, paid for his things and stepped outside. The booby pond reek hit him again. How did people live at this end of the island? He set the grocery bag in the shade of a bent palm tree, sat on the nearly-horizontal sweep of the trunk and pulled out his phone. Kat should be at the shop now. And furious he hadn't called. He tapped Kat's number on the screen, waited. Nothing. He checked the screen. A weak-but-decent signal. He checked the settings. All looked good. Cal stepped back inside the store.

"Is there a trick to calling here?"

"Oh, the useable service doesn't *quite* reach us, I'm afraid," Peachy said. "Most resorts are in range of the tower, though." She waved her hand vaguely southward.

"So you don't have a phone?"

Peachy lifted a cracked, yellowed corded princess phone from under the register, white line running from the phone to a wall jack behind the counter.

"Wow. Look, I need to call . . . my wife . . . let her know I got in okay. Can I give you a credit card or cash for a short call to the U.S.?"

"Sure. Here, I'll dial a discount code for you."

She punched a series of numbers into the push buttons, then handed the phone over the counter to Cal.

He punched in the clock shop's number under Peachy's watchful gaze, handset screeching with each button pushed. The phone rang three times, then Kat's voice snapped in his ear.

"It's Cal," he said.

"I wondered if your plane crashed. Whose phone is this?"

"The store's. No cell reception where I am," Cal said. "Or internet. No idea what this'll cost, but I called as soon as I could."

Peachy smiled at him from across the counter.

"Fine. How soon can you sell the house, Cal?"

"It may take a few days to sort that out."

"They don't have realtors down there?"

Antonio wandered down the nearest aisle and stood next to Cal. He tapped his chest, mouthed, 'Tonio says hello.' Cal ignored him.

"Chasing down a lead on that."

Cal had no idea where to find this Cobia person. Marina wandered up, stood beside Antonio. Great. All three of them eavesdropping. He needed to make an attempt at small talk.

"You know, I never realized how much I missed the place." Another lie, but his listeners all smiled.

"Then why'd you never go back 'til now?"

Cal smiled at his audience.

"Waiting for Rhodes to make the first move, I suppose."

Peachy shook her head, clucking like one of the angry chickens at the house. Antonio looked as if he had a toothache. Marina threw up her hands, walked away.

"Well, he did that, alright. Get back up here, Cal. All these chiming clocks are making me batty."

Cal glanced out the window at a car speeding past. A Land Rover. With the Maples in what looked like a heated argument inside.

"Kat, my ride just left. I need to call you back."

Cal hung up before she could reply. He ran outside, waving his arms at the retreating Maples.

"Should've warned you about that." Antonio had followed Cal out. "Not getting a ride back with Frank and Helen. Need to get that car of Rhodes' running."

"The Sight tell you how I *do* get home?"

"Don't need The Sight. Here comes Linford."

A rusty station wagon limped down the road from the north, music blaring out its open windows. Antonio waved it down.

"Linford, this's Cal. Needs to get back to the Batten place. You going that way?" Antonio shouted to be heard above what sounded like a cross between reggae and gospel music.

"Yeah, man." Linford nodded, bushy beard shaking, eyes hidden behind dark glasses. He dragged his arm across the passenger seat to clear it of plumbing parts and electrical supplies.

'*Jesus is strong, strong, strong . . .*' the radio blared.

Cal gathered his groceries and climbed in. The car lurched down the road with a syncopated rhythm not quite in time with the music.

"You Rhodes' boy?" Linford steered with one hand and dangled the other out the window to keep smoke from a cigarette stub out of the car.

"Yep. I'm Cal.

'*I was so wrong, wrong, wrong . . .*'

Linford nodded, whether at Cal or the music, Cal couldn't tell. The man took a long drag off the hand-rolled cigarette stub. Wind swirled the smoke through the car. It smelled nothing like tobacco. Cal stared straight ahead, said nothing. Linford was driving fine, and he was Cal's only option for a ride home, even if he was under the influence of whatever.

'Jesus is with me all along, long, long . . .'

· A white pickup approached from the opposite direction, a light bar across its roof. The police truck.

"Uh oh," Linford said.

He put the joint between his lips, slowed to a near stop and fumbled to connect his seat belt. Once it snapped into place, he stuck the joint out the window again and sped up. He waved at Rafe as they passed. Rafe waved back and kept going, not seeing, or ignoring the joint.

"That . . . um . . . seatbelt important?" Cal said.

"Oh, yeah, man," Linford said. "Rafe sees me without it again, he'll write me up."

"But he's not worried about . . . umm . . ." Cal eyed the joint, trying to phrase it diplomatically.

"Worried about what?"

"Nothing."

They rode the rest of the way to Batten's Down without talking, any chance at conversation drowned out by the music.

Linford dropped Cal at the house, then continued on in a cloud of dust. Cal walked across the gravel yard. The front door was open. Odd. He remembered closing it. Maybe he had been in such a hurry to flag down the Maples he forgot? He stepped inside, set the groceries on the kitchen counter in a clatter of cans and bottles.

Rosie's head appeared in the doorway.

"What the hell are you doing here?" Cal said.

"Finishin' up. You got in the way yesterday, you know."

"No. It's *my* house. *I'm* not in the way. *You* have to go."

Rosie chuckled, retreated to the dining room, knelt and scrubbed at the chalk pentagram on the floor.

"Leave now and I won't call the police," Cal said.

"Can't call from here." A hint of a smirk played across her face. "And I'm not breaking the law. Just doing my job. Go to jail if I *didn't* come clean house."

"No. My old man's gone. So's your agreement. It's over, done with, no more. Go home! Here's severance pay."

Cal pulled out his wallet, held out all his cash to her without counting it.

"No, sir," Rosie said. "Gave my word to Mister Rhodes. Ain't going back on that. I honor his memory, even if you don't."

Rosie went back to cleaning, stacking small piles of papers on top of others to expose other dusty surfaces. Cal felt his face reddening, his anger rising. He would pick her up and carry her out, wedge the door shut behind her.

A misfiring engine clattered outside. Tires crunched on the gravel. Cal stepped from the house to see who was there and to let his anger cool. An SUV covered more in rust than its original white paint. Rusty door hinges creaked and Antonio stepped out, a screwdriver and a roll of duct tape in hand.

"Me and that car go way back, y'know," he said. "She can't breathe—choke's stuck closed."

"You can seriously get that contraption running?" Cal's spirits lifted.

"Short term. Gimme five minutes."

Antonio stalked to the lean-to.

Cal stepped back inside, mood lighter. He was calmer now. And thinking clearly. Physically carrying Rosie out of the house could land him in legal trouble. And from her stance and the look in her eye, she would probably lay him out cold if he tried. But he would have it out with her. Cal found her in the main room, sorting file folders into piles, glancing inside each one.

"What the hell?" Cal yelled. "Rifling through papers is part of cleaning?"

"Got to put like papers with like, you want to make order out of this." Rosie waved her arm to indicate the clutter. "And I seen you looking at everything, eye twitching."

"Make order out of *this . . .*?"

Cal stopped himself. She was trying to make him angry. Why? Cal had still seen no sign of any legal papers. Or cash. Did she want Cal flustered to distract him from that? Cal's anger surged back.

"You have no business looking through anything! Cleaning may not be illegal, but . . . trespassing is!" He caught himself before he said 'theft.'

Rosie straightened, squared her shoulders, eyes hard.

The sound of a small engine coughing to life came through the open window, followed by a blue cloud of engine exhaust. The engine revved. Exhaust poured in thicker. Cal and Rosie ran out of the house, gasping for air.

"She going now, Cal!" Antonio beamed at them. "That choke does like to stay closed. I opened it up and taped off the lever." He waved the roll of duct tape at Cal. "She'll run a little lean, but she'll run. I'll get Dermott to fix her proper."

Inside the shed, the Thing was gurgling like an oversized coffeemaker, shaking non-stop, but still running.

"Antonio, you're a champ," Cal said. "Anything else I need to know about this jalopy?"

"Treat her gentle—she's older than you, you know. And her brakes are worn. You want to do most of your braking with the gears."

Cal started to laugh. He could barely drive a stick shift, and Antonio wanted him to brake with the gears? Something moved at the corner of Cal's eye. Rosie. Slipping back toward the house.

"Oh, no you don't!" Cal quick-stepped to block her way. "Antonio, would you mind helping Rosie off the property?"

Antonio gave him a blank stare.

"You don't want her to clean?"

"Bingo! Finally, I'm getting through to someone." Cal had a vision of Antonio tossing Rosie into the back of his SUV and driving away.

"Mister Rhodes paid me in advance," Rosie's voice came low, forceful.

"Oh. All right, then," Antonio said. "You got yourself a cleaner, Cal. A good one."

"But I don't want one!"

"Rosie's the best on Blacktip," Antonio said. "And honest as the day is long. Trust her with your money *and* your life. Could've fixed that car, too."

Defeated, Cal switched off the ignition, walked slumped-shouldered back into the house. As if wanting to spare him further loss of face, neither followed him.

Behind him a car door slammed. Then a second. At least he had that. Rosie, for whatever reason, had decided she was done for the day. Or was retreating until tomorrow.

Cal opened a beer, sat on the couch, scanned the piles of papers for a likely spot to find Rhodes' important papers. Things had to turn his way eventually. He would wander over to the Maples place later, meet the locals, maybe find Jack Cobia and see what he knew about Rhodes' affairs. For all he knew, the will was on file in a courthouse somewhere. Tiperon Island, maybe, or with Cobia. This couldn't be *that* complicated.

He stared at the Tesla coil. Orion and the Hyades arced across the ceiling next to an oil lamp of green glass. Maybe Rhodes *had* been a mad scientist. And had invented some sort of secret filing system to hide his valuables.

Cal found a blank sheet of paper and a pen. Then, with a book as a straightedge, he made a rough sketch of the house's floorplan. Next he drew a grid pattern across it, dividing the house into twenty-five squares. Tomorrow he would search the place methodically, not overlooking a single inch. He sat back, admired the sketch, calmed by the grid squares with their right angles, the order to be imposed on the place.

3

The sun had long set behind the bluff when Cal, showered and dressed, stepped out his front door, feet chafing in a pair of Rhodes' least-worn flip flops. He hadn't worn flip flops since he was a kid, but he hoped to fit in with the locals. Beyond the palm trunks, the Maples' house glowed yellow with outdoor lights. The faint sound of jazz drifted through the trees. Cal worked his way across the uneven ground, picking up his feet an extra inch and putting them down tentatively, still adjusting to the unfamiliar shoes.

The Maples' place stood on eight-foot pilings above a broad, arcing brick courtyard, now filled with assorted autos. Steps led up to a wide sandstone-tiled verandah, ringed with guttering torches and packed with locals dressed fancier than anyone Cal had seen on the island. Many stared at Cal but didn't introduce themselves. Then Frank and Helen Maples appeared, wine glasses in-hand. Helen had swapped her amber bracelets for gold ones.

"Cal, dear boy! So glad you could come!" she called out. "We'll get you a drink and introduced to everyone."

Helen wrapped her arm around him and guided him into the crowd. She stopped at the makeshift bar, where a thin, balding man was sloshing spirits and mixers into highball and lowball glasses so fast Cal couldn't make out what the man was mixing in what.

"Here we are, then! A vodka gimlet, a gin rickey, and a sidecar!"

The man pushed three drinks across the sopping-wet bar top toward a couple to his right, grinning like a schoolboy.

"This is Reg Gurnard," Helen said. "One of our Tiperon Airways pilots. Reg, this is Rhodes Batten's son, Cal."

Gurnard splashed a last bit of lime juice into two glasses and across the bar, half-wiped his hand and extended it to Cal.

"Come down to wrap things up, eh?" His blue eyes bored into Cal's. "Or did your father leave you his elixir's formula? Maybe a map to the source?"

"Elixir?" Cal stared at Gurnard's wet hand, hesitated, then gritted his teeth and took it.

"The old fox found the Fountain, or Spring, of Youth, you know. Replicated it in his lab. Shipped it out in small batches."

"Oh, that. Sure. There's vats of the stuff."

Gurnard stared, eyes wide and mouth open. Whiskey spilled from the glass in his hand, splattered on the bar.

"A joke," Cal said. "Riffing off your . . . You *seriously* think Rhodes found the Fountain of Youth?"

"Difficult to say," Gurnard said. "Your father was . . . ah . . . one of a kind."

"He certainly seemed to attract strong emotions." Cal needed to change the subject. Though there *had* been pages of scribbled chemical formulas in the house and glass bottles with rubber stoppers. Rhodes had been a mail fraudster?

"Ha! Everyone has a story. Ask Clete Horn about him and your papa having a row about docking space. Clete's boat caught fire the next night!"

Cal started to laugh, then realized this wasn't a joke, either. Rhodes had torched someone's boat after a minor argument? Cal had fond, if hazy, memories of Rhodes as a concerned father, protective of Cal and his friends. It was troubling to hear people speak negatively about him.

Frank Maples, stone-faced, excused himself.

Gurnard flung ice, rum, and a splash of cola into a lowball glass faster than Cal's eyes could follow, then added a lime wedge.

"One Cuba libre as a welcome!" Gurnard slapped the glass into Cal's hand.

Cold rum flowed down Cal's arm. His left eye started to twitch. Cal grabbed a fistful of bar napkins, dried his arm as best he could.

"Yeah. Thanks," Cal said through his teeth. He sipped at his drink. The rum burned, Gurnard had mixed it so strong.

Helen caught Cal's elbow, pulled him into the crowd, sending more rum and cola down his arm, introducing him to people as she went.

"Dr. and Mrs. Tang." The Tangs smiled a greeting, he in blue, she in yellow.

"Is your father's alcohol distiller still functional?" Dr. Tang said.

"Don't tell me you believe the Fountain of Youth nonsense, too," Cal said.

"Oh, no," The doctor laughed. "Your father made his own hooch and sold it on the sly. Never had a chance to sample it. If there happens to be any sitting around . . ."

"The only signs of liquor I've seen are store-bought rum bottles."

Cal wasn't sure he would know a still if he saw one, but there was nothing in or around the house capable of producing spirits. The doctor looked disappointed.

Helen pulled him away.

"Here are George and Belinda Graysby," Helen said. A younger couple in matching polka dot shirts nodded to Cal.

"We're so sorry for your loss," Belinda said.

"Are you in finance, as well?" George said. "Inherit any of the genius?"

"I . . . No. I fix clocks. Mechanical armatures. And set gemstones."

The Graysbys stared at him, faces blank.

"I didn't know he was so good at finances." Cal hadn't seen any financial papers in his fumbling through the house.

"An absolute wizard at real estate and investments, they say. I tried to broach the subject several times, get his advice, but he played things close. Kept his hands in a bit of everything, it seemed."

"Legal and otherwise," Belinda said.

"B'linda!"

"Well, it's true."

"And here's Sergeant Major Beaugregory Damsil." Helen spun Cal to face a small man with a peppery moustache.

"Retired, my boy. Retired." Damsil peered up at Cal as if inspecting a new recruit.

"Sergeant Major Damsil owns a house just down the coast," Helen said. "You're nearly neighbors."

"You'll be taking over your father's duties, I assume?"

"Duties?"

"Ah, say no more." Damsil waggled a finger at Cal. "Loose lips and ships, eh? Just visiting the old homestead, then?" Damsil winked, spun on his heel, and was gone.

"What'd I miss?" Cal said.

"Your father kept to himself. Beau's pet theory is Batten's Down was a CIA listening post."

Cal laughed.

"The place doesn't even have a phone. Or cages for carrier pigeons." Cal was still thinking about the Graysbys. If what they said was true, Rhodes *had* to have records. Computer files. A computer.

"It's a small island. People do invent all sorts of ideas to amuse themselves," Helen said. "Some say your father killed a man and was hiding out under an assumed name." She studied Cal, gauging his reaction.

"The only thing my old man killed was bottles of rum."

"But was he really your old man?" A shaggy-headed man in shorts and a wrinkled, teal button-down shirt with rolled-up sleeves joined them. Drink in hand, he swayed from side to side, as if on a rocking boat. "Looks be damned. *That* would make a great rumor!"

"Cal Batten, Payne Hanover," Helen said. "He has a place up the east coast."

"Oh, I'm his, all right," Cal said. "I brought a birth certificate, just in case."

"Ah. 'Then may there be no moaning of the probate bar.'" Hanover's bloodshot eyes sparkled as he spoke, quoting something Cal knew he should recognize, but didn't. "So, the family fortune's all yours, huh?"

"Sure, if 'fortune' means an ugly house and a broken-down car," Cal said. "Both for sale if you're interested."

"Oh, I already have Toad Hall. No need for another. There's a small market for a house like that. It'd prob'ly interest someone in the . . . import/export trade. Keep it in the business."

"Import/export?" Why did everyone on this island talk in riddles?

Helen shook her head at Payne.

"So, where's home, Cal?" Payne's words slid against each other as he spoke.

"Chicago suburbs. Naperville."

"Swapping Windy City adventures for tropical ones?"

"People in Naperville don't have adventures," Cal said. "It's the law. It's the *draw*."

Payne half-smiled, eyes unfocused, then refocused. He pointed to Cal, as if about to say something, then wandered away.

"Don't mind Payne," Helen said. "He's convinced your father was a drug runner or smuggler or some such piratical thing. Frank and I have seen no evidence of . . . that."

Helen studied him then, eyes reddened, as if she were several drinks in to the evening.

"Why did you ask about large animals yesterday? In the car?"

"Someone was playing a practical joke last night. Stomping around the house and growling." Had it been Frank, and Helen was gauging how Cal had reacted?

A worried look played across Helen's face.

"There *has* been the occasional . . . vandalism in the area. We hoped that would have stopped with . . . well, apparently not."

"What sort of vandalism? And why would it stop?"

"Oh, noises. Thrown rocks and branches. Rummaged-through outbuildings. And someone leaving dead fish somewhere, up on the bluff from the smell. When the northeast wind died, it was awful." Helen spoke low, so only Cal could hear her. "We had thought it was your father and his hijinks. He had that sort of sense of humor. But apparently it wasn't."

"So someone else's . . . hijinks?"

"One can't be sure." She smiled then. "But no worries. No one's ever been hurt."

"By who? Or what?" Had Helen bought into Antonio's mersquatch nonsense? "*Are* there large animals on the island?"

"Look! There's Rich and Sandy. You'll want to meet them if you're selling."

She led Cal to where two neatly-dressed men were talking.

"Rich Skerritt, owner of Eagle Ray Cove resort." Helen Maples nodded to a heavyset man with graying hair. "Sandy Bottoms, owner of Sandy Bottoms' Beach Resort." She turned to a balding, portly man with a too-tight dress shirt. "This is Cal Batten, here to see about his father's estate."

"Bottoms as in Rosie and Peachy and Dermott?" Cal said.

"Cousins, all." Sandy Bottoms chuckled, setting his belly rippling. "The family tree doesn't have too many branches here on

Blacktip." Then, more serious: "You find any of that old rascal's pirate treasure yet? He was prospecting for years, you know."

"Treasure? I . . . no. Old books and moldy papers, but no treasure." Was Rosie treasure hunting under the guise of housekeeping? Was the entire Bottoms clan made up of modern-day pirates?

"And him with no visible means of income?"

"Word is you're looking to sell." Rich Skerritt's voice cut in. Comforting and predatory at the same time.

"I . . . yes. Once I take stock of everything and tally up an inventory." Cal needed the will and deed. Soon.

"I don't care about the chattel." Skerritt smiled, reassuring. "But I *would* like to talk to you about the land. It's a nice parcel, and maybe worth a pretty penny."

"Maybe lots of pretty pennies," Cal said. "Give me a chance to sort out how many, exactly, and we'll get together." Skerritt and Bottoms both thought there was treasure hidden in the house. And were eager to buy. A bidding war would work in Cal's favor. They would laugh if they ever set foot in the junk pile. And Cal wouldn't care once the place sold.

Skerritt stepped away. Bottoms pulled Cal aside.

"If it's a quick sale you're after, I could certainly help with that." His voice was low. "Slightly under market value, for the sake of convenience, you understand."

"I'll keep that in mind," Cal said.

A quick sale might be possible, after all. Both men were eager. Too eager? And what was 'market value?'

Helen had wandered off. Cal excused himself, downed the rest of his drink. Reg Gurnard gamboled past, tray of drinks held high. Cal grabbed another rum and cola as he passed.

"That's the spirit!" Gurnard barked, then disappeared in the crowd, glasses clattering.

Cal rubbed his hand on the glass' condensation, using what moisture there was to clean the drying cola from his fingers. The music shifted to an upbeat tune heavy with saxophone and drum.

A short man with a shock of white hair, bright eyes, and a green linen shirt approached. Despite his hair, he didn't seem much older than Cal.

"I wanted to convey my condolences," he said. "I'm Jerrod. Your old man supplied parts and pieces for multiple art projects. And I helped him with his trebuchet."

"His . . .?"

"Siege engine. For flinging big rocks. It was pure hell calibrating the throws."

"Oh. The catapult. Why'd he build it, anyway?"

"Testing a theory. He was always working on something."

"So . . . you're an artist, then?"

"Among other things. I gave the eulogy at the little service we had for him."

"An artist *and* preacher?"

"Former. The Church and I had a . . . difference of opinion. Or two. They cut me loose. But the island minister wouldn't do it, so I stepped in."

"Why . . . wouldn't the minister . . ."

"A while back Reverend Grunt made an unannounced stop at your dad's place. Rhodes chased him down the street with a shovel, yelling about hellfire and damnation." Jerrod grinned. "Nearly smote him, too. Some of us saw the humor in that. Pierre Grunt, not so much."

"Well, thanks for stepping in. At the service." Cal had never heard anyone use the word 'smote' in conversation, but the man *was* an ex-preacher. And seemed the most normal person on the island. It was nice to meet someone who didn't have a crazy theory about Rhodes. "And any parts or pieces you need, you're welcome to them."

The second drink was kicking in nicely.

"You enjoying being back on the island?" Jerrod's eyes darted around the room as he talked, as if changing focus as thoughts bounced through his head. "You're taking time to do some scuba diving, I'll bet."

"Oh, I don't dive," Cal said. "Just here to sell the place, then zip back home."

Surprise played across Jerrod's face.

"Well, what a great time to learn!" he said.

"Not a chance. I don't even swim. I get queasy standing on the dock."

"Scared of sharks?" Jerrod half-laughed.

"No, just of being eaten by one."

"Marina and Rafe've talked about the three of you swimming when you were young," Jerrod said. "Marina, now, s*he* could teach you scuba."

"That was another lifetime." Cal said. "And Marina's not so friendly these days." There was a twinge of something that could have been regret, but it passed.

"Have you found your dad's stash yet?" Jerrod switched subjects again. "That should keep you here a while, just digging for that."

"There *isn't* a stash." Cal grimaced. So much for Jerrod not having crazy theories. "Of anything. Just the house and land."

"No clues?" Jerrod kept on, as if Cal hadn't spoken. "No gold dive weights? He was working on that, you know, turning lead to gold. We talked about it."

"The only clues I'm looking for are how to get rid of a housekeeper who refuses to be fired." Cal tried to steer the conversation to sane ground. "It's a dump. You should see the place."

"Yeah! I'd love to!"

Around Cal, heads turned, nodded.

"It . . . needs some straightening." Cal gave a half-hearted laugh, mentally kicked himself. He had spoken without thinking. Of course they all wanted a peek at the island's biggest mystery and newest gossip. "Like, maybe a month or three. Rosie may be cleaning every day, but it never looks any tidier."

Cal excused himself, drained his glass. All the talk of scuba diving and sharks had rattled him. He exhaled, made himself relax. Was everyone on the island so credulous about what Rhodes did? Fountain of Youth? Alchemy? Cal made his way back to the bar, grabbed another drink to settle his nerves.

He scanned the crowd. Anyone interested in the house knew it was for sale. Now he needed to find Jack Cobia. He checked the verandah for either of the Maples, but didn't see them. He looked for anyone who looked lawyerly, trying not to seem too obvious. If he didn't run into Cobia soon, he would go home, get some sleep, track him down in the morning. A big swallow of the fresh drink and his tension eased. The music picked up again, a ragtime tune now. Several couples started dancing in the center of the room, including the Maples. Something old fashioned. The Charleston?

Cal turned, found himself face to face with a shoulder-high man with a bushy moustache and shaggy gray hair.

"Cal Batten?" The man held out his hand. "Frank said I should track you down."

Reek of cigar smoke. Two-day stubble. Small eyes and a slight under bite. Rumpled shirt, as if he had just rolled out of bed after an all-night party still wearing the same clothes.

"And you are . . ."

"Jack Cobia."

Cal hesitated, then shook the man's hand. This was Frank Maples' recommendation for legal advice?

"Nice piece of property you're sitting on . . ." Cobia let his voice trail off.

"I was hoping to talk to you about that," Cal said. "Privately."

Cobia raised an eyebrow, led Cal to an uncrowded corner of the verandah.

"I need some advice from someone who knows the local laws and customs and that sort of thing," Cal said.

"I can help with that," Cobia said. "For a moderate fee, of course."

"Of course. Sure." Cal took a deep breath. How to find out what he needed to know without starting the rumor mill turning. "I'd like to keep this as quiet as possible . . ."

"Oh, I'm as discreet as the next person on Blacktip," Cobia said. "More so than most."

"That's what worries me." Cal's stomach tightened. There was nothing to do but dive in. "Do you know who handled my father's legal affairs? Maybe kept his important papers?"

"Rhodes handled his own affairs . . ." Cobia looked puzzled. Then both his eyebrows went up. "Any important papers in particular?"

"The property deed," Cal whispered. "And his will."

Cobia whistled faint.

"I *really* need to keep this between us," Cal said.

"Yeah, you do! Why'd you tell me at all?"

"I need help, and Frank says you're the closest thing to an honest attorney on this island." Cal winced at his phrasing. "That didn't come out right. I've had rum. No disrespect."

Cobia studied Cal for a long moment, reddened eyes locked on Cal's.

"You *need* that will. You don't want this thing going to the Treasury Solicitor. Tiperon Islands' law says someone dies intestate, every last thumbtack goes to the government. No will, they'll pluck you like a *pollo*, son. There's a tight window for getting it proved in court, too. Thirty days, I think. I'll find out."

Cal nodded. Took a long drink of rum and cola. He *had* to find the will. Fast.

"You find his laptop?" Cobia studied Cal's face.

"No computer, no tablet, no phone," Cal said. "No internet, either."

"That doesn't sound right." Cobia paused, thinking. "Well, keep an eye out for any flash drives, discs, things like that. I can use my computer to check them out."

"I have my laptop."

"Yeah, but I'll know what I'm looking at. And for. And how to stonewall the Treasury folks. They'd love to get their hands on your old man's assets. They tried, time and again, but old Rhodes was always too slick for 'em. If there's a will, he'll have it stashed close by somewhere. The deed, too. Rhodes was a world-class pack rat."

Cal winced, glanced toward Batten's Down.

"In a good way," Cobia said. "No disrespect."

"No, that's the nicest thing anyone's said about him all night," Cal said. "He was that much of an ogre?"

Cobia's eyes locked onto Cal's.

"Years ago, Rhodes and I had a . . . disagreement," Cobia said. "Couple days later, someone strung a clothesline across the road, neck-high, where I rode my motorcycle into town every morning."

Cobia ran a finger along a faint scar on his throat, like a faded tattoo.

"But hey, that's ancient history," he said. "I guarantee that will's in the house somewhere. Let me know if you need help looking."

"No, thanks. I have a search grid plotted, and it's a small place."

"Suit yourself. Rhodes was a devious one. And don't forget to enjoy the island when you need a break from searching."

Cal nodded, unexpectedly nostalgic after talking to so many people who had known Rhodes, who had known the younger Cal. He should get to know them, get back in touch with this odd little place he came from. No! He shut that thought down hard. He was here to sell the property. Period. Not get all misty eyed on memory lane. Cobia was staring at him strangely.

"Look, I had one too many of these." Cal waved his now-empty glass at Cobia. "I need to get home. To the house, I mean. Can we talk tomorrow?"

"You know Sandy Bottoms resort?" Cobia said. "My unofficial office. By the bar."

Great. Just the sort of attorney, or whatever Cobia was, Cal should have expected on this Godforsaken little rock.

Cal picked his away back across the broken ground between the Maples place and Batten's Down, head spinning from the rum and eyes struggling to adjust to the darkness after the party's brightness. Jack Cobia's warning echoed in his head. He had to find the will, soon. Cal quickened his pace. Howled in pain when he stubbed his toe on a rock outcrop he couldn't see. He kept on, more slowly, and high stepping, toward the misshapen lump of a house. He would tear the place apart to find the will. Tomorrow, when his head had cleared.

4

Back at Batten's Down, Cal was too agitated to sleep. He needed to find Rhodes' will. He sprayed bug fogger, lit two mosquito coils, then studied his grid sketch of the main room. Cobia said Rhodes would have 'stashed' the will. That meant it wouldn't be lying around in plain sight. A safe? A strongbox? Tucked away somewhere no one would suspect, but where Rhodes could get to it quickly? 'Pluck you like a *pollo*' echoed through his head.

Cal started on the room's east side. He flipped over the couch, the armchair and looked underneath. Nothing. The closet in the main room held no papers, either. Cal had never had a safe, but tried to think of where people hid them in movies. He pulled pictures away from the walls, tapped the drywall behind each one. No telltale 'thunk' of anything hidden there. He checked the bedroom-turned-science lab, but saw no obvious hiding places. He quartered the floor, stomping as he went, but everything sounded solid.

Cal moved to the kitchen, checked all the cabinets but found only dead cockroaches and old ant baits. The fridge hid nothing. He was in a bind, all right.

Was he overthinking this? Cal thumbed through the folders on the big table, half-seeing their contents while he racked his brain for possible hiding places. Geological studies. Weather forecasts and charts. Property surveys and lot layouts on the other side of the island. Stock market printouts. Rhodes could have died a millionaire, or he could have died destitute, yet Cal wouldn't have known which.

One folder contained sheets filled with chemical formulas. 'Au' had multiple references. Gold. Had Rhodes been into alchemy after all? No. Cal wasn't going down that lunatic rabbit hole. He started to sort the folders by subject, stopped himself, settled on stacking them in even-height piles, straightened their edges with the table's edge.

There was still no sign of cash or anything else of value in the house. No one had *no* valuables lying around. He wished he had known Rhodes, known how the man thought, what sort of hidey-holes he would use.

Rosie would know. She knew Rhodes' habits, how his mind worked. Cal shook his head. The island was getting to him. Now he was thinking about asking Rosie for help.

Suspicion surged back. She could have already found all Rhodes' valuables and was cleaning the house to cover her tracks. Or she was searching for Rhodes' valuables while she pretended to clean. He would have to watch her. Maybe even make peace with her long enough to figure out what she was up to. And she would be back. He had lost that battle.

In front of him was the head-high bookcase. Cal pulled books out one at a time, checked to see if any were hollow, shook each one while he rifled the pages, seeing if any papers were tucked inside. Plenty of scrap-paper bookmarks fell out, several notecards, some covered in more bad haiku, but nothing important.

One end of the bookcase was stuffed with rolled-up maps— nautical charts for Blacktip Island, the Tiperon Islands, Cuba, the Caribbean, and the Central American coast. Rhodes had no boat. Did he use someone else's?

Cal jammed himself between the armchair and the bookcase, ran his finger along the spines of the books in the bottom left shelf. The shark books. Touching them, it felt like a rope had tightened around his chest. He remembered them from when he was little. A false memory? No. The memories were vivid. The hand-painted illustrations with their bright reds and blues and greens. And the titles:

The Hungry Ocean by Amp Lorenzini
Shark Attacks and How to Avoid Them by Nash Thresher
The USS Indianapolis: A Survivor's Tale by Bull Hammer
The Illustrated History of Shark Attacks by Sandi Tyger
White Death from the Deep by Mako Bleu

They had been the stuff of his nightmares. And he remembered how well he had slept when he and his mom had first left the island, even living in relatives' spare rooms and basements until they found their own place.

Cal went to the kitchen, poured a glass of rum, downed it, then returned to the books. Were these the monsters Antonio had been rambling about? Great. Just what he needed to think about before sleep. Sharks. And shark attacks.

On a whim, Cal pushed each wooden knot on the bookcase, hoping one would make the bookcase swing away to reveal a hidden room. No such luck. Outside, a rooster crowed. Cal yelled, rattled the window. He smiled at the sound of flapping wings and chicken feet scrambling through the dry sea grape leaves. He needed sleep. He could search more tomorrow when his brain was fresh. And sober.

Cal put the cushions back on the couch, then grabbed the pillow and blanket. He stretched out, closed his eyes against the acrid smoke from the mosquito coils.

The roosters crowed, but kept their distance. Boat engines sounded offshore, raced closer, louder, as if a big speedboat were buzzing the coastline, then receded. Was that what Frank Maples had complained about? After a few minutes there came scuffling sounds outside the door, then outside the window. Cal ignored them, put Helen Maples' worries about wild animals out of his mind. Someone was trying to rattle him, scare him off. Get him to sell quick and cheap. He finally dozed off, but slept fitfully, dreams filled with slashing fins, flashing teeth, eager snouts, while he struggled to swim in darkness.

At sunrise Cal woke, tried to sit up on the saggy couch. Pain shot through his lower back. He collapsed back, waited for the pain to ease. He took a deep breath, rolled onto the floor, then pulled himself upright. He couldn't take another night on the couch. Peachy's store had to have beds, however overpriced. Probably standing on end between the canned tuna and garden hoses.

He had put off searching the master bedroom the night before, not wanting to be near the bed where Rhodes had died. But he had to search the room. And the bed had to go. Rafe had said that the island dump was up the east coast. He could haul the mattress and springs there, now, before Rosie arrived to stop him.

Cal grabbed a big black trash bag and went to Rhodes' room. It was more chaotic than the rest of the house, crowded by bins overflowing with work clothes, heavy boots. Orange life vests and mesh bags full of rope and what looked like climbing gear hung from the rafters. Empty, suitcase-sized black plastic bins were stacked in one corner, gray lids stacked beside them. Jars held rock samples, dead lizards, and random tree leaves. Cal blocked it out, focused on the bed. A light blanket, the sheets and pillows were still strewn across the mattress. Cal held his breath, stuffed them all into the trash bag. He took another deep breath. The mattress, gray and stained, looked decades old. He gritted his teeth, grabbed the top edge, then paused.

Stuffing poked out along one seam. Cal looked closer. The mattress had been cut along the stitching, a foot-long slash, straight and fresh, not a ragged rip with edges tattered over time. Who would make such a deliberate cut? And why? There were similar cuts on the other side, and the head and the foot, stuffing leaking out of each of them. Someone had searched inside the mattress. Cal went cold at that.

Rosie was the only other person who had been alone in the house since Rhodes passed. She kept cleaning and rearranging things, shuffling papers and folders without any apparent progress. Was she working with her cousin Sandy? Or . . . she and Rhodes had been sleeping together. Did that maybe make them common-law spouses? If there was no will, if she found it and destroyed it, would the property go to her?

Cal sat on the bedside chair, letting the possibilities click into place. If that was Rosie's game, what was his next move? Confront her? Leave a fake will where she would find it, see if she took the bait? He needed to talk to Jack Cobia. Jack knew the players, the playing field and the rules.

But first, Cal needed to get rid of the bed. After he made sure nothing was hidden in the mattress, farther in where Rosie's shorter arms couldn't reach.

The mattress smelled of mildew and stale sweat. Cal gritted his teeth, ran his hands across the surface, feeling for any hint of paper crinkling inside. Nothing. He flipped it over and felt all across the other side, more stained than the reverse. Still nothing. Rosie had probably done the same thing. But he had to be certain.

He held his breath and shoved his hand through the first cut in the mattress. The filling inside slid thick, cool around his hand. Cal worked his arm in as far as he could, trying not to think about what might be in the stuffing. Cal shuddered, gagged, but kept groping.

After several interminable minutes, Cal pulled his arm out, scraped nylon fibers from it as best he could. He would take the longest shower of his life when he got back, yellow water be damned. He dragged the mattress out to the car, returned for the box springs. He flipped the springs frame, wasn't surprised to find the bottom cover had been sliced open.

Cal dragged the frame outside. How to attach the springs and mattress to the Thing? They were as wide as the car, and nearly as long. He propped one end of the springs on the windshield frame, let the other rest on the rear seatbacks. He would have to drive hunched over, but he didn't see any other way. Cal took a deep breath, held it, and bear-hugged the stained mattress. He lifted it as high as he could, let it fall on top of the springs, then lashed them both to the car with cord from the lean-to.

Cal crawled into the driver's seat, shoulder blades sliding across the box springs and chin brushing the steering wheel. The mattress reek was thick now, and he fought down the rising vomit.

After what seemed a lifetime of coaxing and cursing, the Thing sputtered to life. Cal coughed, enveloped in exhaust, ground the transmission into gear, and backed through the blue cloud. He ground gears again, shifted into first and, herky-jerky, pulled onto the dirt road. The wind blew away the exhaust and the mattress stench.

He drove north, car clattering over washboard ridges, bed bouncing on his back with every bump. He passed the cut-over road at the bluff's northern end, kept going past a group of low buildings marked 'Toad Hall,'—it had to be Payne Hanover's place—and soon spied a sign that read 'Island Landfill.' Below was a smaller sign that read 'No Burning of Household Waste.' Cal followed the dirt track inland. Ahead was a long mound of scrap metal, junked cars, rusted appliances, and broken furniture. To one side was a pile of yard waste, crushed boxes, and smoldering wood scraps. No one else was there, though a beat-up dump truck with 'Sanitation' stenciled on its door was parked near the scrap metal.

Cal untied the mattress, stared at the rough slashes along the edge, clumps of filling dropping from the cut fabric. Anyone who saw that would know it had been rooted through. Would wonder why. Would ask awkward questions.

He dragged the mattress to the smoking pile, let it fall with the gashed side down, then stacked the box springs on top of it. No one would think to flip over nasty bedding, and with luck, what was left of the fire would singe the slashed edges, make them look scorched instead of cut. He flung the bag with the pillows and sheets as high on the trash mound as he could.

Cal turned the key to start the Thing. There was a clicking sound, but it wouldn't start. So much for Antonio fixing it. He needed to get back to the house before Rosie arrived. He turned the key again. More clicking.

He had heard of push-starting manual-transmission cars by popping the clutch. The Thing was facing down a slight incline. It was worth a try. Cal put the shift in neutral and pushed on the door frame and steering wheel as hard as he could. The car slow-rolled, then gained speed moving down the slope. When Cal was nearly running, he jumped in the open door, stomped the clutch to the floorboard, jammed the shift lever into what he hoped was a gear, then snatched his foot off the pedal. The Thing shook as if it were falling apart. The engine coughed, sputtered, and roared to life.

Cal stomped on the gas and careened down the track, not daring to let the engine stall. In his rearview mirror, flames flickered, already licking around the mattress. He reached the road. A thin spiral of black smoke rose above the tree line behind him. A moment later, a black mushroom cloud erupted from the dump, climbing a hundred feet into the cloudless sky. Whatever the mattress had been stuffed with, it was damned flammable.

Cal passed the 'No Burning' sign in a blur. A siren wailed in the distance. Cal pressed the gas pedal to the floorboard, hoped the dust from his passing settled before the fire department, or Rafe, got to the dump.

There was no sign of Rosie when Cal reached Batten's Down. Good. He grabbed a soda from the fridge and sat on the couch, catching his breath. His gaze locked onto the coffee table.

The folders he had left with their edges straightened had been shifted. The stacks were of uneven heights, too. Someone had moved them while he was at the dump. Rosie wasn't here yet. Who, then? And why? Someone looking through folders meant they were looking for papers. Cal smiled thinking of a would-be thief looking for Rhodes' will and finding God-awful haiku.

Bike tires crunched on gravel. The door swung open. Rosie.

"Were you here earlier?" Cal said.

"Just got here, didn't I?" She looked at Cal as if he were crazy.

"You didn't stop by, leave for a few minutes, then come back just now?"

"Why would I do a fool thing like that? You still asleep?"

"I've been up. I went . . . out. But I straightened these folders before I left. Now they're not straightened."

Rosie started to laugh, then studied him for several seconds, face serious.

"Someone been in here?"

"Folders didn't move themselves. If it wasn't you, and it wasn't me . . . Who the hell just walks into someone's house and goes through their things?"

"We can't leave the place unattended." Rosie's voice lost some of its island lilt.

"'We?' There is no 'we.'"

"You got to go out, I'll be here." The lilt returned.

"I can trust you?"

"Got a choice?"

"Yes. What do you know about Rhodes' mattress getting sliced up?"

Rosie looked surprised for the first time. She stared at him, mouth open. He had her now, the little rat!

"You want to sell this place, you need Mister Rhodes' will," she said.

It was Cal's turn to look surprised.

"I . . . have the will . . . I . . ." Cal tried to form the words, but they wouldn't come.

"You see-through, Cal. You wanna sell this place so bad, if you had the papers you'd be doing it." Rosie swept her eyes across the files on the coffee table. "No worries. Whoever got in didn't find nothing."

"You *have* been poking through things . . . For your cousin Sandy?"

"This's your place, Cal. Where you belong. Your daddy said. No will, you can't stay. Finding that will's my last act for him."

"And you know . . . whoever . . . didn't find it in all this mess because . . . you've already been through all of them."

Rosie nodded.

"And in the mattress," Cal said. "And box springs."

Rosie's face took on an expression that could have been a faint smile.

"Little bit of Mister Rhodes in you, after all." She motioned toward the bedroom. "Know most of his hidey places. Checked 'emall. Most likely in there."

"This is where 'we' comes in?"

"Somebody besides us is after your daddy's papers. They'll come again. You don't want to find that will first?"

Cal hesitated, not eager to go back in the bedroom.

"Where, then, do you think?" It was odd, asking her advice, but if she was sincere about helping him, Cal would be foolish not to accept.

"He stashed things where it looked like they weren't," Rosie said. "Prob'ly staring right at it. Or past it."

Rosie stepped to the master bedroom and stopped.

"Burned that bed, didn't you?" she said. "Dump smoke this morning was you."

"Not intentionally."

"Folks'll know it was you. No secrets at the dump. None."

"That's a problem?"

"That'll rile Rafe Marquette," she said. "You don't wanna rile Rafe."

Cal started to argue, stopped himself.

Rosie circled the bedroom, sliding her fingers across the nightstand, the window ledge, pressing on the edge of the closet door. After a moment of watching her, Cal upended the nearest storage bin, looking for any kind of envelope.

They dismantled the bedroom but found no will.

"Okay, so we know where it's *not*," Cal said. He glanced at his watch. Eleven o'clock. He needed to call Kat. And find Cobia. "Rosie, were you serious about staying here if I have to be gone?"

She nodded once.

"I need to run into town, make a phone call. Then track down Jack Cobia."

"I'll be here." She tensed at Cobia's name.

Cal pushed the Thing across the gravel, popped the clutch, and rumbled up the road, mentally absorbing what had just happened. Rosie had gone from being a thorn in his side to an ad hoc ally. Why? He would ask Cobia about her and Rhodes.

Sandy Bottoms' Beach Resort was three stories of bright pink stucco and teal balconies that ran in a long wall between the west coast road and the sea. Tall palm trees lined the stone walkway running the building's length. In the center an arch rose fifteen feet high to form a breezeway. There, double glass doors led into the resort lobby. Cal pulled into the parking area and turned off the ignition. The engine kept running, chattering for ten, fifteen seconds before it finally died. Resort guests walking past swatted at the blue smoke, pulled their shirt collars up over their noses and mouths.

Cal pulled his phone out, pleased to see the bars of a strong wireless network. He dropped into a wide, padded wicker chair in the breezeway and dialed Kat's number. A series of high-pitched tones squealed from the phone. Then a computerized

British voice said, "The number you have dialed cannot be accessed on this cellular network." Cal scowled at the phone, dialed again, holding it away from his ear this time. The computer voice repeated its message.

He walked into the lobby, paused as the air conditioning washed over him. A bored, red-haired receptionist gave him a halfhearted smile from behind the counter. A nametag identified her as 'Dusty Goby.' Cal wondered if that was her name or a description. Below that, in smaller type, was 'Ireland.'

"There something I need to do to call the U.S.?" Cal waved his phone at her.

"Oh. Right! Mobiles on U.S. carriers can be dodgy." She pursed her lips to one side, weighing whether to say more. Her eyes crinkled. "If you need, you can use the courtesy computer. It's *ancient*, but it'll connect to the real world."

She waved her hand toward an alcove off the reception desk, doorway blocked by a curtain of multi-colored bamboo beads. Cal pushed the beads aside. Their clatter sounded like a soft rain. Inside was an older desktop computer on a rickety table. On the screen was the icon for an online chat program. Perfect. Cal clicked on it, typed Kat's number, and a moment later Kat's face appeared on the screen.

"The store let you use its computer, too?" She had the annoyed look Cal knew too well. Her eyes slid to the still-swaying beads beside him. A suspicious look crept across her face. "Where are you?"

"Sandy Bottoms'."

"You've got what?"

"A hotel. Kat, my phone won't work here."

"Convenient."

"No, not at all. Look, I may have to be down here longer than a few days. There's loose ends to tie up and . . ."

Feet scuffled in the lobby beyond the beaded curtain. Was eavesdropping the island-wide hobby?

There was no way Cal could tell Kat he couldn't find Rhodes' will, not here where anyone could be listening. He motioned for Kat to wait, then stepped to the reception desk and borrowed a pen and yellow legal pad. Back in the computer alcove he scribbled:

'*People listening. Don't respond out loud.*'

Kat looked dubious, but gave him a nod.

"Things down here don't work as smoothly as they do in Naperville," Cal said. He scribbled again, held up the pad:

'*Can't find will. No will = govt gets all.*'

Kat's face hardened.

"Cal, do what you need to sell that place. Hire someone. Just get back up here. I'm not babysitting your damn shop much longer. I have a life. And all this ticking and chiming is making me bug-nutty."

"I always found them comforting." It was the wrong thing to say.

"Cal Batten, I'm doing you a favor. I'll shutter this place and let it rot!"

There was a noise from beyond the bamboo curtain, feet scuffing soft across linoleum. Was it just Dusty the receptionist, or were there others, too?

A clattering came from the computer speaker, as if someone were rummaging through the cabinet behind Kat.

"What's that noise?" Cal said.

"Oh . . . that's . . . the dog. He knocked over some stuff. Gotta go."

The screen went blank. Cal leaned back, exhaled. He had known there would be hell to pay, but it couldn't be helped. It wasn't like he was lounging on the beach sipping piña coladas.

He stepped from the alcove, set the bamboo beads clattering again. Dusty made a point of looking away from him, bored eyes staring at a computer screen. She had heard everything, Cal was sure. He needed to find Cobia.

57

"The bar?" Cal stepped to the reception desk.

Dusty pointed her pen out the glass doors and on through the breezeway, a hint of a smile now.

Cal walked out onto a wide limestone verandah, its tiles filled with fossilized seashells. Across the verandah, by a pool, was the outdoor bar. At the far end Antonio was talking with Jerrod.

"Trouble back home calls for a drink!" Antonio waved him over. "Won't make the wife happy, but it'll do the trick for you."

"So that was you in the lobby."

"Been right here." Antonio chuckled.

Jerrod and the bartender nodded.

"The Sight, y'know." Antonio tapped the side of his head. "And people do wonder what you gonna do with that place. Keep telling 'em you're staying."

"Your Sight's still off," Cal said. "And that car won't start again."

"I'll send Dermott by. He's the best."

"If your wife came down, she'd be hooked," Jerrod said.

"She's not his missus anymore . . ." Antonio said. "And she's not coming to Blacktip."

Jerrod looked as if he might say something, but didn't.

"Right on both counts." Cal wouldn't encourage Antonio by asking how he knew about the divorce. "Kat's not . . . outdoorsy."

"She don't like outdoors, she sure won't like that mersquatch," Antonio said.

"She'd get a good laugh from it, though," Cal said.

Marina wandered across the verandah. She shot Cal a dark look as she passed.

"Ouch," Jerrod said. "That for you?"

"I . . . we had a misunderstanding," Cal said.

"You work fast," Jerrod laughed.

Jerrod and Antonio exchanged looks, then grinned. Cal was about to ask what the joke was when Cobia stepped onto the deck, nodded a greeting, and took a seat at one of the umbrella-covered tables away from the bar.

"We're not through here," Cal said to Antonio and Jerrod.

He joined Cobia in the relative privacy of the far table.

"No sign of Rhodes' will on file over on Tiperon." Cobia spoke low so the others at the bar couldn't hear him. "You have any luck?"

"No. But I have an odd question," Cal said. "Did Rhodes and Rosie Bottoms have any . . . legal standing?"

"Didn't know they had anything but a professional standing." Cobia gave Cal a wary look. "Why?"

"If she . . . stayed over . . . occasionally, would they have a common law marriage?"

"No such thing in the Tiperons. You worried she wants the house?"

"I'm worried she has a hidden agenda."

"Why not ask her?"

"Ask Rosie a direct question?" Cal laughed. "She says she's looking out for me, but . . . ."

"Well, there you go. You need all the help you can get. And Rosie's not one to spill secrets. Or share her business with anyone. You have thirty days from the date of death. Clock's ticking."

Cal nodded, excused himself. At the bar, Antonio elbowed Jerrod. Cal shot a warning look at both of them. They grinned back, too quickly, in unison. Cal didn't have time to deal with them. He needed to get back to the house, keep searching.

A passing resort guest helped him get the Thing rolling across the parking lot. Cal popped the clutch, and the car spat out a gout of blue smoke and clattered to life. He drove back to Batten's Down, mentally running through non-obvious places the will might be.

Rosie stood in the doorway, hands on her hips, when he arrived at the house, apparently still angry at him for burning

Rhodes' bed. A bed. He had forgotten to check to see if Peachy's store had a bed. And he didn't want to drive back in to find out.

"Rosie, does Peachy stock beds?"

Rosie shook her head, brushed past Cal and went to the lean-to. She came back moments later with arms full of what looked like a tangled fishing net in reds and blues and yellows. She pressed it into his hands.

"You hang that hammock in the bedroom for now." She continued on inside the house.

Cal stared at her retreating back, not sure if she was joking. Rosie closed the door, leaving him gaping in the sunlight, hands full of wadded hammock.

He stepped back to the lean-to, looking for bolts, screws, a drill. He had to install the hasp on the front door anyway. Two big bolts to hang a hammock from wouldn't be that much more work. But first he would secure the front door.

He installed the hasp in a few minutes. He latched it, then slipped the pink bike chain-lock through it. The flimsy lock looked silly, but it held. In the bedroom Cal drilled eye-bolt sized holes in the walls and strung up the hammock. It wasn't pretty, but it would do.

Cal spent the rest of the afternoon searching the house with no luck. At dusk, with Rosie gone, he sat by the catapult, rubbed his temples to make a headache go away.

After a quick dinner, he turned off the lights, climbed into the hammock, and closed his eyes. The netting creaked, adjusting to his weight. Yes. Much more comfortable. The rooster crowed. Cal cursed, wrapped the pillow around his ears. He swayed in the darkness, his only visible reference the starry sky through the window.

The window frame shifted. There was a lurch, a sinking sensation, then Cal crashed to the floor, eye-bolt clattering beside his head. Wincing, Cal knelt, fumbled for the light switch. The bolt had pulled out of the crumbling wall stud. Great. He shuffled back to the living room, stretched out in the armchair. He drifted off to sleep with the scent of the burning mosquito coil beside him.

5

C al's shark-filled dreams gave way to the sound of dragging feet. He opened his eyes. Complete darkness. No sounds but the tree frogs' high, reedy '*skreee.*' Cal relaxed. The scrapuffling sound came again, near the window. Feet, or paws, on dirt. Not a dream. Then a low grumbling, as if a bear was rooting under the window. He would find out what, or who, was making the noises.

Cal felt for the big flashlight on the floor next to the chair. His other hand found Rhodes' golf club leaning against the bookcase. The scuffling was under the front widow now. Cal tip-toed to the front door. In one movement he flung the door open, clicked on the light and leaped outside, pitching wedge held high overhead to whack whoever, whatever might be there.

There was no one. Cal spun, shone the light the opposite direction. Still nothing. A faint scuffling came from the house's sea side. He charged around the house, yelling. He rounded the pointed end. His light beam caught a fist-sized land crab scuttling along the foundation. Focused on the crab, he caught his bare foot on a rock and fell face first onto the ground. The flashlight rolled away, its beam shining across the gravel and along the back of the house. Chickens clucked, scuffled away through the sea grapes.

Something larger rustled in the dry leaves. Cal scrambled to his feet, snatched up the golf club, raised it like a baseball bat.

The rustling stopped. The back of the house was as deserted as the front.

He picked up the light, hobbled to the spot outside the window. The dirt along the house's foundation had been scraped away by more than a crab, revealing the rough limestone ironshore the house was built on. Something had been trying to burrow under the house? What would try to dig through rock? Whatever it was, it had cleared dirt from a long swath, as if looking for a gap between the foundation and the ground.

Cal stepped back inside, hands and knees stinging, flipped on the lights to make sure whatever hadn't snuck inside. All seemed fine. Blood welled up across his knees and palms. His left big toe left blood spots on the floor. Cal washed the grit away with bottled water, wrapped his toe with a paper towel, then stretched out in the chair again, alert for any sounds outside.

A faint clanking outside woke him at sunrise. His back ached. The heels of both hurt hands burned. He moved the blanket, winced at it scraping across his knees. Cal stood, grimaced. Dried blood crusted dark on his bandaged toe and the skin not covered in blood was a faint purple. The fall, his mad charge around the house, came flooding back. The island was getting to him. He was an idiot, chasing non-existent boojums.

Cal stepped outside to recheck the foundation in daylight. A rooster and three chickens strutted past, clucking at him. A clanking again, louder now, from the lean-to. Cal froze, heart racing. Then scuffling feet. And a grunt. Something metal clattered in the lean-to. He hadn't imagined it. Whatever was there, it was big. Cal pushed Antonio's mersquatch stories aside, grabbed the pitching wedge from inside the door, and crept to the lean-to.

More banging and grunting. Cal peeked around the corner. Something big, shaggy was hunched over the Thing's open hood, growling. It was on its hind legs, shoulders half-again as wide as Cal's. Each bare foot was the size of both Cal's feet together. It lifted a paw, or hand, wrapped around a power cable. Whatever it was, it was tearing apart the car's engine. Cal inched forward, heart booming, barely daring to breathe, wedge held high.

The figure straightened to its full height. Shaggy black hair hung to its shoulders. Biceps bulged from a sleeveless shirt. It turned, stared down at Cal in the half light. Stepped toward him.

"You Cal, I guess," the thing rumbled. "I'm Dermott. Prob'ly don't remember me. 'Tonio said you got car trouble."

"Dermott! Yes! Good!" Cal exhaled, lowered the club. Antonio had mentioned Dermott. "You've . . . grown."

"Stopped on my way to work." Dermott waved a socket wrench toward a big red dump truck under the roadside trees, 'Skerritt Construction' blazoned in yellow letters across its side. "Old Mister Rhodes' buggy can be cranky, 'specially when she's not run for a bit. Swapped out a starter wire for you. Cleaned up your solenoid post, too."

"Dermott, were you out here working last night by any chance?"

"Just got here. Soon as there was light." He gave Cal an odd look.

"Would Antonio have been here, then?"

"No reason I know of." Dermott's eyes went to Cal's bloody foot, to his knees, then to the golf club. "What happen last night?"

"Nothing important." He wasn't about to ask about big animals. "Like some coffee?"

Dermott shook his mane.

"Got to get to work."

"Well, what do I owe you?"

"We settle up later." Dermott headed for his truck. "Beers at the Ballyhoo be fine."

Cal watched him go, wondering what 'the Ballyhoo' was.

He walked to the kitchen, wincing with every step. The yellow sink water would do more harm than good, and bottled water was expensive. Salt water was supposed to cure cuts. And a beach walk might unkink his back. Cal started the coffee maker, fastened his bike lock across the door and headed for the Spider Bight beach.

A hundred yards north of Batten's Down an ironshore arm jutted out into the sea, creating a broad, sheltered cove behind it with a broad sand beach. The sun above the eastern horizon tinted the flat cove water a dull copper. Waves pounded on the ironshore breakwater, growling as they rushed through the eroded hollows. Was that the sound he kept hearing? There was the low, voice-like wail again, too, of wind in the bluff's caves.

Cal hesitated at the water's edge. Would sharks come into knee-deep water? He had never heard of them doing that. And with the water so clear, and the sand bottom so white, he would be able to see them from a long way off if they did. He waded in, winced as the salt water lapped over his toe, then his knees. He gritted his teeth, lowered his hands into the water, scrubbed the scrapes. It stung, but that was part of the healing. Cal relaxed in the calm water. For all the aggravation on Blacktip, the island had its moments.

He waded the quarter mile to the far end of the cove, letting the seawater wash his wounds. On shore, coconut palms filled the space between the beach and the road in neat lines, rings of dried coconuts around the base of each trunk like tiny skulls. A coconut farm gone to nature? He would ask next time he was in town. He laughed at himself, thinking of the resort strip as 'town.'

Cal's stomach grumbled. Breakfast would be good. He waded back toward the house. At the end of the cove where the sand gave way to ironshore, he left the water and walked up the beach. From this angle, Batten's Down looked like a giant bean with windows set into it. It was also obvious the bulge on the end was off center, its farthest point set forward, toward the front of the house. A construction necessity, maybe. Asymmetrical, but not totally unappealing from here.

He walked closer and the stripes became visible. Then the rooftop laces. Cal rounded the house's north point, had a fresh view of its face, and the pretty illusion dissipated. It was the same ugly house. Cal didn't remember Rhodes even liking football. Cal pushed open the front door, paused. The open bicycle lock dangled from the hasp. He had locked the door before he went on his walk. He stepped inside.

What order he and Rosie had established the day before was gone. The neatly-stacked manila folders were strewn across the main room, scattered over the tables, the couch, the floor. Books had been pulled from the bookcase, left on the floor where they landed. The couch, the armchair, the coffee table had all been moved. Cal stepped back outside, glanced to either side of the doorway. No sign of Rosie's bike. This wasn't her doing, then. And no animal, mythical or otherwise, would have taken the time to pick a lock.

Cal, jaw clenched, studied the mess. He had been gone less than an hour, and in that time someone had rifled through the place. He stepped to the bedroom. That seemed undisturbed. Whoever it was had been in a hurry. And didn't care that Cal knew he, or she, had been there. Anger rising, Cal stepped outside, made sure the door was bicycle-locked shut and stormed to the Maples' house. He needed Rafe Marquette, now, before the intruder got too far. He could use the VHF, but then the entire island would know. If the Maples' satellite phone wouldn't work, he would drive into town, find the constable and bring him back.

There was no answer when Cal banged on the Maples' door. The Land Rover was not under the deck. They had left early, then. Fine. Batten's Down was secured now. He would drive into town, find Rafe. And he hadn't touched anything inside the house, so Rafe should have no trouble getting fingerprints.

Cal picked his way back to Batten's Down, toe throbbing and knees aching. Stopped. The door stood open, bike chain again hanging unlocked from the hasp. Cal bounded inside to confront the intruder.

Rosie was shoving books back in the bookcase. She glared at Cal.

"Said the will's not in here," she said.

"How'd you get in?"

"*Phffft.* Those locks open easy. Used to play at who could pick one fastest when we were little. Waste of money, y'know." Her glare hadn't subsided. "Why you tear this place up?"

"*I* didn't. I went for a walk and it was like this when I got back."

Her glare faded.

"Somebody watching for you to go. Watching for you to come back."

A chill shot down Cal's spine. He hadn't thought of that, of someone lurking in the underbrush, or up the bluff, spying on him, waiting for him to leave.

"So, where's that leave us? We can't stand guard twenty-four, seven. And the lock . . . doesn't."

"I'll think on it." She looked at his scraped knees. "What'd you do to yourself?"

"I fell. Last night. Outside." He glanced toward the window. Imagined or not, the sounds had seemed real. "Are there any animals besides chickens and iguanas on the island?"

She gave him an odd look, as if she knew exactly what had happened.

"Last night it sounded like there was something outside the window, scratching and rooting around and . . . Probably just waves on the ironshore."

"Prob'ly." Rosie watched him, face expressionless.

Cal switched tacks.

"Is there a trick to getting the water to run clear?" He waved toward the kitchen.

"Cistern needs cleaning." She shrugged. "Messy job. I see if I can find someone willing to climb down in there. But right now we got to clear all this mess out the way so we can see where to look next."

She gathered an armful of folders and carried them to the front door. Cal stuffed papers back into folders and made a stack of his own, forced himself not to organize them into categories as he went. If someone could get in at-will, anything he took the time to organize would get strewn around again. Instead, he made his stacks as even as he could, arranged them square with the wall when he set them down.

Rosie, with an occasional glance at Cal, piled papers in ragged mounds as quickly as she could. Soon her rough stacks towered over Cal's few orderly ones. Cal's eye twitched.

"You've still found no cash, no computer, anything like that?" Cal said.

Rosie straightened, glared at him.

"You think I found something and kept it to myself?"

Cal held her gaze for a moment, then looked away.

By midday the place was in as good a shape as it was likely to get until Cal hauled all the junk away. He retrieved the drill from the lean-to, found a more solid beam and hung the hammock with a larger eye-bolt. Rosie watched, with a dubious look, as Cal filled the hammock with all the books from the living room.

"It gets a weight test before I get back in it." Cal rapped on the wall. "Make sure that anchor's solid."

A knocking echoed the front room. Someone was knocking on the door? No one had ever knocked on the door. People just let themselves in. Or broke in. Curious, Cal swung the door open. Rich Skerritt stood there, sweating in the sun, button-down shirt dark, wet across the stomach.

"I come in?" Skerritt blinked, shaded his eyes.

"Sure." Cal motioned him inside. "What brings you way out here?"

"I was driving past some property down this way and thought I'd stop by." Skerritt blinked, eyes adjusting to the dimmer light inside. "Ol' Rhodes never did hold with air conditioning, did he?"

"Tell me about it. Something to drink?"

"Oh, no. I can't stay long." A quick glance took in all the room. His gaze stopped on Rosie, watching him from beside the bookcase. "Rosie." His voice tensed. "Always good to see you."

Rosie crossed her arms, said nothing. Cal smiled inwardly. Good. He wasn't the only one who didn't care for Skerritt.

"Rosie, you mind stepping out for a few minutes?" Skerritt said. "Give me and Cal here a bit of privacy?"

Rosie stepped past them and out the door, eyes on Skerritt. A moment later the sound of a broom scraping across bare dirt came in through the open window.

"I can see why you're in a hurry to get out," Skerritt said.

"Get out?"

"Be rid of this rat trap."

"It's not so bad once you—"

"Cal, you want to sell. I'm on the lookout for property over this way, near the Spider Bight beach and Rosalita Flats where— this doesn't leave this room, now—I can build an offshoot boutique resort. A mini Eagle Ray Cove, if you will."

"Seems like a small piece of land to build a resort on." What was Skerritt really after?

"I'd have to buy up the surrounding lots, but this'd be a start. A big start." Skerritt studied Cal, as if wondering how much information to share. "Thing is, as soon as folks realize what I'm planning, their asking prices'll go up. Can't be helped. But if I can get this piece for a reasonable, get-Cal-Batten-back-home-with-a-fair-profit-in-his-pocket price, it'll offset all that."

"You came here to lowball me?" Cal said it as casually as he could, as if the property deed were in-hand and in his name.

"I came here to help you out of a sticky situation. This place isn't worth much as-is. And word is you may not be Rhodes' son."

"I brought all the papers to prove that." Cal was starting to dislike Skerritt.

"I hope you did. For your sake." A dismissive glance around the room. Skerritt's voice dropped lower, smoother, as if he were talking to an old friend. "Any buyer'll be tearing it down and rebuilding. They'll have to figure that demo and rebuild cost into their offer. You could be waiting a long time to sell. This way, though, it's win-win. You have money, your . . . wife . . . is happy, and I have a beachhead."

"I'm still waiting for the official property valuation." Cal trusted Skerrit less with every word.

"I can give you a good ballpark number, off last year's valuation."

"I don't doubt that, but once I get the current number, I'll be happy to revisit."

"I wouldn't wait too long," Skerritt said. "Sounds like you got pressure to get back home quick as you can."

Skerritt left. The door had barely closed when Rosie came back in, looking over her shoulder at Skerritt's car.

"Mister Rich smells blood," she said.

"He has a good nose." Did everyone on the island know about Cal and Kat?

"Careful he don't get you to sell out like that."

"You heard all that?"

"Window was open."

"So back to our hunt."

"I got to leave for a little bit," Rosie said. "Go into town."

"What, just like that?"

"Got to make some calls. About your visitor. Be back later. Or in the morning, more like."

She threw her bag over her shoulders and left. If she didn't come back today, he would have to wait until tomorrow to talk to Cobia. And check in with Kat. Hopefully keep her watching his shop. He had to find Rhodes' will.

Cal pulled out his grid-covered floorplan, circled the inside of the house. If there were hidden spaces big enough for a computer or strongbox, Rhodes had disguised them well. There was no attic or crawl space or basement. He paced off each room inside, then again outside, hoping to find some unaccounted-for space that might be a hidden nook or cubby. His stiff knees made his steps uneven. He needed a tape measure to know for sure, but there seemed to be no extra area.

He checked the hammock. It was holding, books bulging out of it. A bit of paper stuck out from a biology text. A hand-drawn map of the island. Cal started to set it aside, then looked closer. Straight-edged across the southern end of the island, a loose grid of thin lines at random angles had been penciled in, like headings on an orienteering chart, their intersections marked with small dots. The dots were all in the island's interior, up on the bluff. Lot lines? Had Rhodes bought up land, waited for values to take off? Was that what Skerritt was sniffing around about?

Steps shuffled outside the door. His nighttime visitor was back? Cal slipped the map on top of the bookcase and flung open the door.

Rafe Marquette filled the doorway, arms crossed.

Cal blinked, surprised. Had Rosie run into Rafe, told him what happened?

"Good! You're here!" Cal said. "Someone broke in this morning."

"You know anything about a burning at the dump yesterday?"

"Burning? Someone broke in my house."

71

"Anything missing?" Rafe sounded annoyed.

"How on Earth would you tell? Things were moved all over the place, though."

"That's not illegal. Burning is, except by dump personnel. Everybody on-island knows that." Rafe looked past Cal, his eyes scanning the room. "No fire department here. A fire gets out of control, the whole island could go up."

"You think I burned something?" Rafe had suspicions, but he had no proof.

"Somebody burned a *bed* yesterday." Rafe's eyes cut to the bedroom door.

"Bed burnings worse than regular burnings?"

"They burn fast. That's dangerous." Marquette frowned down at Cal. "Everybody here knows that, too. And you're the only one who'd want to get rid of a bed."

There was no way to deny it. Batten's Down was probably the only bedless house on the island.

"Okay, look, I hauled Rhodes' bed there yesterday. He died in it. I couldn't sleep on it. I didn't even want to be in the house with it," Cal said. "But I didn't know it'd catch fire."

"Ignorance's no excuse. That's a fine and possible jail time. I'm in my rights to arrest you. I ought to arrest you . . ."

"Rafe, I didn't know. And no harm came of it."

Marquette glared at Cal. Then his eyes went back to the living room, tracked over the folders piled by the door.

"Got more of your daddy's things you gonna burn?" His voice took on a more menacing tone.

"No! And anything I take to the dump I'll make sure it's far away from any flames." Cal would leave all the crap in the house and the dump far behind once he found the will.

"Best just leave it be." Rafe looked like he wanted to come inside, but Cal didn't budge. "This house, the stuff in it, got historical significance."

"This place? It's a junk yard. Rich Skerritt wants to tear it down."

Rafe stared at Cal for a long moment.

"This house has value." The constable pointed a warning finger at Cal's chest. "You be cautious. Things going on you don't understand."

"I haven't understood a thing since I set foot on this crazy island."

"Rumor is you don't have the will." Rafe watched Cal's face for a reaction.

"The will's being handled according to Rhodes' instructions." Cal kept his face neutral. Was Rafe fishing, or were there truly no secrets on this island?

Rafe gave Cal another dark look.

"You want to stay away from M'rina, too," he said.

"Marina? What's she got to do with anything?" Did Rafe think Marina was the mystery trespasser? And that's why he wasn't investigating that? She *had* been overly interested in the house.

Rafe's eyes bored into Cal's.

"I'll give her a wide berth." It was like they were twelve again, fighting for Marina's attention. That was the last thing Cal needed now. "I guarantee."

Rafe nodded once, then walked back to the police truck.

Cal closed the door, studied the room. Yes, there was more going on with this house than the missing will. But what? He pulled the map from the top of the bookcase, studied the pencil lines again. Did this have anything to do with Rafe's warning? With Skerritt's over-eagerness? Or was it just more of Rhodes' craziness?

He stared at the empty bookcase, the wall beside it covered in nautical charts and the reading nook with its skylight. A thought shot through him, an electric shock. Beyond the nook was the northern end of the giant football. Could it be that simple?

Cal rummaged through the lean-to, found a rusted tape measure. He measured out the reading nook's exact depth, then measured outside to the bulge's farthest point. Sure enough, it extended nearly two feet beyond the inner wall. Plenty of space to hide a box of papers or cash or a laptop. He measured the house's southern tip, found another two feet of unaccounted-for space beyond the stove's inset. Cal tapped on the outer wall. It sounded solid. But if the secret space was small, there would be plenty of room for insulation.

This was Rhodes' secret, then. And why he had modified the house into such an odd shape. Cal went back inside, tapped on the end walls. They sounded as solid as the others, but that could be from added insulation. Rhodes' valuables, his personal papers, they all had to be stashed in either end of the house.

But how to get into them? Rhodes would have built a way to access the spaces without demolishing the wall every time. Cal ran his hands over the nook's drywall, the kitchen's tile, feeling for any hidden handle or catch. No luck. He went outside, checked the exterior walls. There was no hint of an opening or access point or even an indication the point was hollow.

The sun was dropping behind the bluff then. The mosquitos were starting to swarm. Cal swatted them away, went back inside and studied the nook's wall. He didn't want to demolish a wall. Or destroy what was hidden inside while trying to get it.

Cal found a pad of paper, a pencil, a ruler and sat at the dining room table. If he could sketch an accurate Batten's Down floor plan, he would be able to *see* the dead space behind the walls and better grasp the puzzle. In half an hour he had a to-scale map of the house, with the ends free-handed as accurately as his half-remembered high school calculus allowed.

He stood the books back in the bookcase, eyeing the reading nook beside it for any clues, anything that might be a latch or a panel or a door. His brain was foggy after two nights of marginal sleep, otherwise he would be able to sort this out.

The house vibrated from a big wave slamming the headland. The wind moaned in the sea caves. In his hand were the shark books. Cal shuddered, slipped them back onto their shelf. If he hadn't figured out how to access the spaces by morning, should he tell Rosie about them, let her have a try? No. He would keep this to himself until he knew more about her motives.

6

"Caaaal! Caaaal!"

Cal jolted awake.

His name. Screeched. Piercing. He clawed at the hammock webbing, rolled, dropped to the floor, heart racing. A fire? A murder? Someone sprawled in a pool of blood?

"I found it! Cal! I found it!"

Rosie was balanced on a chair by the bedroom door, waving a yellowed legal-sized envelope above her head. Something, a thin sheet of wood, maybe, extended from the top of the door.

"Door top didn't sound quite hollow yesterday. Worried at me overnight. Climbed up just now, saw the slot." Rosie was grinning at her own cleverness. "Your daddy built him a mini-drawer in the door top."

"It's barely sunrise . . ." Cal rubbed his eyes, stepped closer, made out the frame of the insert that slipped vertically into the door's top edge.

"Came to me sleeping. Had to come check soon as I could."

"And you just let yourself in?"

"It's the will."

Cal snatched the envelope from Rosie. The clasp was already undone. He glanced at her.

"Had to see what it was," she said.

Cal scanned the papers inside. A thick stack of papers whose opening statement was, 'The last will and testament of Rhodes Sayle Batten . . .' Underneath the will was the property deed.

76

Relief washed through Cal. He thumbed through the will. What few possessions Rhodes had went to Cal's mother and several other relatives Cal had never met. The house and property, though, were left solely to Cal. The place was legally his to sell.

"What you gonna do with it?" Rosie's brown eyes bored into him.

Cal paused. He hadn't thought of how he would file the will, or where. There was no courthouse on Blacktip. He would have to fly to Tiperon. Find the probate court. Figure out what legal hoops he needed to jump through.

Or he could get Jack Cobia to handle it. Cobia knew the ropes, had all the contacts. And would certainly have a safe to keep the papers in until he submitted them.

"I'll take this to Jack Cobia," Cal said.

"Mister Jack, he's a funny one." Rosie's face was expressionless. "Lots of things go in that office never come back out."

"You mean I can't trust him?" A twinge of panic at that. Cal had confided in Cobia. And needed him to navigate the details of selling the place.

"I suppose he *is* the one to get it to court for you, make it legal," Rosie said.

"And handle the sale."

"Can't sell this house."

"You just watch me."

Cal would copy the papers at Sandy Bottoms, give the originals to Cobia and let him take things from there, making sure Cobia knew Cal had copies. He needed a secure place to store the copies.

"Rosie, do any of the island resorts have safes?"

Rosie gave him a curious look.

"Eagle Ray Cove, Sandy Bottoms got lock boxes in the lobby." She shook her head. "Jimmy 'emopen with a screwdriver, though." A long pause. "Seen it done."

"Do you know of anyone who has a safe?"

"People got safes don't usually talk about 'em."

"The Maples, maybe?"

"Maybe."

Rosie's face was noncommittal. He would check with the Maples after he got back.

"I'm going to Sandy Bottoms to find Jack," he said. "And make sure word gets out we found this so people'll stop breaking in the place."

Rosie shrugged, as if none of it concerned her anymore.

"Thanks, Rosie. For finding the papers, for letting me know, for . . . well, for having my back."

"Can't sell this place."

Cal ignored her, made a quick breakfast. Rosie went back to her never-ending dusting. At the table he dropped the envelope on top of his floorplan sketch, hoping Rosie hadn't seen the drawing. She had found the will and turned it over to him, and he trusted her to a point, but not completely. He would take the sketch with him when he went to meet Cobia.

Will in hand, Cal stepped outside, scanned the bluff face for any sign of anyone lurking there. Hopefully he wouldn't have to worry about that anymore.

The day seemed brighter, the island less dirty as Cal drove up the coast and past the reeking booby pond, buzzing with energy he hadn't felt since long before Blacktip. All was right with the world. He had a free claim to the property. He could sell it and go home. His time on this crazy little island was coming to an end, his clock shop would be solvent and his bank account would be fatter.

At Sandy Bottoms, Cal asked Dusty to photocopy the original papers. There was no sign of Cobia at the bar.

"He might be down at Eagle Ray Cove," Dusty said. "He needed to talk to Jerrod about something."

Cal thanked her and headed for his car. A door opposite the reception desk opened. Sandy Bottoms stepped out belly-first. He smiled at Cal.

"Just about to track you down. Saved me the trouble." His voice was the deep bass of the waves in the sea caves around Batten's Down. "Wanted to talk more about that place of yours."

"I'd be glad to, as soon as I know what it's worth," Cal said.

"That's easy enough to find. Cut you a check today if you want. Or you more of a cash man?"

"You keep that kind of cash lying around?" Was Bottoms seriously offering six figures in cash?

"I can get it. If need be. Know you want to get home."

"I'll . . . let you know after the place gets appraised. I'm off to talk to Jack Cobia now."

"Jack's a good one. Talked to him myself. You let him handle things, he'll get taken care of, too." Bottoms stepped closer, grabbed Cal's arm. "I can put down a retainer with you or Jack. Make sure I get first option."

"You have plans for it, then."

"Oh, just like to have a little place over that way. Quiet. Peaceful. Nice escape from the hubbub here." Bottoms waved his hand around the empty lobby, as if the place were Times Square.

"I'll let you know."

Cal pulled his arm from Bottoms' grip and walked to the car. He coaxed it to life and headed down the coast toward Eagle Ray Cove. Bottoms' explanation made less sense than Skerritt's, and both rang hollow. There was more to the house, the property, than met the eye. But what?

He passed Club Scuba Doo, its brightly-colored cottages clustered among sea-grape thickets, the sea flashing through the leaves. Five minutes farther on the trees thinned, revealing low, wooden bungalows on stilts spread throughout the grove. Cal pulled into a dirt parking lot in front of a single-story building marked 'Eagle Ray Cove Resort – Surface with A Smile!' When he asked about Cobia, the receptionist waved him toward the outdoor tiki bar.

Cobia sat at a table with Jerrod, empty plates in front of them.

"Thanks for breakfast, Jerrod," Cobia said.

"The Lord does provide."

Jerrod slapped Cal on the back and walked to the bar, shuffled through last night's receipts.

"Jerrod's still got the religious bug, but he's all right. Mostly." Cobia shook his head. "Manages this place now." He lifted a folder from the chair next to him, pulled out a sheet of paper and handed it to Cal. "That's the official valuation for your lot. House doesn't affect it, but . . ."

Cal studied the form, scanned down to the bold-faced figure at the bottom. He sat, looked at the number again to make sure he was seeing it right, then looked up at Cobia.

"Yep. Not saying you can *get* $2.5 for it, especially in a quick sale, but that's the sticker price." He eyed the folders in Cal's hands, raised an eyebrow.

Cal grabbed a stack of napkins from the bar, wiped off the tabletop to make sure it was dry then set the envelope in front of Cobia.

"The will. And deed. Found them this morning. Can you file them with the appropriate authorities?"

"Sure, sure," Cobia murmured. He flipped through the papers, skimming the contents.

"And we'll settle up on any fees once the place sells?"

"Mmmm." Cobia was focused on the papers.

At the bar, Antonio had taken a seat next to Jerrod, still tallying receipts. After a quick exchange, they both looked over to Cal and Cobia, then grinned at each other. Gossiping about the house? Had Cobia told Jerrod its value? About Cal's hunting for the will? Or was one of them the person who had been making animal noises at night? Or who had been rifling through the house? Both of them? No, he was being paranoid.

"What else you got there?" Cobia's question pulled Cal back.

"Copies." Cal waved the other papers at Cobia. "One set stays safe with me."

"It's only the originals that count, but a copy's good to refer back to." Cobia's eyes met Cal's, serious now. "Ah. Smart. Trust, but verify. And make sure I know it."

Cal eyed Cobia's empty mug. A beer with breakfast was island-standard, apparently.

"You want me to drop those at your office later?" Cal said.

"Ha! Worried I'm sauced?" Cobia downed the last of his beer. "Don't be. And I'm headed to the office right now, anyway."

Cal hesitated, uncertain for some reason he didn't understand. Rosie's warning echoed through his head. Could he trust a semi-stranger with something this big? Did he have a choice?

Marina crossed the deck, wearing a staff shirt and visor. She shot Cal a sour look without breaking stride. Jerrod waved her over and she joined him and Antonio by the cash register.

"You want to sell the place? The will's got to be proved before it's a legal document. Even if you weren't selling, that has to be done." Cobia waved the sheaf of documents at Cal.

"Right," Cal said. It was Cobia or no one. And this was no time for cold feet. "And I'll have copies if we need them."

"I'll hand-carry these over ASAP and keep you posted." Cobia laughed. "It'll take a couple weeks, at minimum."

"How does this process work? Exactly?"

"I file the will with the court. A judge looks it over, checks for liens, creditors, any money owed. If it's all good, he signs off and Bob's your uncle."

"Nothing else to it? That takes two weeks?"

"At least. More if it's challenged."

"Challenged? Rhodes left it to me. It says so right there."
Cal's heart rate quickened.

"There's still plenty of pirates in the Caribbean." Cobia gave
him a half-smile. "Especially in property proceedings. This seems
pretty cut-and-dried, but allow some extra time just in case."

"I need to get back to the States. If I give you my U.S. phone
number, can you let me know when everything clears?"

"You may want to hang here. Anyone contests anything,
you being on island—and occupying the house—strengthens
your claim."

"Seriously? Stay here for weeks? I have things I need to get
back to. Yesterday." He needed cash to stay, too.

Cobia started to say something, stopped himself. He
couldn't hide a smirk.

From the bar, Marina was studying Cal, eyes narrowed. She
was still angry Cal was selling the house. That he was talking to
Cobia about it. Antonio and Jerrod were grinning again, looking
like a pair of schoolboys hatching some practical joke. Winding
Marina up so she would tear into Cal. Or maybe the joke was on
Marina, if they had made up some phony buyer to annoy her.

"Staying'd give you time to clean out the place." Cobia's
voice brought him back. "Or you could relax and enjoy life on a
tropical island. People pay good money to do that kind of thing,
I hear."

"People who don't have businesses to get back to."

Cobia raised an eyebrow. So he, along with everyone else on
the island, knew Cal's shop *and* marriage were shot.

Cal left, keeping the bar between him and Marina and her
suspicious glare. Cobia would take care of the paperwork. He
didn't want to know what Antonio and Jerrod were stirring up.
He was sure to find out soon eventually, since this was Blacktip
Island, but with any luck he'd be gone first.

The Thing started after a few seconds of grumbling, though
it still left a blue cloud of burned oil behind it. Dermott had done

well, but he wasn't a miracle worker. Cal headed for Batten's Down. He wouldn't call Kat just yet. He needed to come up with a way to tell her all this that wouldn't piss her off. Plus, Cobia's suggestion to stay until the transfer was complete made sense. That would take some careful wording with Kat.

$2.5 million. Was it worth staying even longer to get that full price, or should he get what he could now and be done with it? What did he have to get back to? A failing business? A cramped apartment full of still-packed boxes? It *would* be nice to haul all the junk out of Batten's Down, give the inside a good cleaning. And with the will safely in Cobia's hands, Cal could throw out all the other junk papers in the house. Or leave them for the next owner.

Sandy Bottoms' talk of Cal getting home came back then. And Bottoms' lowball offer. He was too eager for Cal to sell. Rich Skerritt, too. Both were successful businessmen who didn't throw money around without good reason.

They knew, or thought they knew, there was something valuable hidden in the house. That had to be their angle. They knew there was more to the house than met the eye. Or they thought there might be, and it was worth buying to find out. He still needed to get into the house's dead spaces, see what they hid. Two weeks would give him time to do that. Without anyone knowing. Not even Rosie.

Cal turned onto the crossover road, sped up as the booby pond's stench hit him. He wouldn't miss that part of the island.

Back at the house, Cal found Rosie leafing through a handful of papers. Rhodes' haiku.

"You that bored?"

"Never saw this side of Mister Rhodes," she said. "All this about mouths and teeth and being buried. He was one of a kind, no denying that."

"I'm still not sure what that kind is."

Rosie gave him a sour look.

83

"Your daddy left this for you, and you're throwing it out?"

"It's gibberish."

"Only thing in this house with your name on it." Rosie shook her head, as if more disappointed by this than anything else Cal had done.

"Do whatever you want with it," Cal said.

Rosie beamed.

"You get things sorted with Mister Jack?"

"He says I should stay on island until everything's finalized." Cal would have to put his on-island expenses on his credit card and deal with the fallout later.

"He's not wrong." Rosie nodded, as if Cal had asked a question.

"It'll give me a chance to clear out a bunch of the junk in here, too. And out there." Cal waved a hand toward the junk-filled lean-to.

Rosie's lips tightened.

"Need to go through all this slow, make sure nothing worth something gets thrown out."

"Like wacky poetry?"

"That was close to your daddy's heart."

"Okay. How about anything I throw out is fair game for you. Take what you want, so long as you don't bring any of it back."

Rosie tucked the haiku folder under her arm.

"I'll set this aside for you."

"And you don't have to be here so much now, what with us finding the will. There's no reason for anyone to be breaking in anymore."

Rosie gave him a dubious look.

"Going for lunch now," she said. "Be back soon."

With Rosie gone, Cal spread his floorplan sketch on the table, eyed the reading nook. There was no door to hide a drawer, like where the will had been hidden. He pulled a chair to the bookcase, climbed up and inspected the top edges. There were no secret panels he could see.

A knocking came from behind him. Jerrod, standing in the open front doorway, knuckles on the door frame, a question on his face.

"Making sure there's no papers up here," Cal said.

"Because you wanna make sure you find every last one." Jerrod glanced around the room at the mounds of papers. "I wanted to see if Rhodes . . . you . . . have any kind of copper pipe I could use for a project."

"Take anything you want. Please." Cal climbed down, walked Jerrod to the lean-to to get him out of the house.

Jerrod grinned at the trebuchet.

"You get a chance to crank that puppy up?"

"I lean against it to watch the sunrise," Cal said. "No clue how to work it."

"You pull it back into firing position with the car," Jerrod said. "Then load a storage bin with sand, duct tape it shut and pop it in the sling. Let the cable go and WHOOSH! Physics takes take of the rest."

"Why would Rhodes build something like that?" Cal admired the precision of the catapult, but couldn't image the time, the cost, involved in building such a useless device.

"Your old man loved playing with numbers," Jerrod said. "He fiddled with arm length, projectile size, and counterbalance weight until he had it just the way he wanted it."

"To repel invaders?"

"To keep his brain active. And to scare the crap out of any boaters dumb enough to come too close. That thing swivels 180 degrees to cover the entire stretch of coast, and it's on gimbals so he could move it by himself."

"It actually works?" Cal had a mental image of Rhodes, dressed in Crusader garb, catapulting rocks at fishermen.

"Sure. Grab one of those bins and some duct tape."

Cal fetched an empty storage bin and the roll of silver tape from the lean-to. Jerrod scooped the bin full of sand, wrapped the lid on with tape.

"Pull the car down here," he said.

Cal eased the Thing to within a few feet of the trebuchet's base. Jerrod fitted a hook at the end of a long cable and slipped it into an eye bolt on the Thing's front bumper.

"Back up 'til I tell you to stop," he said.

"And how far will it throw that box?" Cal said.

"Roughly thirty pounds of sand, with that much counterweight, right at 200 yards," Jerrod said.

Intrigued, Cal backed the car up until the arm stood at a forty-five-degree angle and Jerrod hollered to stop. At this, he set the parking brake, then climbed out. Jerrod took the slack from the lines leading from the leather pouch to the throwing arm, heaved the bin into the pouch, then walked up to stand beside Cal.

"Yank the pin on that hook whenever you want," he said.

Cal pulled the pin. The cable flew from the bumper. The trebuchet's counterweight thundered down, shaking the ground and rocketing the throwing arm up, snatching the sling and bin backwards down the polished ramp. Then, as the arm reached vertical, the sling moved in a giant loop, arcing the bin high into the blue sky.

"WOOHOO!" Jerrod's whoop startled Cal.

The black bin hung for what seemed like minutes, a diminishing blot in the blue sky. Then it plunged with a resounding splash hundreds of feet offshore. It bobbed there, waves radiating out from it in white-capped rings.

"Rhodes said thirty-pound missiles worked the best." Jerrod laughed. "He stole dive weights from all the resorts for months to get the counterweight heavy enough."

"So that was the noise Frank Maples was complaining about?"

"Probably. If I lived next door and was trying to sleep, I'd be pretty hacked off."

"Rhodes used this a lot?"

"Only when fishing boats got too close at night."

"What's the draw for boats along here?"

"Deep-water drop off, maybe? Currents bring the big fish in? Whatever, Rhodes didn't like company."

"Why storage bins?"

"He could load them on site. And they usually wash up on shore later, so he could reuse them."

"Seems like a lot of work just to scare fishermen away."

Jerrod nodded, walked to the lean-to. After several minutes of rummaging in a box of scrap metal, he pulled out six twisted lengths of copper tubing and a motorcycle gas tank.

"These'll work great. Building a giant Cootie for the art show."

"Cootie?"

"You know, the kids' game, where you build the bug?"

"Of course. Hey, take that whole bin, if you want."

"I just need these bits. Thanks." Jerrod started toward a bright green scooter, then stopped. "Marina was asking about you. After you left."

"Marina was looking death at me."

"That's just her way. She keeps people at a distance at first. Give her a chance."

"Right." Was this the joke Antonio and Jerrod were cooking up? Getting Cal to approach Marina so they could watch her dismember him publicly? "If she starts a conversation, I'll be as polite as possible. From a distance. With a table or two between us. How's that?"

"Just a suggestion, brother."

Jerrod put the pipes in the scooter's basket and rode away.

Cal went back inside, spent the afternoon poring over the walls and floor at either end of the house, running his hands over ever surface searching for any irregularity that might indicate a hidden compartment. There was nothing out of the ordinary, though. Maybe the ends were merely decorative.

He stepped into the lab, his former bedroom, eyeing all the gizmos there. He could probably sell some of the gadgets if his money ran low. The underwater scooter alone had to be worth several hundred.

Cal looked through the window to the trebuchet. The functioning trebuchet that flung objects with a precise weight a precise distance. Then he looked to the sketched floorplan. No. Rhodes hadn't been one to build anything without a practical application. There had to be a way into the house's ends.

7

The next morning Cal set out to inspect the house ends from outside. He peered out the front window at the bluff, looking for anyone lurking there. The cliff face was pocked with plenty of hidey-holes, and there were vertical seams a person could wedge into, but he saw no sign of anyone.

He stepped outside and walked to the back of the house, out of sight of the cliff. He rapped his knuckles on the wooden planks of the house's northern point. The wall sounded as solid as it did from inside. He went to the lean-to, dug through jumbles of tools until he found a rubber mallet with an oversized head.

Cal carried it behind the house's end, smacked the wall with it. The boards gave a dull thud but sounded as solid as ever. He moved down a few feet, hit the wall harder. Then again. Still solid sounding. Bits of paint flew off the wood with each blow. Near the bulge's end, he swung the hammer as hard as he could. The wall boomed with the same solidity.

Should he try a different spot? A different angle? Cal checked the southern end. That blob was off center the same way as the one at the other end. By design rather than by mistake, then. To help the house withstand wind and waves? Or to hide hollow cavities? He needed to test the front of the house but couldn't if someone was watching from across the road.

"What you whacking with that hammer for?"

Cal jumped at Rosie's voice. He had been so caught up in testing the walls he hadn't heard her footsteps.

"Nothing . . . just tapping some planks back into place."

"Uh huh." Rosie gave him her suspicious look. "Regular hammer'd work better for that, y'know. Nails'll tear that rubber up."

"I was trying not to damage the planking." How much of his wall pounding had she seen? Had he given away the ends might be hollow?

"This house, she's built to last." Rosie kept eyeing him. "Your daddy was married to the idea of her standing through anything."

Cal's stomach did a slow roll. Married. Kat. He needed to call her. Tell her . . . something. He would have to pick those words carefully. That thought drove worries about Rosie from his mind.

"Rosie, I need to call Kat. About the will. You don't need to stay, but . . ."

"I'm gonna keep cleaning." She put her fists on her hips, fought back a smile. "And make sure that wall don't fall down."

"Fine. Fine. I'll be back soon as I can."

Rosie shrugged, went inside.

Cal quick stepped to the Thing, wrangled it to life, and clattered north for Sandy Bottoms, racking his brain for the best way to ask Kat to watch the clock shop a while longer.

The Sandy Bottoms lobby was full of people—tourists and locals alike. Perfect. Cal would make sure they all overheard him telling Kat about the will. The news would spread around the island twice before he got back to the house. *That* would put an end to the Batten's Down break-ins.

Dusty, behind the counter, was swamped with arriving guests. She waved Cal toward the computer nook. The beaded curtains clinked together behind Cal. He parked himself in front of the desktop. Moments later he was facing Kat on the screen, sitting in their, her, bedroom, hair disheveled, looking annoyed.

"Tell me you've sold the place," she said.

"Not yet." Why was she not at the shop? Cal raised his voice so it would carry into the lobby. "But the will's off to probate court. No more reason for anyone to ransack the house here."

"I don't care about that. When are you coming back?"

"That's the thing. Stuff takes longer to get done on this island," Cal said. "The guy handling things says I need to be on hand until things clear probate."

"So have The Guy handle everything. Double his commission."

"It's not that. If I'm not here, the property, everything, may get pirated." Cal took a deep breath, lowered his voice. "And I may need you to transfer some money down. Temporarily."

"Oh, no you don't!" Kat's lips tightened. A scuffling came from behind her. Something moved in the background.

"You have company?" Cal said.

"No." Kat snapped the word.

"That looked like Buddy Leshlce's head."

There was a long pause. Kat didn't move. Had he lost the internet connection? Then Kat spoke again.

"Buddy's not *company*. He's here to *fix* the dishwasher."

"Then what's he doing in the bedroom?"

"Really, Cal? He's showing me the broken part, the one that needs fixing. Replacing. Since I have to be talking with you."

"What needed to be replaced?"

"Don't change the subject." She shifted her computer screen so it faced the wall. "You need to get back up here and deal with *your* clocks and *your* bill collectors yourself. I'm not sending money and . . ." Her face hardened. "You know what, Cal? Take as long as you need. Have a little tropical vacation. The clocks'll get along just *fine* while you're gone."

Kat smoothed back her hair, then the screen went blank. Cal stared at the monitor for a moment, unsure of what had just happened. Was this one of her 'fines' that meant just the opposite? And what the hell was Buddy Leshcle doing upstairs in the bedroom?

Cal stepped from the alcove, set the hanging beads clattering. The lobby crowd had thinned, with only a few arriving tourists remaining. Behind the reception desk, Dusty made a show of not noticing Cal. She shuffled papers, intent, as if trying to memorize every detail of every page. She had heard everything. Good. That meant news of the will would be spreading already.

His mind went back to Kat. To her odd reactions. To Buddy. It was only 10 a.m., but Cal needed a drink.

At the near-empty bar, he ordered a rum and cola and settled into one of the high-legged chairs. Was he reading too much into his talk with Kat? Her messy hair, her not being at the shop, Buddy being in the bedroom . . . The divorce had come through, and she could do what she wanted. But the knot in his stomach wouldn't go away. Why had she been so defensive? And how long had she and Buddy been seeing each other? Pre-divorce? Cal downed the drink in two gulps, ordered another. Antonio crossed the deck, levered himself into the chair next to Cal's.

"Treasures sometimes wrapped as something else, y'know," Antonio said.

"Treasures?"

"Your missus. That house of yours. Good things ahead for you."

"Well, I can sell the house now, so you're partly right."

"No selling gonna happen." Antonio shook his head. "You and that place are part and parcel."

Cal sipped his drink. He had no idea why Antonio wanted him to stay so badly. And he didn't care.

Rafe Marquette wandered onto the patio, sat across the bar, and ordered a soda. He nodded a greeting to Cal and Antonio, then spoke low with the bartender.

"Any sign of that ol' mersquatch?" Antonio said.

"Haven't noticed anything unusual." Cal kept his tone casual. Whatever was happening around the house at night had to be some bizarre practical joke of Antonio's. He had probably been making the noises around the house to mess with Cal.

"He'll make himself known. Surprised he hasn't already. Right, Rafe?"

"Got no time for foolishness." Rafe shot them a dark look, went back to his conversation.

Marina stepped from the lobby, a scuba regulator system coiled in one hand, and headed across the patio towards the Sandy Bottoms dive shop. She gave Cal a sour look as she passed.

"She's got eyes on you, boy." Antonio was grinning now.

"Not good ones."

"No. You're all right. She's just making sure she can trust you. Give her time."

"She can have all the time she wants."

"Shame. She's nice, you know." Antonio paused, studied Cal. "Says nice things about you."

Cal shook his head, took another sip of his drink. First Jerrod, now Antonio. But between Cal staying on the island, the mersquatch, and Marina, Antonio was zero-for-three.

"I'm just saying." Antonio winked at him. "Got you on her radar. You wanna catch a mermaid, you gotta think like one."

"I don't want to catch anyone."

Marina walked back up from the dive shop without the regulator. She stopped to talk with Rafe.

Antonio elbowed Cal in the ribs. Was the man serious about Marina? She smiled as she talked to Rafe. Cal hadn't seen her smile since he had been back. He had forgotten how her face lit up when she did. She noticed Cal watching. The smile faded.

Cal gritted his teeth. He had apologized. He had been polite ever since. Her over-the-top hostility was getting old.

"So, no diving with her then?" Antonio's voice drew him back.

"No diving with anyone," Cal said. "Or snorkeling or swimming."

"Don't like water?"

"In a glass." The rum was kicking in nicely.

"You're a Blacktipper. Sea's in your blood."

"Not anymore."

"Something spooked you." Antonio nodded slow, as if remembering. "But I seen you diving. Just like I seen you staying here."

"I'm just not tempting fate."

Cal tuned out Antonio. His mind was on Kat and Buddy. At the house. On a Saturday morning. That meant the clock shop wasn't open. The shop didn't do a ton of business, but still . . .

"Time to kill on Blacktip. Got to at least try diving."

"'Kill.' Good word to use with 'diving,'" Cal said.

"Just need the right teacher, is all."

"That teacher doesn't exist."

Rafe and Marina were still talking.

"Hey, M'rina!" Antonio yelled across the patio. "Cal here doesn't think you're much of a scuba instructor."

"I never said . . ." Cal started.

"I could teach a monkey to dive." Marina squared her shoulders, eyes boring into Cal's.

"Put up or shut up, girl. Here's your monkey." Antonio jerked his thumb at Cal.

"That's not a monkey," Marina said. "That's a sow's ear."

"Hey!" Cal's anger surged. "You don't think I can?"

"Not in a million years."

"When do we start?" It sounded like his voice. And his lips had moved. His vocal cords, too. But it couldn't have been him.

Across the bar, Marina looked at him strangely. Rafe glared. What had he done? A smile crept across Marina's face, but not a smile that brightened anything.

"I'm off tomorrow." Her voice was too low, too sweet. Crocodile-tear sweet. "Nine o'clock. Eagle Ray Cove pool. It'll be *fun*."

Cal's bar stool seemed to tilt. How to get out of this? He could fake illness. Food poisoning, maybe. Or hurt himself so badly he couldn't swim . . . No. He had to go through with it. Witnesses had heard him, seen him. It was his childhood all over again, with charge-ahead Marina getting him in trouble and by-the-rules Rafe looking on.

"See you there," Cal heard himself say.

"Bring any gear you have." Marina turned back to Rafe.

Cal stared at Antonio, the realization of what had happened settling over him.

"You set me up."

Antonio grinned.

"She's gonna drown me, and you're laughing about it."

"You'll do fine," Antonio said. "M'rina, she's more fish than human. You two spend a little time together, it'll be like old times."

"I need out of here." Cal struggled to breathe, as if there were no air around the bar. First Kat and Buddy, now Marina and diving.

He walked toward the lobby on shaky legs, ignoring Antonio calling after him. Rum. On an empty stomach. What had he been thinking?

The Thing coughed, shuddered, then finally started. Cal backed onto the road, oblivious to the cloud of blue exhaust. He had to get away, far away, as fast as he could. The problems at the house would be a welcome relief from the dread of scuba lessons.

Marina had said to bring gear. There was bound to be some of Rhodes' old scuba equipment around the house, though he hadn't seen any, other than the underwater scooter, in all his searches. Maybe in the lean-to with all the other junk. But what exactly did someone need for diving? Goggles, of course. And some flippers. A knife. Definitely a big knife. Shark repellant, too, though not in the pool.

At the house, under the sagging workbench in the lean-to, Cal found a big plastic storage bin packed with dusty snorkeling equipment. Still queasy, Cal pulled out a mask with a crumbling rubber strap, another orange mask with two upside down j shaped snorkels built in, a caged ping pong ball at the end of each. Stubby, bright yellow flippers that could have been stolen from a giant duck costume. A dive knife the size of a butcher's blade, with rubber straps to lash it to his leg. A pair of baggy orange swim trunks with hula girls and 'Aloha' all over them. The mask fit well enough. So did the flippers, silly as they looked. The shorts, though . . . Cal hadn't brought any swim shorts of his own, and he hadn't seen any while searching the master bedroom. The 'Aloha' shorts would have to do.

He needed a tank, too, though. And a regulator with all its hoses, like Marina had been carrying. Cal dumped the bin upside down so he could sort through everything in it easier. Cal sat to pick through it all. Fins with broken straps. Masks with broken lenses. Salt-crusted neoprene booties of all sizes. A tangle of hoses attached to nothing. Why had Rhodes saved all this junk?

Then Rosie was staring down at him, arms crossed. Giving him the suspicious look he had come to know.

"Is this all the scuba-diving gear there is?" Cal said.

"You going in the sea?" From her tone, she could have been asking if he was going to flap his arms and fly.

"Sort of. The pool. Are there any better goggles and flippers around here than these?" Cal waved the orange snorkel mask and duck fins over his head, setting the ping pong balls rattling.

"Why you all of a sudden want to go diving?" Suspicion filled her voice.

"I don't." Cal sat, looked up at Rosie. "But Antonio . . . I've been . . . I backed myself into a corner. Now I have to follow through."

"That 'Tonio, he gets the devil in him sometimes," Rosie laughed.

"With Marina." Should he tell Rosie about Antonio saying Marina secretly liked him? Get her opinion? Or would she just laugh?

Rosie studied him a long moment, then smiled.

"M'rina gonna drown you, y'know."

"Yes, but there's nothing for it." That seemed to settle any question of whether Marina liked him. "Is there more diving stuff here or not?"

"That's all Mister Rhodes' scuba gear." Suspicion filled her face again. "You gonna be going through all the stuff in this shed, too?"

"No. I just need enough equipment for this stupid lesson. Course. Whatever it is."

Rosie glanced at the shorts. Smiled again.

"Tread careful with M'rina," she said. "She knows her business, but she don't suffer fools."

"Yeah. I picked up on that."

Cal set the snorkel mask, flippers, shorts, and dive knife aside. He scooped up the rest of the junk and dropped it back in the bin.

"Any of this crap salvageable?" he said.

Rosie wrinkled her nose.

"Fair enough."

Cal snapped the lid shut and dragged the bin to the roadside trashcans. It was a minor bit of junk gone, but it felt like a victory to get rid of something without Rosie protesting. He walked back to the lean-to, collected the gear he had set aside, and tossed it in the Thing's back seat.

Inside the house Rosie had gone back to sorting through folders and adding them to the stacks by the door. With the furniture cleared of papers, the place looked almost livable.

"I made sure the entire island knows we found the will," Cal said. "There shouldn't be anyone rummaging through here anymore."

"We'll see." She sounded doubtful.

"You could work half days, if you want, now the place doesn't need so much minding." Cal needed time to search inside the house, but couldn't if she was there. "You could come in later, leave earlier, have time to do other things you need to do."

"I'm gonna keep tending this place the way it needs to be." Her voice hardened, antagonistic again.

"Think about it." Cal held up his hands in surrender. He would have to search in the evenings and early mornings, then. "I'm going to start hauling some of this clutter out to the road."

Rosie watched him for a moment, then nodded.

Cal grabbed an armful of stacked folders, carried them outside, and dropped them in one of the trashcans at the road. Between the scuba junk and the papers Rosie had approved for removal, the garbage collector would have his hands full.

From the road Cal studied the house's ends. It looked less like a football the more he looked at it. Rhodes could have made the ends pointed, exactly like a football, but didn't. Why? He glanced back at the bluff, half expecting to see some shadowy figure with binoculars lurking there. Cal strolled back to the house, eyes still on its bulging ends. Access to any hollow spaces *had* to be inside. Something obvious he had seen, but hadn't recognized. He needed to examine each end, to narrow the possibilities in a logical manner so he could find the most likely options. That could be his mental task this afternoon while he hauled out junk. And he would study his grid-lined floorplan that night.

That would take his mind off tomorrow's scuba session, too. He needed to be searching the house, not take diving lessons. But he couldn't search while Rosie was here. He would let Rosie do whatever it was she did in the house while he waited for word on the will.

The scuba lesson would give him an excuse to get away from Rosie. And at least tomorrow he would only be in the pool.

Maybe he would do so badly Marina would give up, call it off. It was a slim hope, but the only one he had.

Cal spent the afternoon hauling out banker's boxes of useless papers, the tacked-out iguana skin, the Tesla coil, and other junk. Then, after Rosie had gone, he studied the reading nook walls inch by inch, looking for a latch, some disguised button to push to free a secret panel like the one in the bedroom door. Nothing. He checked for lines in the paint that might betray a hidden door. Still nothing. He moved the armchair and hardbound books leaning against one wall—*Keys of Arithmancy* and *The Hidden Gateway: Modern Theosophy and Ancient Wisdom*—but no hidden compartments were behind them. What was he not seeing?

He retreated to the dining room table, pulled out his sketched floorplan. He sat, pored over the reading nook's curvature. The answer *had* to be here somewhere.

The shifting breeze blew the front door ajar. Cal ignored it, intent on his drawing, on the reading nook's far wall. Beyond that wall was where most of the scuffling noises came from at night. What if that wasn't Antonio joking? Someone else might be looking for secret compartments, too. That made more sense than some animal. Or Antonio's mersquatch. And they searched at night, when Cal was asleep—the only time they could do that without getting caught. Maybe Rosie was right to doubt the break-ins would stop. He had the will, but he might still have to deal with someone creeping around the house every night.

A scratching came from behind him. Cal jumped, spun, stood, sent his chair crashing backwards across the tiles. The open door was empty. Something moved on the threshold. A dark red crab the size of both Cal's fists together scuttled in through the open door, its armored feet clattering on the floor tiles.

Cal grabbed a couch cushion, threw it at the crab.

"Shoo! Get out!" Cal yelled.

The crab stopped, raised its hand-sized claws in defiance. Claws big enough, nasty enough, to take off a toe. Cal cursed himself for being barefoot. He put the edge of another cushion on the floor, pushed it at the crab like a plow to scoot it out the open door.

The crab scuttled to the side, around the cushion. Cal jumped to keep his feet away from it, repositioned his cushion. No, this would never work. He grabbed a second cushion and, cushion in each hand, tried to herd the crab back out.

The crab scuttled one way, then the other, before retreating enough to scoot around the cushions and under the kitchen table, leaving a trail of something as it went. Cal eyed the golf club by the door. No, that wouldn't herd any better than the cushions, and he couldn't hit the crab with it among the chair legs. He looked closer at whatever the crab had spread on the tiles. Then the smell hit him. The crab had pooped across his floor. Wonderful.

Cal stepped back. He was smarter than a crab. He hoped. This shouldn't be that hard. But he had never imagined being in a standoff with a giant crab. He closed both bedroom doors to keep the crab in the main room, stacked cushions to block off the kitchen and nook, then turned back to his opponent. Plowing hadn't worked. Herding hadn't worked. What then?

Cal circled the table. The crab moved with him, its claws still high, eager for a fight. All right then. Cal could use that. He grabbed a long-handled wooden spoon from the kitchen counter and jabbed it at the crab's eyes. The crab lunged forward, clamped a claw tight on the spoon. Cal lifted the spoon, crab still attached with a death grip, flung them both outside and slammed shut the door. He would get the spoon later. Or toss it on the roadside junk pile.

Cal scanned the cliff face again in the dying light. Still no obvious signs of a lurker, but he was certain someone was there, watching, waiting for Cal to drop his guard. He would take his drawn floor plan with him to Eagle Ray Cove the next day to make sure the intruder, or Rosie, didn't get it.

Back inside, Cal gave the reading nook another once-over, then let it go. He would let his brain work on the puzzle overnight, while he slept, and would probably have an answer in the morning. He started dinner, pulled down Nash Thresher's *Shark Attacks and How to Avoid Them* from the bookcase and prepared himself for the next day's scuba ordeal.

8

The next morning, Cal sat beside the Eagle Ray Cove pool, frowning at the liability waiver in his hand. Frowning at the scuba gear strewn across the deck in front of him. A big black vest with plastic clips and bright metal D-rings. A tangle of hoses and gauges and regulators with multi-colored mouthpieces. A gray metal cylinder that looked like something a military jet would drop on an advancing enemy. He dug his flippers and twin-snorkel mask from his bag and set them on the deck next to him. The ping pong balls in the snorkels rattled in their cages.

Marina, still laying out scuba gear, burst out laughing.

"Where did you get *that*?" She pointed to Cal's mask.

"My goggles? In a bin of Rhodes' stuff at the house."

"Well put it back. Quick as you can." Marina sat on the cement deck, laughing hard. "No, wait," she gasped. "Let me get a picture of it first!" She reached for her phone, but fell back laughing again.

Cal stuffed the snorkel mask back in his bag, on top of the folder with the Batten's Down floor plan sketch, before she could photograph it. His face burned.

"Here. I always bring spares." Marina handed him a clear silicone mask with a neon yellow frame. "It's ugly, but it won't block your airway with plastic balls." She glanced at Cal's dive bag, giggled. Then her face and voice went serious. "Now, you don't like to swim. Do you know *how* to swim?"

"If I fell off a boat, I could get to shore." Cal bristled. "But it's just not something I'd do for fun. Or anything short of an emergency, really."

"Think of this class as an emergency."

"Already there." Cal eyed the pile of gear.

Marina paused, as if reappraising him.

"This is your mask and fins—*not* your goggles and flippers. That's your buoyancy compensator." Marina tapped the black vest. "It lets you float at the surface."

She lifted the bundle of hoses.

"This is your regulator system. It lets you breathe underwater. Simple, once you use it a few times. Here's how you connect it all to your air cylinder. *Not* a tank. Tanks fought at the Battle of the Bulge. Do it with me."

Marina stood a cylinder upright, clamped her buoyancy vest to it with a wide strap. Cal did the same with his vest. She kept up a steady commentary as she set the rest of the gear up, explaining each step as she went. The regulator went on the cylinder valve like so. Hoses hooked up to the vest here. Gauges clipped onto the vest like this. Cal copied her, more nervous by the second, mind ticking off what could go wrong with each step: a regulator breaking, a hose bursting, the tank exploding. All underwater.

Marina's hostility disappeared while she was teaching. Whether that was her in instructor mode, or Antonio and Jerrod were right about her softening toward Cal, he wasn't sure.

"So, any questions?" Marina knelt next to the assembled scuba unit, eyes on his.

"Um . . . no." Had she guessed what he was thinking? "What calamities are we likely to encounter?"

"Calamities?"

"They're a concern."

"Who mentioned calamities? Who talks like that?"

"Your waiver." Cal flipped to the second page, pointed to a line near the bottom. "'I absolve Eagle Ray Divers from responsibility for any accidents or *calamities* that befall me on a dive . . .'"

"So, what do *you* think 'calamity' means?"

"Something bad happening. To me. My regulator blowing up. My tank running out of air. A shark eating me. Who needs 'calamity' explained? It's a calamity."

"Worst that'll happen is you get stung by a jellyfish."

"There!"

"That's not a calamity."

"It is if you're the one who gets stung!"

"You sure you weren't adopted? You look like your old man, but—"

"I just need to understand every step of this process."

"You will. Now grow a pair, grab your gear, and get in the pool."

"We'll be using shark repellant? In the ocean?"

"Sure. Your wetsuit comes pre-loaded with the stuff."

Cal let it pass. He would press again when—if—they made it out of the pool and into the sea. He had read *Shark Attacks and How to Avoid Them* cover-to-cover the night before. Marina could laugh it off all she wanted, but Cal knew the dangers, the risks, back to front.

The pool was chilly. Cal gritted his teeth as he inched down the steps. Marina's face was expressionless, as if the cold water didn't bother her. He could play it that way, too. When they were waist-deep, Marina helped him slip on his scuba unit.

"Right. First thing you do is stand here and breathe through your reg." Marina handed Cal the black regulator with a blue silicone mouthpiece. "Exhale first, to clear out any water."

Cal put the regulator in his mouth, exhaled, inhaled hard to get the air to flow. The regulator vibrated. Cal snatched it out, flung it as far as the two-foot hose would allow.

"It does that in the air." Marina laughed again. "It's made to breathe underwater."

Cal didn't believe her but put the regulator back in his mouth.

"Now we're going to kneel down, so our heads are underwater, and just breathe," Marina said.

Cal followed her lead, slipped beneath the surface, both hands clamped on the regulator to make sure it didn't escape. Sure enough, it stopped vibrating. After a few breaths she signaled to stand.

"See? No problem. Now I'm going to show you what to do if that reg pops out of your mouth."

"There. Calamity."

"Not even close. Watch me."

They knelt again and Marina led Cal through a series of skills, each in sensible, easy-to-follow steps—recovering his regulator, clearing water from his mask, breathing from her secondary regulator if he ran low on air.

Cal clutched his gauge console in his left hand, checked it every few seconds. The order of it, the precision of the needles showing him exactly how much air he had used, how much he had left, how deep he was, was calming. He had finally found something reliable on this chaotic little island.

Marina was a good teacher, and patient. He found himself going through the drills smoothly, whether because of her skill or his being able to calm himself. Or both. Maybe this wouldn't be so bad. In the pool.

Marina tapped him on the forehead to get his attention. Her brown eyes bored into his. Cal flashed her a quick 'okay' sign. Marina pointed to her eyes, then to herself: 'watch me.' Cal gave the 'okay' sign again. Marina pulled off her mask, held it to one side, eyes open, as if saying, 'see? no big deal.'

Without the mask on, her eyes took on an unfocused look. Cal stared, as he hadn't dared to do when she could look back, looking for a hint of the Marina he had known. Dark brown, with greenish flecks. Yes. They were the same. And not filled with contempt. Wisps of black hair drifted around her face now that the mask strap wasn't holding them in place, as if Marina's head was surrounded by a dark halo.

Marina drew her hand across her face, slicking the hair back against her head, slipped the mask back on. She tilted her head down, then up, exhaling through her nose to clear the water. Her eyes, focused now, stared into Cal's. Had she caught him staring? She motioned for him to take off his mask. He did.

Water rushed up Cal's nose. He opened his mouth to gulp air. His regulator shot out. Cal lunged for the surface, coughing when he reached the air. Marina stood beside him, waited for him to stop hacking.

"What was that?" she said.

"Water up my nose."

"So?"

"I almost drowned!"

"Not until you spit your reg."

"I just—"

"No. Never spit that regulator out. And *never* bolt to the surface. Do that on a dive, *that's* your calamity. You'll be dead. You get spooked, you sit on the bottom and signal to me what's wrong."

Cal nodded. All he had done was stand up, but he saw Marina's point.

"Good. Now let's try that again."

Cal's teeth were chattering an hour later when he crawled from the pool. He dropped his gear and wrapped himself in towels. Marina toweled off, eyed him with what almost looked like approval.

"For someone who doesn't like water, you picked this stuff up fast."

"Osmosis. Or from when I was little," Cal said. Never mind concentrating on each step of every skill, and on his air gauge, kept him from freaking out under water.

"So, I'm off tomorrow," Marina said. "You good to do your first checkout dive then?"

"In the ocean?" Cal's stomach tightened.

"No, in a palm tree."

"Why so soon?"

In the pool the skills had been a sort of intellectual exercise, not something he'd ever put to practical use. He knew the ocean dives were coming but had pushed that aside. Now an actual day had been set.

"Because. Now, no boats're going out, so we'll go in from shore. You got a car, right?"

"Sort of."

"Meet me here at nine."

Marina gave him a thin smile, then knelt to break down her scuba gear. Cal copied her, disassembling his own equipment. Maybe Antonio was right, she was softening.

A shadow fell across Cal's gear. Rafe Marquette towered over him, arms crossed. He shot a dark look at Marina, then focused on Cal.

"Look like you're settling in," Rafe said. "Taking a break. Learning to dive."

"Killing time while the house paperwork goes through," Cal said.

"Spending time with M'rina." Rafe's face held a hint of his warning for Cal to stay away from Marina.

"Trying not to drown."

Neither Rafe nor Marina laughed.

"You finish up quick as you can."

"Rafe, he's my student. We'll finish when we finish."

"And he's leaving the island quick as he can, too," Rafe said. "That'd be best."

"Rafe. Enough." Marina's voice took on the tone she had used with Cal in the store. The tone Cal remembered from childhood.

Rafe gave Cal a hard look and walked away.

"What was that about?"

"In the back of Rafe's mind, he and I should be a couple." Marina shook her head. "Facts be damned."

"I'm not going to get between you two."

"There is no 'us two.' Except in Rafe's imagination."

"Great. So his imagination'll beat me senseless."

"Rafe's fine. You worry about keeping your reg in your mouth. And if you're hungry, the bar food's decent here."

She loaded the equipment on a cart and wheeled it toward the dive shop. Cal retreated to the bar and ordered a burger, then a beer. He pulled the house floor plan from its folder, studied it. No solution about how to find whatever secret chambers there might be had presented itself that morning.

"You and Marina get on okay?" Jerrod settled into the chair next to Cal, grinning. White hair slicked back under a red Eagle Ray Cove visor.

"I survived," Cal said. "The diving and Rafe."

"Yeah, Rafe can be a little intense." Jerrod glanced at Cal's drawing. Then cocked his head sideways, looked at it closer, eyes narrowed.

"Ooo! Cool. Fibonacci diagram." He stood to get a better view. "Something you're making, or just playing with the numbers and shape?"

"Something . . . from back home." Cal had no idea what Jerrod was talking about, and wasn't about to tell him the sketch was Batten's Down. "What's a fibbo-whatsit?"

"Diagram based on the Fibonacci number sequence, you know—one, one, two, three, five, eight, thirteen, twenty-one. Add the last two numbers to get the next one. Golden ratio. Golden spiral. The Mayans used it for all their buildings."

Cal looked at his sketch. He didn't see anything that looked like a number sequence or spiral.

"Here. I'll show you. This big square in the center? Its sides correspond to one of the numbers." Jerrod grabbed a separate sheet of paper, pressed it over Cal's sketch, and traced the house's outline. Then he drew a series of ever-smaller squares in one bulging end, the outer ones neatly bisected diagonally by the curve of the house end. Then he continued the curve inward through the smaller squares he had drawn inside the bulge. He held the overlapping drawings up to the sunlight.

"See? The big block in the center's your 'thirty-four' square. Then that curve cuts right through your 'twenty-one,' 'thirteen' and 'eight' squares and curls right into the 'one' square dead center. Or close enough not to be a coincidence. What is it?"

"The . . . uh . . . neighbor's putting in a pool and wanted input. Just trying to visualize it." Cal's mind raced. The house wasn't a football. Rhodes had changed the shape of the house, put extensions on both ends that fit this pattern, then put the stripes and laces on as distractors. Could the 'one' or 'two' squares represent where small compartments were concealed, toward the front of the house?

"Huh. Fibonacci cutouts." Jerrod's voice cut into Cal's thoughts. "Cool idea. Ugly pool, but cool idea."

Cal's burger arrived. Jerrod was still studying Cal's drawing, turning it one way then the other. Cal slid the drawing back in its folder as nonchalantly as he could and asked for a to-go box. If Jerrod was sharp enough to figure out the numerical pattern, it wouldn't be much of a jump for him to recognize Batten's Down outline.

"I need to run, but good talk," Cal said. "It'll impress the neighbors when I call them."

Cal cut through the resort lobby, nodded to the receptionist and to Rich Skerritt, who was studying something on the reception computer. Skerritt stepped around the counter, blocked Cal's way.

"Heard about the will," he whispered, voice oily smooth. "Give any more thought to my offer?"

"Not 'til it's through probate." Cal eyed the outside door. He needed to get back to the house. "Legally, it's not mine yet."

"It will be. And I know Sandy's been pestering you."

"Look, I need to run."

Cal stepped around Skerritt and headed home as fast as the clattering Thing would take him. He had to see if Jerrod's number sequence was the answer. After he got Rosie out of the house.

His mind drifted back to everything he and Marina had worked on in the pool. How each skill was done. How he and Marina had gotten along. How the flecks in her eyes were the same green as the palm fronds waving overhead. How he had never thought about Kat's eyes like that.

Rosie's bike wasn't leaning against the house when he arrived. Good. He had the place to himself. He stepped through the front door and stopped.

All the books in the bookshelf had been thrown on the floor again. Vials on the chemistry table were overturned. The couch, coffee table, and armchair had been moved. The contents of the kitchen cabinets were strewn across the counter, and the refrigerator had been pulled away from the wall. Cal collapsed into the closest dining room chair, mind spinning. By this time everyone on the island had to know Rhodes' will had been found. This wasn't about the will.

Someone was looking for something else. Like Cal was doing. Only whoever was doing this was getting bolder, taking bigger risks. And didn't care if Cal knew it. Or Cal had surprised them by coming home early. Who had known he would be at the pool all morning? Marina had agreed to teach him so quickly, had kept him in the pool a long time, had suggested he have lunch at the resort. Was she in on whatever was going on, keeping Cal occupied while an accomplice ransacked the house?

Cal shook his head to clear it. There was no reason for Marina to do that. The island, the situation, was getting to him. It would be good to sell, to get back to the real world.

But what in the house could be so important? Something made Skerritt and Bottoms eager to buy the place. If two of the island's richest people were so interested, there must be something incredibly valuable here.

Someone stepped through the door behind him.

"What you been doing?" Disbelief filled Rosie's voice.

"I just got back."

"Anything missing?" Her voice lowered, concern replacing disbelief. Her accent shifted.

"Seriously?"

"Somebody went through here but good." The lilt was back, but her voice was still serious. "Looking for something. Letting us know it."

Cal studied her. Her eyes did a slow scan of the room, as if cataloguing everything in it. She was the closest thing to an ally he had. He needed her input, whether he was sure of her motives or not.

"Rosie, what was Rhodes mixed up in? What would someone be looking for in here, and why are people so eager to buy this place?"

She eyed him, as if debating what, or how much, to say.

"Your daddy had his fingers in a little bit of everything. Legal and otherwise. And got credit for being involved in way more than he ever was. Folks' imaginations are running wild with dollar signs. Thinking there's some fortune in here."

"That doesn't answer my question."

"You don't want to know everything your daddy was mixed up in," she said. "Bottom line, this's gonna keep happening 'til someone finds what they want, or they tear the place down trying."

"So, if I were to look for whatever it is that's supposed to be here, what would I be looking for?" Did he dare ask her about hollow compartments in the ends of the house?

Rosie's face went blank.

"Okay." He was out of options. He needed help. "You ever see, or hear of, him stashing anything in either end of the house? Messing with things in the reading nook or by the stove? A small cubby hole he could access from inside?"

Rosie's eyes locked on his, but she still said nothing.

Cal spread his sketch and Jerrod's tracings on the table.

"Here's what I'm talking about. Any way there could be a hidey-hole here or here?" He pointed to the 'one' squares on Jerrod's sketch.

Rosie leaned over, studied the drawings, then looked at the walls at either end of the great room. She nodded.

"Never seen Mister Rhodes messing with either place, but we need to find out. Whoever's searching's getting braver. You best find what they're looking for first. Or find a new place to live." She looked at the sketches again. "What're these curlicues?"

"Some math thing Jerrod drew. Represents a number series."

Cal stepped to the bookcase, picked up the numerology text he had re-shelved multiple times. He leafed through the pages until he found a diagram like the one Jerrod had drawn.

"There you go." He passed the open book to Rosie. "I finally found a clue."

"What you gonna do with it?"

"Don't know. But it shows we're on to something. Whatever it is."

"How you gonna get back in there." She tapped the sketch's 'one' square. "That's a foot-and-a-half, two feet in."

"He'd've got at it from the inside. For secrecy. Something fairly easy to access, like the slot you found in the door."

Cal stepped to the reading nook, even with where the 'one' squares were on the diagram. There was nothing that looked like a hidden door. He pushed the chair aside to see the entire wall, looking for anything that might hide a seam. He knelt, tugged at the baseboard under the return air duct. It was solid. He eyed the air vent, then sat back, laughing.

"What's so funny?" Rosie was looking over his shoulder, watching his every move.

"The house doesn't have air conditioning."

Cal tugged on the vent cover. It came away in his hands, a magnet behind each corner matching with screw heads in the drywall at the corners of the rectangular hole. He grabbed the flashlight from beside the chair, lay on his stomach, and shined the light into the hole. Inside was an empty space a little more than elbow deep lined with black-painted drywall. The light glinted off something small at the far end. Cal reached in, grabbed what felt like a cabinet knob and pulled. The back of the compartment swung up on bright hinges. Cal reached farther in, felt the handle and sides of a metal box.

Fingers tight around the handle, Cal pulled the box out. It was an old steel filing box just smaller than the hole in the wall. Rosie knelt beside him, eyes bright, but saying nothing. The box was latched with a rusty clip with a tiny keyhole.

"What are the odds Rhodes kept this locked . . ." Cal said to himself.

He pushed down on the clip, tugged on the box's top, and it opened as if it were brand new.

"We found out what Rhodes did for money," Cal said.

Inside were bundles of cash, green U.S. currency beside bright-colored Tiperon bills. Two passports, one American, one Tiperon. Both Rhodes'. Cal lifted the cash and passports out. Beneath them was a shiny aluminum laptop and a half-dozen thumb drives. A key ring with dozens of padlock keys. He flipped through the stacks of twenty-, fifty- and hundred-dollar bills, mentally tallying each denomination. $2,770 in U.S. dollars, $1,320 in Tiperon dollars. More than enough to finance a few weeks on Blacktip. If it was his to keep.

"So, this was Rhodes' money?" Cal said.

"In his house."

"So, now it's my money?"

"Your house."

"So it's okay for me to use it for food and gas and other expenses? If it was his?"

"Who else you think it belongs to?" Her tone was neutral, giving away nothing.

"If he was holding it for someone?"

"If he was holding it for somebody, they might come looking for it, you mean?"

"Why would he . . . enough. I'm going to see what he was up to."

Cal carried the laptop to the table, powered it up. On the desktop screen were dozens of documents. The first four he clicked on were password protected. The fifth, labeled 'South End Sailing and Holdings' was a spreadsheet of some sort showing money flowing into and out of the account, but no indication what the transactions were for. All the files concerned real estate, small companies, and banks with unfamiliar names. Cal didn't understand any of it.

"Does any of this look familiar?" He looked to Rosie for help. "Any of it make sense?"

Rosie's face was blank.

Cal tried each thumb drive, but everything was password protected.

"Well, maybe I'll run all this past Jack Cobia tomorrow. If I survive my scuba lesson."

"Be careful showing Jack all your cards," Rosie said.

"Any idea what these keys go to?"

"Only lock in this house is your child's toy on the door, and it don't need a key."

"I'll run that past Jack, too."

"I'll be in late tomorrow." Rosie gave him a warning look at Cobia's name. "Got errands to run. I'll ask around about your daddy's business, too. Quietly."

Cal slipped the laptop and drives back in the storage box, pulled several hundred Tiperon dollars from the stack and slid the box back in its hiding place, securing the false wall and false grate in front of it.

"That'll keep it hidden until I figure out what to do with it. Safer there than anyplace else I can think of."

He slid the chair back in front of the vent and went to the kitchen. There, the stove blocked the wall opposite the fake vent, where the corresponding 'one' square would be. With Rosie's help, Cal pulled the stove from between the countertops. Behind was a plain wall, with nothing but grease stains on it. The baseboard was solid. Cal took the turkey drawing off the towel hook, jiggled the hook, but it didn't budge. There was nothing in the cabinet above the stove.

"Maybe Rhodes just had a secret compartment in one end of the place."

It sounded hollow as Cal said it. Rosie looked dubious, but said nothing. Together they slid the stove back into place. Cal hesitated, then rehung the picture. He was getting sentimental, or the pace was growing on him.

"Think I'll go ask questions now," Rosie said. "Find someone who knows about computers."

She collected her things and left. Cal set to straightening the room, his brain in overdrive wondering what real estate deals Rhodes might have been involved in. And how, if, that related to the island map with its crossing lines and dots at each intersection.

9

The next morning Cal tried not to think of his upcoming scuba session. He straightened furniture in the main room. He rechecked the wall behind the stove again for any hint of a hidden compartment. He double-checked the fake vent was in place and slid the armchair back in front of it. Then he studied the bluff face through the picture window. Something moved high in one of the vertical fissures. Cal tensed. Then relaxed. A clump of bushes, ruffled by the rising sea breeze. He stepped closer to the window for a better view, stumbled over his dive bag. Right. He had delayed meeting Marina as long as he could.

Cal stepped out and locked the door, if only for show. Rosie would be there soon and would let herself in. He tossed his dive gear into the Thing's back seat and headed for Eagle Ray Cove. He imagined Marina's face when she saw the car. She might refuse to get in it, cancel the dive. No. She would take it out on him. Doubly, since he was late. But there was no hurrying in the Thing.

The Eagle Ray Cove shuttle van was idling in the parking lot, half-full of resort guests and their bags headed for the airstrip. Its sliding door stood open, waiting for more passengers. Behind the van stood Marina, surrounded by scuba gear and looking annoyed. Cal pulled up in a cloud of blue exhaust, set the guests in the van coughing.

"I'm not doing this for fun, you know." Marina snapped. "There's a ton of things I'd rather be doing."

"I got here fast as I could." Cal patted at the Thing's dash. "It has a mind of its own."

He slung the two cylinders into the back of the car, avoiding Marina's eyes.

"This P.O.S. get us two miles up the road?" Marina cast a doubtful look at the Thing. She fought back a smile at the shredded convertible top. "What do you do when it rains?"

"Hasn't come up yet."

The lobby door crashed open behind them. A brown carry-on bag sailed through the air and tumbled down the wooden steps. Jerrod, red-faced, leaped through the doorway, held the door open.

"Out! Don't come back!" Jerrod shouted into the lobby.

A portly man in a red Hawaiian shirt stormed past him, his resort bill wadded in his hand. He spun to face Jerrod, waving the bill under his nose.

"You haven't heard the end of this! I have every right to—"

"You *lied* about a lost bag! You *lied* about vermin in your room! And now you want your stay comped? Because of your *lies*?"

Jerrod took a step toward the man. The man retreated down the steps.

"I, my friends, will *torch* you on every review site—"

"Be gone, imp!" Jerrod snatched up a rattan stool by one leg and advanced down the steps, shaking it at the man. "Get out or I *will* smite you!"

The man snatched up his bag and dove for the van's open door.

"Now would be a good time to get out of here," Marina whispered.

Cal coaxed the Thing to life. He pulled out of the parking lot, leaving Jerrod and the van in the dust and exhaust, Jerrod still shaking the stool at the van.

"What the hell was that?" Cal said.

"Jerrod does that. On occasion," Marina said.

"He seemed rational every time I've talked to him."

"Oh, he is. And smart, but lying and cheating are two of his buttons. And when he starts spewing Bible-ese, look out. He, well . . . just don't lie to him."

"Does this island have a big-ass crazy magnet buried somewhere? There's no way all these nut cases can be on the same island by coincidence."

"You'd be surprised." A smile played across Marina's face. "And you're one, too, now."

Cal replayed everything he had said to Jerrod the day before. He hadn't lied to Jerrod, not technically. Except about his drawing being a pool instead of a house. If Jerrod found out, would he come after Cal with a wicker stool, too? He smiled at that. Just what he needed. Add a psychotic Jerrod to his worries about people breaking into the house, the will being contested, Kat, the clock shop and diving. He was close to solving the Batten's Down mystery, to getting off this crazy rock. If a defrocked minister didn't whack him with a chair first.

"What are you grinning about?" Marina was watching him. Suspicious.

"Nothing," Cal said. "Just a nice day, is all."

"Right. I *know* you're not smiling about diving."

Her expression softened for a moment. Cal watched the road, focused on driving and tried to ignore his suddenly-burning face. Marina stared at the flapping palm fronds overhead.

"We'll stay over here today," she said. "East wind'll make diving miserable on your side of the island."

Cal drove north, following Marina's directions. They passed Sandy Bottoms and the airstrip. A mile later, at a roadside sign for 'Diddley's Landing,' Marina had him pull off the road onto a broad expanse of concrete with rusted bollards as high as Cal's waist. Beyond the pier, sunlight glinted off the barely-rippling sea.

"Public pier," Marina said. "Not supposed to dive here, but there's no barge coming in, so no one'll care. Easiest entry and exit spot on Blacktip."

Cal nodded, tried to ignore the tightness in his gut. All worries about the house and Jerrod evaporated. His first dive in real water. Hopefully not his last. His last anything.

"You brought shark repellant, right?" He stopped the car, looked at Marina. "None of this 'it's in the wetsuit' crap?"

"Dude, are you a World War Two sailor? No one's used shark repellant for seventy, eighty years."

"Well maybe they should."

"No. Know why? It doesn't work. It never worked. Oh, and sharks aren't a danger." Marina pulled equipment from the car. "Now gear up so we can get this over with."

Cal started to snap back, thought better of it. He attached his BC and regulator to his tank. When that was done, he dug Rhodes' big dive knife from his bag and strapped it to his calf.

"Seriously?" Marina said. "If you needed a knife that big, we wouldn't be getting in the water."

"Works for me."

"No. Take that thing off. Now."

"No shark repellant and no knife? Uh-uh." Cal crossed his arms, squared his shoulders. "I take the knife, or I don't go."

Marina stared at him a moment, mouth half open. Then a sly look crept across her face.

"Oh no. You're not getting out of this *that* easy," she said. "Fine. Take your dive machete. But don't tell anyone about it."

Once geared up, Marina showed Cal the way down wide cement steps and into turquoise water. Cal didn't like the look of so much water, or the idea of getting into it. There was no telling what was under the surface, ready to grab him. He bit down hard on his regulator's mouthpiece to make sure he didn't say anything stupid.

"Giant stride like this," Marina said. She took a big step out and splashed into the water.

He tensed as water lapped over his fins. Ignored Marina watching him, gauging his mood. He needed to get this over with as quick as he could. Without any more thought, Cal leaped from the step, as if he were competing in the broad jump. Marina gasped. He hit the water butt-first, then the sea closed over his head.

After a moment that felt like forever, he bobbed back to the surface. Breathing hard, Cal looked down, past his fins, alert for any danger. All he saw was sand several body lengths below. Some algae-covered rocks. A few thumbnail-sized brown fish darting around them. Nothing looked too deadly.

"Different. But effective," Marina said.

She signaled to go down, then slipped beneath the surface. Cal swallowed hard, dumped the air from his vest, not about to float alone at the surface. He cleared his ears twice and settled feet-first in the sand, trying to catch his breath, bubbles whooshing past his ears. He clutched his regulator with one hand and his gauges with the other. What the hell was he doing underwater? In the ocean? He tried to slow his breathing, told himself he wasn't going to drown. The surface was ten, twelve feet above him. All the air in the world was up there.

Marina hovered in front of him, eyes concerned. She flashed the 'okay' sign at Cal. Then again, more forcefully. Cal nodded, let go of the regulator long enough to signal back. Marina looked less worried, but not much.

She motioned for Cal to kneel, then knelt facing him, a hand on his buoyancy vest. Cal's breathing slowed. Marina motioned him to clear his mask, like they had done in the pool. Eyes focused on hers, Cal let some water seep in, then blew it out. Marina motioned for him to take out his regulator, retrieve it, and put it back in his mouth. Her eyes were calming. His pulse slowed. She had him breathe from her alternate regulator, as if he were out of air. The skills they'd done in the pool came automatically. He checked his gauges. Two-thousand six hundred pounds per square inch. sixteen feet deep. Good. The exactness was reassuring.

Marina's eyes beamed encouragement. Cal relaxed. She signaled for him to follow her, then dolphin-kicked slowly toward a just-visible something in the deeper water.

A few kicks later, the something became clearer. A coral mound, rising like an enormous fang from the sand. Small, neon-blue fish swarmed around it. A larger, banded brown fish rested under an overhang at the spire's base, mouth open, pale purple shrimp darting in and out of its mouth and gills.

Marina pointed to her gauges, then pointed to Cal's. Air check. Cal signaled back: exactly two-thousand three hundred P.S.I.; precisely twenty-seven feet. Cal glanced toward the surface, felt his breathing quicken. This was crazy.

Something grabbed his arm. Cal pulled away. The grip tightened. Marina. Holding him in place. Asking if he was okay. Cal nodded. Returned her 'okay' sign. They swam on, Cal staying so close to Marina their arms bumped every few kicks. A stingray skimmed across the sand in front of them, unconcerned about divers. Marina, graceful as any fish, glided to a bigger stand of coral, her fins barely moving. Cal looked back to his own fins, flailing, kicking up gouts of sand.

Fish crowded the coral, some he recognized from the fish books at the house: green parrotfish, silvery snappers, red squirrelfish staring big-eyed back at him. A lobster under a ledge, all spines and waving antenna. This was good. All stuff he could see on the menu at a restaurant. Nothing that could eat *him*.

A glance at his gauges again. Twenty-one hundred P.S.I. Thirty-one feet. It didn't *feel* any different from twenty-seven. Or from the sixteen feet where he had first stood to catch his breath. Maybe Marina hadn't been underplaying the dangers of diving. Maybe there wasn't anything to be afraid of under the water.

Marina tapped his shoulder, pointed toward a nearby coral head. She held up her thumb and index finger, then put one open hand on top of her head like a fin, then both hands next to her head like she was sleeping. She wanted to nap on the coral? No. The first signal: small. The last signal: sleeping. The signal in between, the fin-on-the-head . . . Shark! Cal lunged backwards, fumbling for his knife and kicking the sand. He wasn't going near a shark, small, sleeping, or otherwise. The damn thing could be faking to draw them closer.

Bubbles spewed from Marina's regulator. Her eyes scrunched tight. She was laughing. At him. She slapped his hands away from the still-sheathed knife, motioned for him to come closer. Cal shook his head, backed away another two feet. Marina laughed again, grabbed his hand and led him back to the coral. A brownish-greenish thing the size of his forearm lay unmoving by the coral, broad-headed and slender-tailed, looking for all the world like a giant tadpole with fins. A shark. But a goofy one. And sleeping, like Marina had signaled.

Marina pulled a white dive slate and pencil from her BC pocket, scribbled something, handed the slate to Cal. 'Baby Nurse Shark,' he read. 'Harmless.'

Cal gave her a dubious look, crossed out 'harmless,' underlined 'shark' and handed the slate back to her.

After thirty minutes that seemed like forever, Marina steered them back towards shore. At the pier a four-foot-long, silver torpedo of a fish sidled up to them, jagged teeth flashing in its half-open jaws. It hung motionless alongside Cal. He would hate to be whatever the thing ate, judging by its fangs. He looked a question at Marina. Out came the slate. She wrote a word, handed the slate to Cal.

'Barracuda.'

Cal jerked away from the fish, from the white fangs. Marina *was* trying to kill him. He needed to get away from those teeth, back up in the world of air. Cal kicked hard for the surface. He slowed. He kicked harder. Went slower, held back by something.

Marina. Clutching his vest. Pressing her hand to his regulator, keeping it in his mouth. Fins flared wide to slow them both. They broke the surface. Marina grabbed his BC's inflator hose, filled the vest with air, then pushed him away from her.

"Dude, what the hell?" she yelled.

"It was a barracuda!"

"So?"

"A *BARRACUUUDA!*"

"They're not dangerous." Marina's voice was calmer. "They're just curious. The only thing dangerous out here is you panicking and bolting for the surface."

"Well . . . you need to warn people about things like that," Cal said. "That barracuda's the kind of thing that comes back to you in nightmares. And therapy sessions."

"Unreal," Marina said. "This dare isn't worth it."

"Call it off anytime you want."

"Nice try."

They were at the pier then. They picked their way up the slippery steps and slid their gear off at the car. Cal reached for a towel. Paused. The towels he had left stacked neatly in the back seat were now piled in the floor. The little ice chest he had wedged in the floor was in the seat, its lid askew. Their t-shirts and shorts were strewn across the front seat. The door-less glove box had been rummaged through. The ash tray hung open. Cal flipped up the driver's-side floor mat. His cash and credit card were still there in their plastic baggie.

"Problem?" Marina looked over his shoulder.

"Someone went through the car. But they didn't take my cash," Cal said. "Or didn't find it. You leave anything valuable here?"

Marina unzipped her backpack, peered inside.

"Not missing anything. You sure the wind didn't just blow stuff around?" Marina fought back a smile. "Or maybe a barracuda did it."

"The ice chest didn't just jump onto the seat by itself." Cal bristled. Then half-laughed. Marina was actually joking with him.

It had probably been someone seeing if there were anything worth stealing, and they'd overlooked his cash and Marina's pack. Or were looking for not-so-obvious valuables. No, that was paranoid. Maybe. Thoughts of Rhodes' computer returned. Cal needed to get back to the house, make sure the place was okay.

"We need to get going," he said.

Marina gave him a puzzled look, but piled their scuba gear back in the car. They headed south for Eagle Ray Cove.

"You did well," Marina said. "Nervous, but you settled down. Mostly. If I didn't know better, I'd think you enjoyed it. Until the barra' showed up."

"It was all right." Cal admitted it grudgingly, partly to himself. He still didn't want to be doing this scuba nonsense. But if he survived these certification dives, he would never have to dive again.

"We just have to find you a reef without any baby sharks or barracudas."

Marina was smiling in the passenger seat. Waiting for Cal to take the bait.

"You did that on purpose, didn't you? You knew there was a barracuda there."

"There's 'barras everywhere," Marina said.

"You're not a nice person."

"I *am* a nice person. Sometimes I just do not-nice things." Then her voice grew serious. "Okay. Sorry. That was partly on me. But I didn't think you'd freak. Doesn't matter what we think of each other—you're my student, I make sure you don't get hurt. And you did so well in the pool."

She sounded sincere. Cal chanced a look at her. Marina's brown eyes studied him. She was smiling, but there was no mockery on her face.

"What?" Cal said. "Another barracuda jab?"

"For you, this is as big a deal as it would be for me to jump out of an airplane with a parachute."

"I'd rather sky dive than scuba dive."

"Wanna quit?"

Something inside him jumped at that. She was giving him a way out? No, a chance to give up. Cal shook his head.

"Good, 'cause we're going again tomorrow afternoon. Wind's supposed to shift tonight, so the east side should be nice." Marina grinned at the look on Cal's face.

"I'll leave my valuables at home," he said.

"If you're worried about your vintage auto getting damaged, why don't we go in by your place?" Marina was still grinning, and her eyes flashed when she mentioned the Thing. "Rosalita Flats. Two p.m."

They unloaded the gear at the resort. Marina put two tanks for the next day in the Thing for Cal to take back with him. Once everything was rinsed and stowed, Cal headed for Batten's Down. He was worrying too much, but he wanted to make sure the house was secure. He clattered across the island, Blacktip Haven on the bluff looming above him to his right, then down the washboarded east coast road, gritting his teeth to keep them from chattering in time with the shuddering Thing.

At the house, the chain lock was still latched on the door's hasp. There was no sign of Rosie. Cal unlocked it, stepped inside. Everything looked the way Cal had left it.

Cal sat, exhaled slow. He was making himself crazy. Some drunk, or kids, had rummaged through the car, and now here he was chasing shadows.

Footsteps sounded outside.

"You out of breath, Cal." Rosie stepped into the room.

125

"Well, yeah. A bit," Cal said. "I thought there might be a problem, but everything seems all right."

"Then why you so skittery?"

"Nothing . . some kids rifled through the car while I was underwater with Marina. At the pier. Shook me up, I guess." It was odd confessing all that to Rosie, but saying it out loud made him feel better.

"No kids on this island," Rosie said.

"Well, a drunk then."

"People don't mess with cars on Blacktip," Rosie said. "Island's too small for that. Take anything?"

"No. My cash was still under the floor mat. Marina's stuff was fine, too. Maybe they just wanted a towel."

"Or weren't looking for money." She gave Cal a long look. "Sending a message, maybe."

"Which is why I rushed back." He hadn't been paranoid after all, if Rosie was suspicious. "And I'm worried about you, too, if whoever is getting more aggressive."

"I take care of myself." Rosie walked to the kitchen and grabbed her feather duster.

"Any luck finding a computer expert?" Cal said.

"Not yet." The words came slow, her voice guarded.

"Well, I'm going to see if I can make sense of the files I can get into."

Cal popped off the vent cover, lifted the false wall, and slid the file box out. He opened the box. A chill shot through him. The laptop was gone. The passports and money and keys were still there. Cal thumbed through the cash. It was all there, too. But no computer. Or thumb drives.

"Rosie, were you here at all this morning?"

"You saw me just get here."

"The laptop's missing. And the external drives."

Rosie stared down at the open box. She glanced across the room to the big window by the front door, then the kitchen window, both in view of the fake vent.

"You think someone was watching us yesterday." Cal said.

"Only thing makes sense. Checked your car, too, I guess."

"So . . ." Cal sorted through the jumble of thoughts swirling through his head. "Whatever's on the computer, or someone thinks is on the computer . . . is more valuable than all this cash."

Rosie's face was expressionless.

"And we showed whoever right where it was. I need to tell Rafe, have him take fingerprints, investigate."

"You *do* want folks tearing this place down stick by stick," Rosie said. "Word gets out you found a hidey hole and something in it, they'll take the house apart with you inside."

"I have to do something."

"Stay quiet," Rosie said. "And calm, if you got that in you. I'll ask around. Coconut telegraph'll turn up more than Rafe Marquette ever will."

Cal's mind was still racing.

"So, Rhodes was involved in real estate and finances and nondescript little companies. When he wasn't catapulting storage bins at boats. Are the files in that laptop the 'treasure' people keep talking about?"

"Island talk says there's gold and jewels here somewhere," Rosie said. "And your daddy was a cash man. That computer's prob'ly somebody else's and they just took it back. That's how they knew to look for it. And watched for where to find it."

Cal studied her. She was serious. And less bothered by the theft than he would have imagined.

"Where's that leave me?"

"Let that computer business be. For now. Poke around too much might not be healthy. You need to stash that money someplace else and not let anybody know you found it."

Rosie scanned the room. She crossed to the lab table in the spare bedroom, pulled the dictionary-sized surge protector and battery backup from under the workbench. She popped the back off, pulled the battery out, then stuffed the cash into the battery compartment and closed the back.

"Temporary, but it'll do."

Rosie moved the few electric plugs to the 'surge protection only' side of the protector and shoved the whole thing back under the workbench. She handed the battery to Cal. "Wrap that in a rag, hide it in your car. Or the back of the lean-to, 'til you come up with someplace better."

Cal wrapped the battery in a ratty bathroom towel that needed to be tossed out anyway. He stepped outside to the Thing, made a show of pulling out his dive gear to cover his slipping the towel-wrapped battery under the seat. Back inside, Rosie was waiting for him.

"Stay dead quiet about that computer, now. Don't want whoever took it to know we know it's gone," she said. "More people know about it, and that you know about it, the more dangerous things'll be for you."

She pointed the feather duster at him for effect, then turned to clean in the kitchen.

Cal stared out the window, processing everything that had happened that day. Was the computer, the information on it, what whoever was after with their break ins? Or was there something more? The mystery gnawed at him. He needed to know what was going on with this damned house. It was a blessing, maybe, the probate process was taking so long. That gave him time to get to the bottom of it. Figure out why people were so eager to get in the place. To buy the place.

He glanced at Rhodes' hand-drawn map with its crossing lines. His eyes strayed to the bluff across the road, its face in shadow. Cal would climb up, see what he could find in the morning.

10

The rising sun tinted the bluff a dull orange when Cal stepped outside the next morning. As ever, he checked the ground around the house for footprints and scuffed dirt. There had been the usual scuffling outside during the night, and near dawn, some kind of howling from the bluff. It was past time to explore up there. After he made the house look unattended, he made a show of putting a box of papers in the Thing's back seat, then drove north, as if headed to the resort strip.

Two hundred yards up the road, Cal pulled into a cleared spot at the bluff's base. He would climb up, double back and see what hiding places there were, if anyone was hiding there, watch the house for a while. With any luck, he might catch the vandal breaking in.

He found a likely route and clambered up the rock face. The jagged rock bit into his hands and knees and through the soles of his sneakers. Cal hadn't expected that. He was scraped and bleeding when he reached the top ten minutes later.

There, too, the ground was rougher than Cal had expected. No trails led through the underbrush, and the pocked limestone rose like rotted fangs ready to shred him if he fell. He picked his way along the cliff's edge, taking small steps to make sure he didn't trip, gripping a branch in each hand to steady himself before each step. It was slow going, but soon he was looking down at Batten's Down.

Waves crashed against the headland, sending sprays of white foam into the air behind the house. The house looked small from here. Isolated. And ratty, as messy on the outside as it was on the inside. The roof needed painting more than the rest of the place. The rain gutters were crooked. The corrugated-tin laces were corroding in the salt air. The place needed major repair. By the next owner. The house would soon be someone else's problem.

There was nothing among the rocks or underbrush to hint anyone had been here. Several openings gave way to narrow caves leading down into the bluff, some big enough for a person to crawl into. Was it possible for someone to use the caves as a way to get near Batten's Down from another part of the island without being seen? Or for a quick getaway when Cal appeared unexpectedly? That could explain a lot.

The morning breeze moaned faint through the openings. The higher wind overnight, blowing through the rocks, could have made the howling sounds.

Two of the lines on Rhodes' map intersected inland, if the map was accurate, and another was south of that, even with the Maples' house. He needed sturdier shoes, and long pants, to explore any farther, though. But he could spy on the house from here.

Cal climbed part way down the cliff face, wedged himself into a crevice and settled in to watch until Rosie arrived.

The island had grown on him. If the house wasn't such a mess, and constantly being ransacked, he would almost enjoy staying there. He was even getting along with Marina. Sort of. He shuddered thinking about their run-in with the barracuda. His pulse quickened. He shouldn't worry so much about getting bit. Yesterday's shark and barracuda weren't the threats he had imagined. And they certainly couldn't bother him sixty feet up the side of the island. He understood it intellectually, but the thought of a shark, a barracuda, still made him break into a cold sweat.

Dust rose from the road to the north. Soon he heard the low hum of tires. A white truck came into view, slipping from beneath the green of the gumbo-limbo branches overhanging the road. A rack, or light strip on top. A broad blue stripe down its side. Rafe, on patrol. The car pulled off the road at Batten's Down and stopped in front of the house. Rafe pulled himself out. Even from up the bluff, the man looked big. Was he finally going to investigate the break ins?

Rafe glanced around the place, hands on his hips, taking in the empty lean-to, the tattered house and the unkempt yard. Cal stayed motionless in his bluff-top crevice, waiting to see what the policeman would do.

Rafe turned, scanned 360 degrees around him. He did another half turn, stopped facing the bluff.

"Cal, what you doing up there?"

Cal didn't move. There was no way Rafe could know where he was.

"Cal, get down here. Got no time for games. And that ironshore crack can't be comfy."

Red-faced with embarrassment, Cal clambered down. The climb reopened the cuts on his hands. His sweat-soaked t-shirt stuck to him.

"How'd you know I was there?" Cal said when he reached Rafe.

"Car stashed up the road."

"And you guessed I was around somewhere."

"You wanna hide, don't wear a yellow shirt." Rafe shook his head. "Blind man could've seen you."

Cal looked down, ground his teeth. He was wearing his bright yellow Schmaltz's Deli shirt.

"You up there for a reason, or you getting island fever so soon?" Rafe said.

"Getting a better view of the place." Marquette gave him a dubious look. "And seeing if I could . . . catch whoever's been going through the house. Making things look deserted so whoever would maybe try again."

Rafe snorted, a half laugh to himself.

"You let me worry about investigations, Sherlock Holmes." The constable studied Cal for a long moment. "You gonna sell the place to Sandy or Rich?" What could have been a calculating edge had crept into Marquette's voice. Was he sizing it up for someone else?

"I'll be open to all offers once the will's proved," Cal said. "Know anyone else interested?"

"I hear rumors. Best you sell it quick, but check with me first. Or hire someone to, if you need to leave the island. Before the will clears. I can look after the place."

"Why the rush?" This had to be about Marina. Rafe had tried threats, now he was trying what passed for charm.

"Heard somebody went through your place again. And your car. Somebody gets desperate, you don't want to be in their way."

"You know who's been breaking in?"

"Don't need to. The way things're picking up, it's not safe you staying here. Somebody's getting bolder . . . and it's awful isolated out here. Not the place you want to get hurt."

The constable's eyes locked on Cal's.

"But you haven't even investigated anything!" If Rafe was trying to rattle Cal, he was doing a good job.

"Healthiest for you if you leave the island quick as you can. Jack can handle the will and sale. And again, I'll keep an eye on the house 'til it's sold."

"What kind of danger do you think I'm in?" Cal's mind raced. "If this is about Marina, trust me, she still hates my guts."

"She's bad news for you." Rafe's eyes bored into Cal's.

"She's mixed up in all this?" He had been right to be suspicious about Marina dragging him away for a scuba lesson.

"You need to stay away from her. And you need to leave this house."

The constable climbed back in his truck and drove away.

Cal went inside, changed into a fresh shirt. Had Rafe warned him or threatened him? Both? This island was squirrely. But Cal was intrigued. By the break-ins, the computer theft, the threats. There was a mystery to solve. Out of curiosity. Out of spite. And he wasn't leaving until he solved it. Maybe there *was* more of crotchety old Rhodes in him than he thought.

How much danger could there be, really? Whoever the would-be thief was, they hadn't done anything more violent than overturn furniture. Rosie was in the house more than he was, and no one talked about her being in danger. No, Rafe was jealous, whether he had reason to be or not. And Cal didn't like to be pushed into making decisions.

He walked back to the Thing, drove home. He was cleaning his cuts when Rosie arrived.

"What you do to yourself now?" she said.

"I climbed the bluff to see where someone might hide. Rougher than it looks from here."

"You wanna be careful up there. Easy to get hurt. Or lost. No one'd know to come look for you."

Her eyes had their guarded look now, and her words were drawn out, as if she were lining them up with care. Cal recalled the map with its intersecting lines, had a sudden hunch.

"Did Rhodes do much exploring up there?" Cal waved his hand toward the bluff, as if making small talk.

Rosie's eyes dissected Cal as if he were a fresh-caught snapper. Her lips tightened. She crossed her arms, but said nothing.

"Just curious." Cal turned his back to Rosie, went back to scrubbing his scrapes. He could feel her eyes boring into his back, but pretended not to notice.

His guess was right, or close enough. Rhodes had been doing something on the bluff. And Rosie knew about it. Whatever truce she and Cal had formed about the house, all bets were off on this new front. He would take another look up there when she wasn't around. See if anything matched the lines and dots on Rhodes' map.

His eyes settled on the dining room table. He had left the map there, in plain sight if Rosie walked by. Cal dried his hands, scooped up papers, worked his way toward the table, glancing at the papers as if sorting through them. He felt Rosie watching him, made himself walk slow so he wouldn't arouse her suspicions.

He picked up a stuffed manila folder, set it on top of the map, then added more folders to the stack, and evened them with the table edge. When Rosie was gone, he would stash the map somewhere safe.

Rafe's warning gnawed at him then.

"Rosie, is there any reason for me to worry about my safety in this house?"

Rosie stopped, a yellow kitchen glove half-on one hand, the other glove on the counter.

"Never know what's safe. Island folks always crossing each other. Like you and Rafe."

"No, I mean, would someone break in with me here? And if they did, would they hurt me?" An image of an enraged Dermott flashed through his mind.

"Depends on the person." Rosie slid on the other glove. "You getting rabbity out here by yourself?"

The sound of a small engine, a motorcycle, maybe, came from outside.

"No, it's . . . am I in physical danger?"

"Only if people hear you found money. Or a computer and drives. Especially that."

"You think there's more hidden?"

"Mister Rhodes hid one thing; he's bound to've hidden more."

"So, I should . . . take precautions?" Cal wasn't sure what he could do other than carry the golf club with him twenty-four hours a day.

Rosie stared at him, lips tight, then started scrubbing the stove counter. Rafe hadn't been trying to scare him, then.

Feet scuffled behind him. Cal spun, ready to fight. Marina stood in the doorway, motorcycle helmet in hand, looking puzzled.

"You're skittish today," she said. "Ready?"

"Does anyone on this island knock?" Cal's heart was pounding. How much had Marina heard?

"Not when your door's open and I can see you standing there. And what's with the kung-fu stance?"

"Nothing."

Marina's expression went from puzzled to concerned. "Sure you're okay to dive?"

"No. Absolutely not. But I'm finishing the damn course."

"You're really not enjoying any of it?"

"The part where I get out of the water. And have a beer."

"That's the spirit." Marina shook her head. "That rust pile of yours get us to the far end of Spider Bight? There's a decent shore entry there at Rosalita Flats. And shallow coral outside the fringe reef. You'll be back here for your lunch beer in no time."

Cal glanced at Rosie. She shrugged, kept cleaning. He would have to leave the map where it was. Moving it, or the stack of folders, would draw too much attention. Hopefully Rosie wouldn't decide to clean the table in the next hour or so.

Marina set her helmet on a red dirt bike next to the Thing. Her dive bag was already in the back of the car. Cal tossed his gear in with it.

"If you bolt for the surface today, I'll leave you out there for the sharks and barracudas and all the other sea monsters," Marina said. "You have any problems or . . . concerns, you kneel in the sand and we'll sort it out. Got it?"

Cal nodded, drove to the north end of the bight where the coconut palms stood in their neat, evenly-spaced lines. He stopped at the top of the beach, precisely between two palms. As

135

ever, the orderly trees gave Cal a sense of calm. He needed to come down here more often. Marina seemed calmer, too.

"I like diving over here," she said. "Some of my earliest memories were here, having fun playing in the water by your house. That's why I'm bummed you're selling. The place'll get torn down so whoever can build something new. That makes me sad."

Cal said nothing. Any of the responses going through his mind would ruin Marina's good mood.

He and Marina geared up in the shade, walked across the pink-tinged sand, and waded into the water side by side, Cal watching Marina for whatever came next. Soon the water was chest deep.

"What?" Marina said.

"I like this better. Wading in instead of yesterday's splashdown."

"Put your regulator in. Let's go."

She slipped beneath the surface. After a moment, Cal followed. They swam deeper. Marina, fins together, dolphin kicked, gliding effortless as any fish. Light rippling through the surface, flickering off the sand, cast a fish-scale pattern on her legs.

Cal pinched his nose, cleared his ears and followed. Soon ragged clumps of coral appeared, then longer coral fingers, hazy in the silty water. Clouds of thumb-sized fish, brown ones and blue ones, swarmed above the coral. Something dull green lurked beneath a coral ledge, mouth open, jaws working. An eel. A tap on his shoulder. Marina. Right. Skills.

She had him kneel, take off his mask, put it back on and clear it of water. She signaled she was out of air, had him pass her his alternate regulator. She handed him a compass, pointed in the direction she wanted him to swim, toward a barely-visible coral head looming in the haze.

Cal set the compass' bezel and swam off roughly northeast, eyes glued to the compass needle and mentally counting his kicks. At twenty kicks he stopped, looked up to see how accurate he had been. Sure enough, the coral head he had been aiming for was dead ahead. Cal barely saw it.

Between him and the coral a fish was passing. A big fish. Nearly as big as Cal. Gray, as if it had materialized from the underwater haze, tail lazing side to side, dorsal fin rising sharp on its back. Mouth barely open. Eye rotating up, down, studying Cal.

Cal hung motionless, paralyzed. He wanted to scream, turn, swim away, bolt for the surface, all at the same time. His body wouldn't move. His exhaled breath roared past his ears. His pulse boomed. He sunk to the sand, immobile as any shipwreck, compass still in front of him as if he were still navigating. The shark swung toward him, taking a closer look, then turned away and disappeared into the haze. Cal followed it with his eyes, unable to move anything else.

Another tap on his shoulder. Cal jumped, spun, sent sand flying.

Marina, her smile obvious despite the regulator in her mouth. She pointed to Cal, then made the 'okay' sign with her thumb and finger inches from Cal's mask.

Was he all right? Not even close, but there was no way to explain that underwater. And there was no way he would let her know how scared he had been. Still was. What had she been thinking, taking him out to a shark-infested reef? Cal gave her a quick 'okay' back. They would talk on shore.

Still grinning, Marina took the compass back, led him on a long tour around the coral heads. Heart still racing, Cal swiveled his head back and forth, looking for any sign of sharks. After what seemed like hours, Marina signaled they were heading back. Cal made himself match Marina's easy pace and not race back to dry land as fast as he could. He glanced behind him every few seconds, alert for the shark, any shark, sneaking up on them. All he saw was sand and water.

When the water was waist deep Marina stood. Cal did, too.

"Oh my God! How cool was *that*?" Marina pulled off her mask, her dark eyes flashing. "You got to see a reef shark, up close, on only your second dive! Most people dive for years before they see something like that."

Cal stared, trying to understand. Marina thought swimming with a shark was a *good* thing. And was unconcerned they could have been eaten.

"And you, with your 'I'm scared of sharks' routine! You didn't flinch. You settled in the sand, just perfect, and let it come to you!"

"Oh. Sure. That." Cal scrambled for something to say that would be appropriate, given Marina's excitement, without letting on he was worried he had crapped in his wetsuit. "It . . . seemed like the thing to do."

"She was a beauty, wasn't she?"

Marina waded toward the beach, Cal followed, glancing behind to make sure more sharks weren't lurking in the shallows.

"How'd you know it was a 'she?'" Cal said.

"Pelvic fins," Marina said, as if 'pelvic fins' explained any question he might have about sharks. About anything.

At the car they shed their gear and dried off. Marina watched Cal, an odd look playing across her face.

"You're all right when you're not being a punter," she said. "The island agrees with you."

"No. It gets under my skin."

"But so does fungus? I can hear your dad now," Marina laughed.

They stacked the scuba gear in the back seat and rattled the half mile back to Batten's Down. Rosie's bike was gone. With the will secure, maybe she would taper off on cleaning a house that was patently not cleanable.

"You want a drink?" Cal didn't want Marina in the house, but not to offer would have been rude. And suspicious. "Water? A beer?"

"Water'd be good."

The front door stood open. Of course. Had Marina kept him away from the house again so someone could ransack it? Cal led the way through the doorway and stopped.

"Something wrong?" Marina said.

"I'm not used to coming back and not finding the place trashed."

Cal crossed to the dining room table. The stack of folders was still there, though uneven and not exactly square with the table's corner. He lifted the folders. The map was still there. Good. Rosie had probably bumped the folders while cleaning.

Marina wandered the room, taking in the jumbled furniture, the packed rafters, the charts on the walls. Cal handed her a bottle of water.

"I like what you've done to the place," she said. "Apocalyptic post-modern's all the rage. This isn't trashed?"

"No, it's . . . Someone keeps getting in, tossing furniture and papers to find something they think's in here. Unless Rosie or I are here to keep an eye on things." He watched for Marina's reaction.

"You tell Rafe?" She seemed genuinely concerned.

"He says there's nothing he can do unless there's a burglary."

"So, what do you reckon they're after?" Marina ran her fingers on the stuffed iguana nailed to the wall.

"Gold doubloons. The Crown Jewels. Who knows? Rafe said it could be dangerous to stay here."

"Danger from what, dust mites? Falling globes?" If her lack of concern was an act, she was doing it well.

"A determined criminal, to hear Rafe tell it. Desperate for astrology equations and bad poetry."

Cal slid the haiku folder to her. She scanned the first two sheets, then laughed.

"That's . . . unexpected."

"Rosie wouldn't let me throw it out. Not sure why I'm hanging on to it. It feels more personal than a lot of the other stuff, maybe."

"Jerrod's weekly open-mike poetry slam's tomorrow. You should take these, read them out loud." She handed the folder back to Cal, face serious. "Weird. I haven't been in here since I was little. It seems . . . smaller. And definitely more cluttered. This whole pile more poetry?"

Marina lifted the top folder in the stack covering the map.

"It's all a jumble." Cal put a hand on the rest of the folders to keep her from digging deeper, or lifting the stack.

"These are electric bills from thirteen years ago." Marina set the folder on the table, glanced at Cal's hand on the other folders, then gave him a curious look.

"Hey, you know anything about caves? On the bluff?" Cal waved his other hand toward the door and the bluff beyond. It was all he could think of to distract her. "Do people ever explore them?"

"Not really. The person who would've left a while back. Why?"

"Whoever's breaking in is watching the place, and I found some small caves up there." Cal walked to the door, pointed, pleased Marina followed him away from the table.

"The person to ask is Hugh at Eagle Ray Divers, but I guarantee he's not your bad guy. He's explored caves on the other side of the island, though."

"He's discreet?"

"You're on the wrong island." She gave him an appraising look. "He doesn't gossip too much or stir up trouble, if that's what you're asking."

"Good enough."

"I'll tell him to be on the lookout for you."

Marina walked to the Thing, slung her dive bag on her back, then pointed to the cylinders in the back seat.

"Can you run those back to The Cove and grab two more? No telling when we're diving again, but probably in a few days. You're halfway there, shark man."

She kick started the motorcycle and roared up the road.

Cal hesitated by the car, not wanting to leave the house unattended. But Rosie had been comfortable doing that. If she was okay leaving the house empty, maybe Cal should be, too. And he needed to talk to Kat. He would make a quick trip. Cal stepped inside long enough to slip Rhodes' map in the folder with the house's floor plan to take with him, then headed for town.

At Eagle Ray Cove he swapped the used tanks for fresh ones. Hugh the divemaster wasn't there, which was just as well. Cal was short on time.

At Sandy Bottoms, Dusty barely glanced at him. Cal ducked into the computer nook and tapped in Kat's number. No answer. He tried the clock shop. No answer there, either. Midafternoon on a weekday. He tried Kat again. It wasn't like her to not answer. She was probably busy with customers. No, the shop was never busy with customers. She wasn't answering. And wasn't at the shop. That was what her 'fine' had meant. The shop was closed until he got back. Which meant the shop bills wouldn't get paid this week. He needed to sell Batten's Down, fast, if he was going to avoid bankruptcy. Until then, though, he was stuck. Stomach churning and throat clenched, Cal rattled his way back to Batten's Down. If there were other valuables hidden in the place, or near the place, he would find them.

At the house, Cal was surprised again it hadn't been ransacked. He spread Rhodes' bluff map flat on the table. He would track down divemaster Hugh, but first he would get a better idea about what was on the bluff top. If the map and lines were to scale, the nearest intersection wasn't too far inland from the edge. He would climb up tomorrow, before it was too hot, and see what he could find. At least there would be no diving the next day. He shuddered again thinking of the shark.

11

The next morning Cal slipped on jeans and heavy boots. The two lines on Rhodes' map intersecting inland from the house were high on the bluff near where he had tried to hide the day before. He would start there, see if the intersection marked anything. He folded the map, stuffed it in his pocket, and grabbed a pair of heavy leather work gloves from the lean-to on his way past.

The sun was barely above the horizon, but the day was already hot. Cal made sure the road was clear, then jogged across the road to the bluff, wanting to start his climb before anyone drove past and asked what he was doing. He slipped on the gloves and scrambled up the crevice he had hidden in, concentrating on the rough rock in front of his nose and trying not to look down. Soon he was at the top of the bluff. His shirt clung to him, already soaked with sweat.

Cal crouched behind a stand of gumbo-limbo trees with their peeling red bark, out of sight of the road, and checked the map again. If it was accurate, whatever was marked was maybe 100 yards inland and forty-five degrees to his right. He guesstimated the angle he should take and forced his way through six, eight feet of dense brush at the bluff's edge. The undergrowth thinned then, and the ground became firmer, though no less jagged. Cal pushed his way through thinner brush. Branches scraped across his arms and face. Sweat dripped from his brow, stung his eyes. He swatted at the mosquitos now swarming around his head.

After half an hour Cal stopped to catch his breath. His shirt and pants were both sweat soaked now. He checked the map. If everything was to scale, he should be near the spot where the lines crossed. There was no hint of a trail or clearing or anything but trees and cactus, though. He pushed deeper into the jungle, clutching tree trunks to keep from falling on the uneven ground. If anyone had been here in the last decade, there was no sign of it. Cal zig-zagged in what he hoped was an arc, looking for anything out of the ordinary.

Ahead and to his left, the trees thinned and the ironshore smoothed into a flat section of limestone free of pocked holes. The brush around it was less dense, as if the level ground didn't collect enough dirt for plants to grow. Cal picked his way to the space, if only to have a patch of solid ground to rest on for a few minutes.

The flat ground beneath his feet felt wonderful after what seemed like hours of rocky spikes jabbing into his boot soles. Cal squatted, resting. His mouth was dry. He cursed himself for not bringing water. Sweat dripped from his face, splattered on the dusty ground.

There, stained darker by the sweat drop, was a regular shape, a man-made shape, round, metal, the size of a silver dollar, set into the rock. A thin '+' was hammered on its face and small figures were scratched around the edge. Cal kicked at it to see if it was loose. No. It was set solid into the rock, held in by some sort of cement or epoxy. He pulled out his phone, took a photo. He would figure out what the markings meant later. Cal knelt, inched around it for a closer look. The scratched figures were numbers and letters stamped around the disc's edge. What looked like latitude and longitude coordinates, and others that didn't look familiar. A property marker?

He studied the map again. This had to be the spot where the lines crossed. To mark what? A tiny clearing in the jungle? With a metal disk in it? There were no trails or tracks leading out from the marker.

Cal stood. The world turned gray. His legs went numb. His tingling fingers found a sapling in time to keep him from falling. He had been stupid, coming out on a day so hot without water. He needed to get back to the house. He looked back the way he had come. The way he thought he had come. There were no broken branches, anything, to show he had passed there. Cal scanned the clearing. There was no sign of his passing in any direction. The sun had been generally behind him coming in. He glanced at the sun, now higher overhead and no longer due east. He hadn't thought to notice the sun's exact angle hiking in. He could guess the direction of the bluff's edge, but that guess could be twenty, thirty degrees off. Enough to make him miss the edge completely if he guessed incorrectly. A wrong decision now could be his last.

The marker was the only point of reference Cal had. He looked at the map again. If the marker indicated the crossed lines, the bluff's edge could be . . . anywhere.

Cal sat, breathed deep, forced himself to think. He was dehydrated and overheated. No one knew where to look for him, or that they *needed* to look for him. The bluff edge was relatively close. But backtracking was impossible. He had to find the edge, find a way down. Once at the road he would have an easy walk back. If he could get there.

Cal knelt over the metal marker. The smaller characters arced around the edge in a semicircle, a small break between the final numbers and the start of what looked like latitude/longitude marks. Had that break been to the left or the right when he had first found the marker? He closed his eyes, tried to remember. To the left, he thought, but wasn't sure. He wasn't thinking clearly.

Then he laughed at himself, pulled his phone from his pocket. When he photographed the marker, he hadn't yet turned around. He had stopped, knelt in place, tapped the camera button with his finger and . . . The saved photo on the phone showed the numerical semicircle open to the left.

145

Cal stood over the marker, shuffled around it until he was oriented the same direction he had originally been. The most direct route to the bluff's edge had to angle to the left. He flipped to the phone's compass. Roughly east and south. Twenty degrees away from the sun.

He grabbed a tree limb for support, eased back onto the jagged ironshore. His head was light. His mouth was parched. He seemed to not be sweating as much as he had before. That wasn't good. Step by careful step he picked his way across the broken rock. Every few minutes he took out his phone, checked the compass to make sure he was still headed in the right direction. The battery was down to eighteen percent. Great. But he only needed to reach the edge. After that it didn't matter if the phone died.

The ground grew more jagged, as if there had once been more of the softer limestone here to erode away. A rock spike crumbled when he put his weight on it. Cal caught himself on a branch before he fell. He pulled himself up and kept going, stepping carefully, keeping a firm grip on tree limbs as he went. Did the crumbling rock mean he was getting close to the edge? The trees grew just as thick. It could simply be a random area of less-dense rock. Dizzy and nauseous, Cal pressed on. He had to reach the road before he passed out.

The underbrush ahead grew thicker, nearly impenetrable under the taller trees. There was no getting around it. Cal checked the phone compass. Yes, he would have to get through it somehow to reach the bluff's edge. Cal gripped two sapling trunks as tight as he could, stomped down the nearest bush and pulled himself into the thicket. The dry branches scraped his arms and face. He grabbed two more saplings farther in and pulled again. At least the trodden-down brush was filling the ironshore, giving him more stable footing. He was breathing hard now, though, and the bushes around him spun. He reached farther again, grabbed two more trees and pulled hard, eyes shut against the raking branches. Limbs scraped against his face. Then a burst of light.

Cal opened his eyes, blinked in the sudden sunlight. Ahead was open sky. An onshore breeze blew cool on his face. Below, the sea glittered, foil-like in the sun, and broke across the ironshore breakwater north of Batten's Down. Closer, the dirt road snaked through the mangroves. The turnout he had parked in the day before lay 100 feet below his toes. Cal clutched the nearest tree to steady himself. He breathed deep, trying to still his spinning head and his roiling stomach. He closed his eyes, took two, three more breaths, savoring his success, then reopened his eyes and studied the rock underfoot. He still had to get down.

The cliff face here dropped sheer, though it was as rough and pitted as the crevice he had climbed up. Cal had never been good with heights, but this was the only way. His head spun again when he looked down, but there were plenty of hand and foot holds. Thankful for his jeans and gloves, Cal lowered himself over the edge and picked his way down, not sure whether his head was pounding from dehydration or the height. Jagged rock bit into his hands and feet, but he kept on, seeing only the ragged stone in front of him. He exhaled a relieved sigh when his feet finally touched the hard-packed dirt of the ground below.

He was breathing heavy now. The breeze wafted cooler here. Cal crouched in the shade beside the road, catching his breath and enjoying the breeze. The pounding in his head was worse. He needed water.

Cal forced himself to his feet and started down the road. The 200 yards from the house to the Thing had taken ten minutes the day before. It would take longer now, with him walking so much slower. His legs wobbled. The road seemed to tilt one way, then the other. Cal forced himself to keep moving. There was a syncopated throbbing in his head now, as if bongo drums were beating in time with the pain. Cal pushed on. The throbbing grew louder, into a clatter surrounding him, drowning out the sound of the nearby surf. The smell of exhaust.

A rusty white SUV appeared next to him, shuddering in time with its misfiring engine. Cal shook his head, blinked to make sure he wasn't imagining it. The car was real enough. Cal stopped. Antonio grinned from the driver's seat. His grin faded.

"Cal, you bright red, y'know." Concern filled Antonio's voice. "You break down or something?"

Cal tried to respond, couldn't, shook his head.

"'Sploring," he managed to choke out.

"Well, you discovered heat stroke." Antonio pushed open the passenger door. "Climb in. I'll get you home. Got to be careful about the heat down here."

Cal nodded, mouth too dry to speak. He pulled himself into the car. Rusty hinges screamed when he fought the door closed. Antonio nodded, ground the car into gear, and they were off. The engine's calypso beat grew louder, more insistent. The air rushing through the open window felt wonderful. Antonio slapped him on the shoulder.

"M'rina said you found some of your daddy's poetry."

Cal stared, not sure he had understood Antonio.

"Poetry slam at Eagle Ray Cove tonight. Got to come read some out loud. Folks'd love to hear Mister Rhodes' rhyming. I got a terzanelle I'm gonna read."

Cal mouthed 'terzanelle?'

"Like a villanelle. But with terza rima rhyme pattern."

Cal gave him the scuba 'okay' hand sign, leaned his head back against the seat and closed his eyes. The man was crazy, and Cal couldn't make sense out of a word he said.

Antonio coasted to a stop in front of Batten's Down. He helped Cal inside, settled him in the armchair, and opened the windows so the sea breeze would blow through.

"Air conditioning's what you need," Antonio said. "And what you ain't got."

Cal didn't respond, concentrated on stopping the pounding in his head.

"Here, sip on this." Antonio pressed a bottle of water into Cal's hand. "Slow. See what your stomach'll handle."

A minute later he draped a wet hand towel across Cal's forehead and another across his throat.

"'M good," Cal managed to croak. "Thanks. Y'can go."

"Nope. Gonna be here 'til I know you're all right. Future's foggy in here right now. You don't cool down pretty quick, I take you to the nurse. Lucky I came along."

Cal didn't, couldn't, argue. He closed his eyes. Concentrated on stopping the pain in his head. Antonio swapped out the hand towels with fresh ones, checked Cal's temperature. The couch creaked, and Cal knew Antonio was sitting, watching him. Breeze through the window was good. Cal's stomach tightened with every sip of water at first, then gradually settled enough for Cal to drink more. Antonio brought him another bottle. The breeze felt cooler. The pounding eased. Cal opened his eyes, sat up straight.

"No need for you exploring out there." Antonio was studying him. "'specially bluff-top. Run into that ol' mersquatch up there, and you don't want that. Anyhow, labyrinth's right here, y'know."

"Had a wild hair," Cal said. Labyrinth? Antonio was talking about caves? Knew about caves? About the top of the bluff? "Got turned around. Took me a while to get back down."

"People die doing things like that. Nothing but trouble up there."

"Just wanted to see the island before I go back."

"That's a good one," Antonio laughed. "You're just getting settled. Too much to do here. Got mysteries to solve and monsters to fight."

So Antonio knew what was going on at the house. Was he the thief? No. Antonio was nuts, but not a thief. His comment about a labyrinth stuck in Cal's mind.

"You're saying there's caves under this house?" That would explain why the house vibrated when big waves struck the headland.

"If there are, you want no part of them," Antonio said. "Old houses like this, got no septic system. Everything goes through that ironshore and out to the sea."

Cal shuddered at that.

"Labyrinth's up here." Antonio tapped his temple.

If Antonio was talkative, and lucid, Cal might get some useful information, though.

"'Tonio, you know of any reason someone might search this house, or who might want to search it?"

"All sorts of folks, good and bad, want in. You the only one matters." Antonio's voice went flat then, a detached monotone. He stared, glassy-eyed, past Cal. Or through him. "Gonna have to go down into the pit, face your fear, find your way back."

"'Tonio? You okay?"

"Monsters down there. But you know that. Nobody can help. Gotta be done."

"'Tonio, what the hell are you talking about?"

Antonio's gaze sharpened, focused on Cal.

"This house's where you belong." His voice sounded normal again. "No two ways about it. Need to have a Batten here. Balance things out."

"Balance what out? Who keeps breaking into my house?"

"Folks not too interested in balance." Antonio rose, set a hand on Cal's shoulder. "Oh, almost forgot. Jack Cobia called. Said to tell you he's still on Tiperon, walking that will of yours through the courts personal. Make sure there's no foul-ups. House'll be yours soon."

"Thanks, 'Tonio." There was a pang at that, some part of Cal that wasn't ready to give up the junk pile of a house.

"That's what I mean." Antonio winked at Cal, as if reading his thoughts. "I reckon you're okay now. I leave you in peace. 'til tonight. Eight o'clock at The Cove."

Antonio walked out, leaving the door open behind him.

Cal lay back in the chair, trying to make sense of what had just happened. Antonio had upped his Sight game with his trance routine, or whatever it was. Some new wrinkle to Antonio's brand of crazy. To him, Cal meant balance and the thief meant imbalance? Cal was more confused now than before.

"What'd 'Tonio want out here?" Rosie stepped into the room, swung off her knapsack. "And what you been doing to get so red?

"I . . . went walking. He gave me a ride back."

"Hell of a walk."

"Yeah. Antonio has this second sight thing going on."

"'Tonio's got his ways." Rosie's suspicious face was back. "What he say to you?"

"Nothing that made any sense. I'm supposed to fight monsters. And read Rhodes' poetry at Eagle Ray Cove."

"Don't know about monsters. That's between you and them. Poetry reading's not a good idea, though."

"You don't think I'm up to it?"

"Those rhymes are personal. Between you and your daddy," she said. "Folks won't understand them. Or they'll get taken wrong."

"People can take them any way they want." Cal's anger surged again. It was bad enough Rosie wouldn't leave the house, that she had told him what things he couldn't throw out. But now she was telling him what he could and couldn't do with his social time.

"I think I *will* go," he said. "Maybe bad poetry will jog peoples' memories. Maybe someone'll share something they know about Rhodes and his business."

"Trouble'll come of it."

Rosie gave him a dark look, then stalked to the bedroom. The sound of storage bins sliding across the wooden floor followed. If only she would take some of them out to the trash bins.

Cal thumbed through the folders on the coffee table, found the one with the haiku. He scanned the first few. He would prove Rosie wrong. The imagery in these would make sense to someone, and that someone could explain it to Cal. He didn't like public speaking, but it wasn't like he would be reading his own work. He would simply be reciting Rhodes' ramblings.

Three or four haiku would be enough. Ones with the most striking imagery would probably be best. The one about the teeth. And bluff-top moonlight sounded fairly poetic. And if nothing else, sorting through bad poetry kept Cal's mind off labyrinths and mersquatches and other imagined boojums.

A strange feeling came over him then, a prickling on the hairs on the back of his neck, as if someone was watching him. Cal looked up. Started. A figure was silhouetted inside the doorway, watching him.

"Mister Cal. Got a message from M'rina."

It was Linford, his stoned ride from town that first day.

"You scared the crap out of me!" Cal said.

"Sorry 'bout that. But M'rina, she said . . ." Linford closed his eyes as if trying to see the message. His eyes popped open. "Said tell you she'll be here tomorrow at two to go diving."

"Thanks, Linf . . ."

The man was gone before Cal could finish.

Marina was coming back to the house, then. Cal was uneasy at that thought, not sure if he could take Marina's new friendship at face value. If she wasn't using that as cover to scope out the house. Whatever the case, Cal's next certification dive would be tomorrow afternoon, whether that was convenient or not. And hopefully would be shark free.

Cal went back to the haiku. His head pounded in time with the swells outside, with the vibrating house. Yes, the one about 'sea cave thunder' would work. And the 'Euler angles' one, whatever a Euler angle was. That would be plenty. He would read one or two, gauge the audience reaction, and save the other two in case they wanted more.

Cal put the poems in a fresh folder and set it aside. He wasn't sure which thought was more terrifying, reading poetry in front of a group of strangers or diving with Marina. At least she had softened towards him, for whatever reason.

Maybe Antonio and Jerrod—and Rafe—were right about her being interested in him. It didn't matter. He had enough to do without complicating things chasing island rumors. Cal pushed those thoughts aside. All they would do is make it more awkward between him and Marina. He would dive with her, try not to piss her off, and hopefully survive. And look for clues of her wanting something more.

Meanwhile, Cobia was making sure the will was handled properly. The odd attachment to the house came back to Cal. Cobia could take his time with the will. Cal had enough cash from the strongbox to cover his on-island expenses for a while. And he was reluctant to sell the place before he discovered why everyone was so eager to buy it. What everyone's motives were. What other secrets it hid.

The only thing he had to get back to in Naperville was whatever was left of the clock shop. Kat was done with him. Meanwhile, the mystery here became more intriguing by the day. He needed more information. Why would Rhodes plot a long-forgotten marker so cryptically on a secret map? That made as much sense as the tacked-out iguana skin or the pentagram in the middle of the floor. Or his goofy poetry.

It was too much for Cal that morning. He needed to rehydrate, get his head to stop throbbing and his stomach to settle. Then read poetry out loud publicly. Never in his life had Cal imagined those words, that thought, would go through his head.

Cal opened the battery backup under the desk, pulled out enough cash to cover an evening at Eagle Ray Cove. He pulled his wallet from his computer bag hanging on the back of the armchair. Something seemed odd, but he wasn't sure what. He ran his hand through the bag's inner pocket where he kept his wallet and passport. The passport was missing. He checked the pocket again, then the other pockets. Had he left it at the Immigration counter on Tiperon? No. They would have tracked him down. And he remembered putting it back in the bag. But he hadn't taken it out since he had been on Blacktip Island.

"Rosie, have you seen my passport around anywhere?" he yelled.

"Why would I?" she shouted back. Then her head appeared in the bedroom doorway. "You don't know better than to look after an important thing any better than that?"

"I do," Cal snapped. "It should be in this pocket in my bag. Where it *always* stays."

Rosie looked at him as if he were a child who had lost a pair of mittens. She shook her head, then walked away.

Cal sat, still in disbelief. Someone had stolen his passport. Not his money or credit cards or other identification, just the passport. That made no sense. Unless someone wanted to strand him on Blacktip. That ruled out everyone except Antonio and Marina. And possibly Rosie. Or it could be someone using his passport to create a fake one. Whoever the thief was, whatever the motivation, Cal finally had an actual theft to report to Rafe, a theft the constable would have to investigate.

He needed to track down Rafe immediately, report the theft. He jumped up, headed toward the door. His head spun. The room tilted. He eased himself to the floor, closed his eyes until the room and his stomach stilled. He couldn't drive in this condition. He would have to wait until that evening's reading and hope Rafe was at the bar so he could report the theft there. If he was well enough to drive by that evening.

12

The Eagle Ray Cove bar deck that night was crowded with a mix of tourists and locals, all seemingly talking at once. Cal scanned the deck, file folder in hand, looking for Rafe. Looking for any familiar faces. Frank and Helen Maples were talking at the bar. On the far side of the deck, Marina and Rafe were joking with a scraggly group in Eagle Ray Divers DIVE STAFF t-shirts. He started working his way toward them when a hand shot out of the crowd, grabbed his arm and pulled him toward the bar.

"Knew you'd be here," Antonio crowed. "Told Jerrod to write your name in, but he didn't believe me. C'mon. Let's get you to him."

Antonio dragged Cal into the crowd, angling for the head of the bar. Cal could see Jerrod's shock of white hair now, then the man himself, microphone in one hand, shuffling through several sheets of paper.

"Jerrod! Told you he was coming!" Antonio shouted.

"We'll put him up right after you, 'Tonio," Jerrod said. "Never pictured old Rhodes as the literary type. It'll be cool to hear what he wrote about."

"You might not say that after I read a couple of his . . . things," Cal said.

"Only one way to find out." Jerrod scanned the crowd, paused, grinned. "Marina's looking nice tonight."

At the back of the crowd, under one of the flickering tiki torches, Marina was watching them, a curious look on her face.

"OK, Welcome to Open Mike Poetry Night!" Jerrod's amplified voice boomed across the deck. "As ever, we have some old favorites, and a few first timers. So without any further ado, here's Hugh Calloway with his latest."

A man about Cal's age, with close-cropped blonde hair and a blue 'DIVE STAFF' shirt took the microphone.

"This one's called 'Quiz Night,'" he said. He unfolded a piece of paper and started reading.

> *"Sitting beside you*
> *In perfect friendship*
> *I catch myself*
> *Wandering beyond our well-tended parameters . . ."*

Cal tuned out the words, watched the man reading. Marina had said 'Hugh' at Eagle Ray Divers knew about the island's caves. This had to be the same person. He needed to introduce himself, see what the man knew about the caves by Batten's Down, find out if someone could sneak up to the house through some sort of cave system. How best to catch anyone hiding in those caves.

"So, which is it, the Rhone or the Rhine?"

The man folded up his paper and handed the mike back to Jerrod. There was some applause, and a bit of laughter. People at the bar were smiling, nodding. Marina and Rafe grinned. Hugh joined a tall, brown-haired woman near them at the edge of the crowd.

"Thanks, Hugh," Jerrod said. "And now, Antonio's been working on a new villanelle . . ."

"Terzanelle!" Antonio shouted from beside Cal.

"Terzanelle," Jerrod said. "My mistake. 'Tonio, take it away."

Antonio took the proffered mike.

"Wrote this about facing the truth, no matter what," he said.

*"Going back down to Chapel Perilous
See if I'm ready for the Grail this time . . ."*

Cal couldn't follow any of it: something about failure and soulless dogma and atonement. He thumbed through Rhodes' haiku. The stuff wasn't any more nonsensical than what Antonio was reading.

*"Raising your own self whole from a half-life
Ain't got time or space to be careless."*

Antonio finished. The crowd's reaction was more subdued than for Hugh. People looked at each other, gauging their neighbors' reactions. A few people at the bar clapped for a moment. Marina looked puzzled. Rafe looked annoyed. At the head of the bar, Antonio beamed as if he had won an award.

"Yeah. A quest . . . terzanelle," Jerrod said. "What we've all been clamoring for. Give it up for 'Tonio!"

Applause came then, and a few whistles. Jerrod motioned to Cal.

"Most locals knew Rhodes Batten, who passed last week," Jerrod said. "But what none of us knew was old Rhodes wrote poetry when he wasn't doing whatever it was he did out at that wizard's workshop of his. Tonight we have his son, Cal, with us. He's going to read some of his dad's haiku."

Jerrod handed the mike to Cal. Cal took a swallow of water, set the folder on the bar in front of him and cleared his throat. Marina and Rafe were watching him, eyes intent.

"As Jerrod mentioned, I didn't write these," he said. Cal pulled the first page from the folder.

*"In times of seeking
Like a soft rain on sea swells
Gold en la boca"*

Cal looked up. Around the bar, the deck, a sea of blank faces stared back at him. Confused tourists. Locals whispered to each other. Here and there a quizzical look. There was nothing to do but press on. His voice came stronger.

> *"Hidden in darkness*
> *Below the teeth, the belly*
> *And sea cave thunder"*

Locals were alert now, hanging on every word. Some muttered to one another. Island imagery that reminded them of the coast? Hopefully that meant the poems were jogging memories they would share with Cal, help him solve the mystery of Rhodes and the house. Rafe stared at him, unblinking. Marina smiled, but she had read some of these the day before and knew what to expect. Cal pulled out the third poem.

> *"To see clearly now*
> *A thorny bluff-top sunset*
> *And Euler angles"*

The whispers among the locals increased. Some made hand gestures, indicating something tall, or on top of something. Several stood, eased off the deck toward the parking lot, side-eying Cal as they left. Rafe followed them. Marina met Cal's eyes, shook her head.

"Okay! Interesting stuff from Rhodes' files!" Jerrod took the mike from Cal. "Who else do we have with something to read tonight?"

The locals still there stared at Cal, but none approached him or spoke to him. They muttered among themselves, so the poems obviously meant something to many of them.

A woman in a Blacktip Haven shirt took the mike, began reading a free-verse poem about eagle rays and sunlight and lost love. Jerrod sidled up to Cal.

"You lit some fuses with that stuff." He stared at Cal, as if trying to read his mind.

"I can't take credit." Cal took a step back.

"Yeah, but you kicked the hornets' nest. In a big-ass way."

"What hornets' nest?"

"That stuff sounded a lot like clues." Jerrod leaned closer, eyes still too bright. "Half the bar just ran out to test their pet theories on where Rhodes hid his fortune. And what he did at that house."

"Great. Someone's probably on their way to trash the place. I wanted to get information about Rhodes, not restart a treasure hunt." Cal paused, studied Jerrod. "Jerrod, what was it Rhodes did for daily expenses?"

"Family money?"

Cal shook his head.

"Huh." Jerrod shrugged. "No way to know, really. Your Pops kept to himself and didn't like people poking in his affairs. You generally crossed him just once."

"What about rumor? Gossip? What was the verdict there?"

"Gossip?" Jerrod laughed. "Yeah, you're settling in on Blacktip. You'll learn not to trust the coconut telegraph pretty quick. If someone doesn't know, they'll make it up."

"But . . ."

"Your old man had a reputation as the nutty professor, out there on his own, doing who-knows-what. You'd see him wandering the road in the middle of the night, watching the sea. He tinkered with home-made contraptions like that trebuchet, but no one knew what most of them were or what they did. Makes for some wild conspiracy theories. Frank Maples about got his head ripped off when he went over to ask one time. And always watching for boats offshore. Your guess is as good as mine. Probably better."

Boats again. And no sign of Rhodes owning a boat.

"Wish I could help . . ." Jerrod paused. "This have anything to do with you being scraped up and dehydrated when 'Tonio found you this morning?"

"I had a hunch. I was wrong."

"Uh huh. Well, take some water next time you have a 'thorny bluff-top' hunch. And maybe a friend."

The woman finished reading her poem. Jerrod left, took the mike from her. Marina wandered up. Jerrod stumbled against Cal when he passed the mike to the next reader, knocking Cal nose-to-nose with Marina.

"Oops. Sorry," Jerrod said.

Marina's brown eyes were startled for a moment, looking into Cal's.

"What was that about?" Marina's gaze went to Jerrod.

"No idea," Cal said. "But at least he's not smiting me."

"Well, you know how to break up a party, don't you?" Marina stepped back a half pace.

"It wasn't on purpose."

"You're a natural, then. Hey, you asked about caves yesterday."

"Is that what the poems are about?"

"Not a clue. They're probably about rum. But the guy I said to talk to is right over there."

Marina led Cal to the edge of the crowd where Hugh, who had read the first poem, still stood. Beside him stood the brown-haired woman with light eyes, drink in her hand.

"Cal, this is Hugh and Jessie. Hugh, Cal was asking about caves and I thought of you."

Marina put her hand on Cal's shoulder for a moment, then glided through the crowd and down to the beach.

"Bottom line about caves here is they're trouble." Hugh studied Cal, as if deciding whether to trust him. "The interior's like Swiss cheese, only sharp and brittle. Treasure hunting?"

160

"I was wondering if someone could go into a cave one place and come out in a completely different place."

"Sure. But you're more likely to get lost, or trapped. And if you fall, or there's a cave-in, you're screwed. Where you want to go from and to?"

"Me? Nowhere. I . . . Could someone go into a cave on the bluff somewhere and come out by my house? Or wait there and watch the place?"

"Possible, but dangerous." Hugh paused, thinking. "Is that what that haiku was about?"

"I guess people think so."

"You're down at Mahogany Row, yeah? Those flats were an old anchorage, back in the pirate days." Hugh's voice was quieter now, his eyes searching. "If Rhodes found . . . there a lot of caves down that way?"

"Not really. No." Cal regretted starting the conversation. Now Hugh would be treasure hunting around Batten's Down. Though that might be okay, if he chased off whoever was watching the house. "Just little ones you'd have to wiggle into. Over sharp rocks."

"Yeah, well, if you go to check any out, tell someone where and when." Hugh looked thoughtful, gave Jessie a quick glance. "And maybe mark your trail so you can find your way out. Or someone can find you. Or your remains."

"Right. Thanks."

Hugh thought Cal was prospecting. Now word would get out. Great. Cal finished his beer and made his way toward the parking area. He needed to get back to the house, try to keep people out. In the morning he would check every cave entrance within sight of the house, see if there were any signs of people crawling through them. Hiding in them.

The stars were bright on the drive home. Rhodes' 'sea cave thunder' and 'blufftop sunsets' were obvious. But he still had no idea what a Euler angle was. Bearings to stars? Something from a compass? The lines on Rhodes' map? If they were clues, Cal still couldn't tell what they were clues *to*.

Cal pulled into the Batten's Down yard and stopped without pulling into the lean-to. The headlights lit up the front of the house. Someone had spray painted 'Get Out!' in two-foot-high red letters across the front door. At least the door was closed.

The chain lock hung open on its hasp. Cal stepped inside, turned on the lights. The place had been tossed again. Furniture was overturned. Books were dumped onto the floor and the bookcase pulled down. The glass distiller and beakers in the lab were shattered on the floor. Someone had pounded holes through the drywall by the bedroom. The glass float balls hanging from the rafters were still swaying in their netting. But the false vent by the chair hadn't been touched. Whoever had been through the house, it wasn't the same person who had taken the computer from the hidden compartment.

Cal hoisted the golf club from beside the door, turned on all the lights, crept through the house to make sure the intruder wasn't still inside. He snatched up the flashlight, went outside, circled the house, and went through the lean-to before turning off the car's headlights. Tiny lights flickered on top of the bluff, though that could have been tree branches waving in front of the stars. Other lights danced on the beach at the far end of the cove. Cal wasn't about to investigate any of that tonight.

He stepped back inside, righted the couch, and set the armchair up by the bookcase. Whoever had been here hadn't been searching for anything. They had simply thrown things around, done as much destruction as possible. As a warning. A threat.

Rafe's warning echoed through Cal's head. Things had gone from trespassing to breaking and entering to threats. That made Cal angry more than anything. Someone was trying to force him out of the house. His father's house. His house. He'd be damned if that happened. He would sell the place. Eventually. But on his terms, not because some anonymous vandal ran him off.

Cal paused. His house. The place was growing on him. Not enough to want to stay, but enough to keep the place until he solved the mystery of what was hidden, or not hidden there. And what Rhodes had been mixed up in.

Cal stared at the kitchen wall opposite the reading nook's fake vent. There *had* to be another hidden compartment there, by the stove. But he had already checked there. Twice.

A noise came from outside. Light footsteps by the kitchen window. Cal snatched up the golf club and flashlight and charged out the door. No one was there. Or had hidden quickly. Cal's being in the house was no longer enough to keep intruders away.

Cal went back inside, latched the door, closed the windows, and drew the blinds so no one could see inside. He slid the couch across the room and jammed its back under the front door knob. It wouldn't keep intruders out for long, but it would slow them down and give Cal a warning. He went to the kitchen, studied the wall where a hidden chamber had to be. Behind the stove. There was only a plain wall there. Above the stove was the back splash of foot-square ceramic tiles, the ceramic towel peg in the center of the middle one. The laminated hand-turkeys he and Marina and Rafe had made hanging from it. An odd place to hang a towel, or anything else. Cal set the picture on the counter, tapped the tile around the peg. It sounded solid. He pulled on the peg, as if it were a drawer handle. Nothing budged. He pushed, then pulled. Still no go. He twisted, pushed it left and right, but it didn't move. Angry, and adrenaline still draining, Cal swung his fist down on it, hoping to knock it off the wall.

The peg slid down with a *snap*. Nothing else moved. Cal pulled on the peg. This time the square tile slid free from the wall, revealing a long, low foot-square crevice.

Cal checked the windows, made sure all the blinds were pulled tight, then shone the flashlight in the hole. Stacks of money, in a half-dozen different currencies. Two passports with

Rhodes' photo in them, but showing different names. A teabag-sized silk bag with a handful of gemstones, blue ones, red ones, and clear ones. There were jewels in the house after all. Cal set the bag on the counter, shone the light deeper in

A blocky, black something. Cal pulled it out. It looked like an oversized walkie-talkie, but with a numerical keypad, like a phone, and a lumpy, fold-out antenna. A satellite phone. Rhodes *had* had direct contact with the outside world. And wanted to keep that as secret as possible, if he hid the phone like this.

Cal shone the light in the chamber again. Something else black and blocky was there. He pulled back, throat tightening. A pistol. Handle toward him, barrel pointing away. A box of ammunition behind it. Whatever Rhodes was involved with, it was dangerous. And certainly illegal if he had a pistol—firearms were banned in the Tiperons. Whoever was searching the house might be armed, too. Cal stepped back from the hidden chamber.

The passports he could burn. The money he could spend. Or throw away. But what to do about the gun and bullets? Tell Rafe? Even having a gun in the house, his house, could land Cal in jail, and Rafe was already pissed at him. And as sure as he took it out to throw it away, Rafe would stop by and catch him with it. Or the Maples would see him toss the gun into the sea and tell Rafe. No, he would have to leave it where it was for now, hope no one found it. And would deny any knowledge of it if someone did.

Cal scrubbed the passports and phone with kitchen cleaner, hopefully getting his fingerprints off them. He put them back in the compartment with the money and gemstones, roughly as he had found them, then snapped the tile in place and rehung the turkey drawing.

Shuffling came again outside, a slow crunching this time, like someone heavy-footed trying to sneak across rough gravel. The intruder was back. Armed? Cal was too angry to care. He eased the couch out from under the door knob and grabbed the golf club and flashlight. The sound came again, just outside the kitchen window.

Cal raised the club, switched on the light, and swung the door open so hard it bounced off the wall. He sprang outside to confront whoever was there. No one was in sight, though the slapping sound of running feet came from the gravel by the sea grapes beside the house. The footsteps stopped. Whoever was watching him? Waiting to see what Cal would do?

"Get back here, whoever you are!" Cal shone the light as the thicket, waved the gold club toward it. "Come back and meet me face to face!"

Silence. Then a fist-sized chunk of broken ironshore landed two feet to his right, tumbled to a stop. Then another, closer. A grunting sound, then a dead branch, as thick as Cal's arm and nearly as long, landed in front of him. Whoever was getting their aim and range down. Cal pushed thoughts of the mersquatch aside, stepped forward, club held high. He would chase down whoever this was before they could throw anything else. His shadow stretched in front of him from the light cast through the open door.

Cal took another step. Stopped. If he went chasing after someone and left the door open, someone else could get in the house. The rock thrower's accomplice, maybe. Was that the plan? Cal lowered the club, backed toward the house, light beam playing across the sea grape leaves, ears alert for any sound of movement.

"Anyone who tries to come in this house tonight is gonna get hurt," Cal shouted into the darkness. He waved the pitching wedge is a slow arc around him. "Anyone who actually gets in will get hurt worse."

A growling grunt came from the ticket. Another chunk of dead wood landed six feet in front of him. Good. At least he had backed off whoever it was. Or whatever it was. Cal backed into the house, club at the ready, and closed the door behind him. He jammed the couch back under the door handle, then made sure every window was latched. It was stuffy inside, despite the fans, but there was no helping it. He would put up with that, sleep in the armchair in the main room, with the lights on and club in hand, in case anyone tried to break in.

13

P ounding on the front door woke Cal. He sprang from the armchair, golf club in hand, pulled the couch aside and swung the door wide. Marina stood there, eyes wide and mouth open.

"I'll come back." She backed away.

"No! Sorry!" Cal tossed the club behind him. It clattered across the living room's wood flooring. "It got a little tense last night. I thought someone was trying to break in."

"I see that." Marina's eyes went from the spray-painted letters on the door to the main room's disarray.

"Rafe was right," Cal said. "Things are escalating. Someone's eager to get me out of here."

Marina gave him a worried look.

"You *are* looking a little wild-eyed. How about we give you a break from the place for a bit?"

"No! As soon as I leave, the place'll get trashed again."

Rosie, walking her bike, appeared behind Marina, eyes scanning the graffitied door.

"Well, here's someone to look after things. Jerrod let me borrow a proper car from the resort." Marina pointed to a once-blue Jeep with scuba gear piled in the back. "How about a dive to clear your head?"

"No. I need to find Rafe. On top of this, someone stole my passport."

Marina looked shocked. Rosie shook her head.

"Told you reading them verses was a bad idea," Rosie said.

"Well, there's nothing I can do about that now," Cal said. "Except go find the constable. And skip diving." The graffiti, the stolen passport were blessings in disguise.

"Oh, no you don't," Marina said. "Rafe's busy processing a bunch of would-be treasure hunters he arrested last night. How about we drive back to where I can get a mobile signal, we call and let him know. By the time our dive's over, he should be free to head down this way? And there's a U.S. consular agency on Tiperon where you can get a new passport in a few days."

Cal hesitated. He didn't want to go diving, but it *would* be good to get away from the house and get his mind off the stolen passport. He also wanted to talk to Marina, find out what she knew about the house and Rhodes and everything going on. Figure out whether she was involved in any of this, or truly just nostalgic about the house. If a dive made her drop her guard, it could be worth the discomfort.

"Sure. We can do that," he heard himself say. "Let me tell Rosie."

Rosie was staring at the graffitied door, her face stern, when Cal stepped outside.

"Going from bad to worse, Cal." Rosie leaned her bike against the house, rubbed at the paint on the door with her thumb. "I get this off with soap and a scrubby."

She went inside. The sound of running water and Rosie rummaging under the sink came moments later. She stepped back outside with a pail and a green scrubbing pad. Cal reached for the pail, but Rosie pulled it away.

"I'll clean this. You got other things to do." She shot a glance at Marina, a hint of a smile playing across her lips. "I'll be here 'til you get back, make sure nothing else gets tore up."

Marina raised her hands, palms up, in a 'what can I say' gesture. Cal changed into the hula girl swimming shorts then shoved his scuba gear into the back of Marina's borrowed Jeep. He would pick Marina's brain on the ride out.

Marina popped the clutch and fishtailed onto the road, sending gravel flying. They blew past the Mahogany Row houses, the car skidding through curves. Cal clung to the seat and door handle, any questions for Marina chased from his mind. The mangroves lining the road grew thick here, crowding into the roadway, slapping at him through the open windows.

"We in a hurry?" Cal yelled.

"Scared?"

"You always drive like this?"

"I forgot. Your car *can't* go this fast."

Marina grinned, coaxed the Jeep faster. The road took a broad curve to the right. The roadside trees thinned, revealing open sky. A gaudy-colored shack whizzed by on the left, a garish sign Cal didn't have time to read over its door.

"That's the Ballyhoo," Marina yelled.

"Great." Now Cal knew what the Ballyhoo was. He still owed Dermott a beer there.

The road turned north, running along the cliff edge. Soon the road sloped down, and they were angling down the cliff face. The rock here was as sharp and broken as on the bluff's eastern side, but shot through with more caves, some the size of water pipes, some big enough Cal could have walked into them.

Then they were at sea level. Marina turned south, rounded a bend, and skidded to a stop on a thinly-grassed verge, barely big enough for the car. In front of them the blackened limestone ended in a broad horseshoe of pink-tinged sand at the edge of the sea. To one side of the cove, palm trees arched overhead, and underneath were sporadic sea grape shrubs, their round leaves littering the shaded sand.

"Welcome to Duppy Cove," Marina said.

"First Antonio's mersquatch, now duppies?"

Marina laughed.

"Don't blame me for the name. Lots of locals believe in them."

As if on cue, a faint moan rose from behind them, wavering up and down with the faint wind. The hair on Cal's arms stood on end. Cal crossed his arms, hoped Marina hadn't noticed.

"There any animals on the island that howl?" Cal said.

"Other than people, the biggest animals on Blacktip are iguanas. And they don't make much nose." Marina's eyes were bright. A smile played across her lips for a moment. "Why do you ask?"

"Just curious." He wasn't about to mention the mersquatch. "Someone's messing with me. Why'd we stop?"

Marina studied him, still fighting back a smile. "That reminds me." She punched numbers into her cell phone.

"Hey, Rafe. Yeah, someone spray painted Cal's house and stole his passport . . . When?"

She looked to Cal. He mouthed 'realized it yesterday.'

"Not sure. He just found out about the passport yesterday . . . Yep. We're diving now . . . Three hours, at his place . . . Gotcha." She tucked the phone away. "Now, this is the most underrated dive on the island," she said. "Most people don't know it's here."

"Probably scared to stop."

"Nope. It's just hell-and-gone from anywhere and people are usually in a hurry to get to the Ballyhoo."

Marina stepped to the back of the Jeep, began pulling scuba gear out onto the rough ground.

"We'll set up here, then wade in," she said. "Just beyond the cove are some incredible coral heads. You don't like this dive, you'll never like diving."

"I thought we'd established that."

"This one'll change you." Grinning, she put a hand on his shoulder.

Cal struggled into his gear. Marina was being far too nice. Were Antonio and Jerrod right, after all? More likely she was getting used to him again. And wanted information about the house, or Rhodes' doings.

He checked his air pressure, made sure everything was in place on the buoyancy vest, and followed Marina down to the sand. Neither wore a wetsuit. Marina's red bikini bottom swayed beneath her tank. He hadn't noticed that before. He stopped that thought, looked past her, to the ocean. He had no business ogling Marina. They were barely friends. And Rafe would have every reason to beat the crap out of Cal if he knew Cal was checking out her butt.

At the water's edge Marina stopped.

"We'll drop down once we're outside the cove. It's about thirty feet deep out at the best part of the reef, so a nice, shallow dive."

Cal followed her, death grip on the gauges in his left hand, focused solely on repeating the insanity of going underwater. When they were chest-deep in the sea, Marina slipped under, barely leaving a trace on the surface. Cal hesitated, took a deep breath, then plunged after her.

The bottom here was pure sand, pinkish-white, with small wave-formed ridges parallel to shore. Cal kicked after Marina, following her black fins and dark legs through the shallow water. A touch of current from the right, cooler water, and the bottom sloped down. They were out of the cove. Marina turned, flashed an "okay" sign at him, then turned back without waiting for a response. They followed the slope, sand giving way to pale rock, then to patches of green coral and purple sea fans. Cal looked back to see if anything big and toothy was following, then kicked harder to catch up with Marina.

Soon larger coral heads appeared, faint at first, then in sharper focus as Cal got closer. A stingray cruised in front of them. Marina used a small flashlight to point out an eel tucked deep in a coral fissure. Cal nodded, scanned behind him and around him, still not over his basic distrust of anything to do with swimming or diving or the ocean. Even with Marina right there with him. He checked his gauges. 2900 psi. Thirty-one feet. Good.

Marina made Cal pass her his alternate regulator, as if she were out of air. They hovered together two feet above the sand, cross-legged, with fin tips in their hands, keeping themselves in place by how deep they breathed.

Marina motioned to follow and they wound their way through a coral maze, with low ledges bristling with spiny lobster. A turtle swam overhead, unconcerned about the two divers. After half an hour Marina signaled to head back toward shore. The bottom grew more shallow.

They rounded a coral head. Something large moved over the sand in the distance. Cal started. A sharp black triangle silhouetted against the sand. The triangle moved, collapsed, then swung up again, wing-like. It was close enough now Cal could see white circles in stark contrast to the black, and a second wing, moving in unison with the first. A ray, but bigger, wider than Cal was tall. It spun in place, dropped to the sand and rooted with its duckbill snout. Marina motioned Cal to kneel. He did, feeling relaxed underwater for the first time since . . . well, ever. The ray circled them, curious, then went back to feeding. After a few more minutes it swooped up from the sand and glided away.

Marina signaled Cal to follow her again and led the way around jumbled coral heads, brown legs flowing graceful as she kicked. Cal looked away, mentally scolded himself. Marina was a friend. Sort of. And there was Kat back home.

No. Kat was gone. He needed to let her go. He needed to let the shop go, too. Without a passport, he couldn't get back in time to save it. That life in Naperville was gone. It was time to move on. But to what? And where? His things were still boxed up. He could have them shipped . . . anywhere. In the meantime, he would try to enjoy this dive. His time on the island. And reconnecting with Marina.

Marina led him back into the shallow water of the cove. Cal did another quick gauge check. 16 feet. 1400 psi.

"What'd I tell you?" she said when they surfaced. "You can't tell me the eagle ray wasn't awesome."

"That was . . ." Cal stopped himself before he said, 'fun.' "… not terrifying."

"You liked it." She beamed at him, in that moment looking like the ten-year-old he remembered splashing beside him in the warm water by Batten's Down.

Cal said nothing. He walked from the water, slid his dive gear into the back of the car next to Marina's. Back on dry land now, his mind drifted back to what Marina might know about Rhodes.

"Here. Relax and enjoy." Marina tossed Cal a towel, then handed him a beer from an ice chest in the back seat. "That dive did you a world of good. Your eyes are back to normal size."

"That's because it's over with."

"Yeah, and you're away from that house of yours. It's not healthy, hanging out alone there so much."

"I need to find out why so many people are so interested in it."

"You're not adding 'so I can sell the place,' anymore."

"It's implied." How to nonchalantly ask why she was so interested in the house?

"So why'd you think somebody keeps tearing through the place and wants you gone?" Marina had a beer now, too, her dark eyes scanned Cal's face.

"I was going to ask you that."

"Me? I steered clear of your old man. We all did."

"Your dad and he were friends," Cal said.

"Your dad didn't have friends. Especially my dad. They crossed swords way back when, and that was that."

173

"Crossed swords about . . ." Cal tried to say it nonchalantly, as if out of pure curiosity. Alchemy? Boat parking at the dock?

"No idea. Your dad was mixed up in some shady business, but I don't know what. It's Blacktip. You don't ask."

Marina's eyes locked onto Cal's, questioning.

"You know more than I do," Cal said. He thought for a moment. "So . . . you're saying a shady business associate is looking for something."

"You here to take over the family business?" She said it casually, her voice low, as if an afterthought, but her eyes bored into his.

"I'm here to unload the place, then go home. Until I can do that, I need to know what's coming at me."

She studied him for several moments.

"The rumor is you came back to pick up where Rhodes left off, doing whatever it was he did. That's Rafe's big concern."

"Well, you can kill that one." Cal said nothing about Rafe's concern being Cal spending time with Marina. "Whatever he was doing, I want no part of it."

"You're not even a little curious?"

It was Cal's turn to study Marina. She was working *him* for information. She seemed to genuinely not know what Rhodes had been up to, but was still curious. Why? To help Rafe with his 'concerns?'

"Is this good cop, bad cop, you and Rafe?"

"You're a jerk." Marina spat the words, but there was something in her eyes that said he wasn't completely wrong. "I'm being friendly because we used to be friends and you're floundering."

She pointed to the fresh scrapes on Cal's arms and legs.

"And Rafe has nothing to do with it?" Cal said.

"He said to let him know if I got wind of what Rhodes had been doing or if you look like you were following in Rhodes' footsteps." Her eyes hardened to the look they had had when Cal had first run into her at the store. "But I'm *here* because I want to be, not because I'm a snoop. I'm *making* the time to hang out with you because I thought it might be fun. I'm re-evaluating that."

"Sorry. With all that's going on, I can't trust anyone." Cal took a long swallow of his beer. "Why's Rafe warning me away from you?"

"Wounded pride." Marina half-laughed. Her features softened. "Also, he blusters. A lot."

She seemed sincere. And Cal wasn't about to ruin a pleasant morning.

"Yeah. I . . . Thanks for the dive. And the beer."

"My pleasure. Look, if something illegal's going on, or someone's in danger I, we, need to tell the police. But anything that happens between us stays between us. Deal?"

Marina stood without waiting for a response, tossed her empty bottle in the ice chest. Cal downed his beer and climbed in beside her.

Marina backed onto the road and headed back the way they had come. The car crawled its way up the steep slope of the bluff. Cal's stomach rumbled, an echo of the straining engine. They reached the top of the bluff.

Ahead of them, a lone figure was walking, back to them, in the center of the road, carrying something in one hand. They got closer, made out the shock of white hair. Jerrod. With a cast iron frying pan. Marina slowed, pulled even with him and matched his pace.

"Jerrod? Everything okay?"

"Doing the Lord's work." He smiled at her, face blissful.

"Which is . . ."

"Hugh didn't succor a neighbor in need. Broke the house water pump and ran off when Cori asked him to fix it. Left her without water. Her and her dogs. He doesn't make that right, he has a smiting coming."

"That's kind of harsh, don't you think?"

175

"Not my place to say. I just mete out the allotted justice." Jerrod spun the frying pan twice with his wrist, as if testing its heft.

"Whacking him with a frying pan seems a bit extreme, though."

Marina kept her tone light, as if they were talking about the weather. Jerrod turned his head toward her without breaking stride.

"You're a good person, Marina, so I know you mean the best. But Hugh's transgressed. There's tribulation due. You know that."

"You could really hurt someone with a skillet like that, though. Hurt them, or worse."

"It's in the Lord's hands. But I'll act with as much restraint as He allows." Jerrod stopped. His voice went low, flat. "Don't hinder me in this. I'm just the vessel of His wrath."

"Wouldn't dream of hindering you, Jerrod."

Marina sped up, eyes on Jerrod in the rear-view mirror. Cal stared at her, mouth open. She pulled out her phone.

"Rafe? Hey, Jerrod's walking down the south bluff road with a frying pan, talking about smiting Hugh. Yep. A mile west of the Ballyhoo, headed east. Five minutes away? Perfect. No worries!"

She shot Cal a bemused smile.

"Jerrod's having a psychotic break and you're laughing?" Cal couldn't contain himself any longer.

"That's just Jerrod being Jerrod."

"He's going to attack a man. With a frying pan! He could kill Hugh!"

"Nah. Rafe's on his way. He'll corral him, talk him down." She half-laughed. "Last time, he coaxed Jerrod into putting the broom he was carrying in the back of the police truck, then drove him home and everything was fine."

"Until now! Jerrod needs to be arrested. And given a psych eval!"

"His spells don't last long, then he's fine again, once someone eases him down. And you've seen him—he's great the rest of the time."

"But he's dangerous. He needs to be locked up."

"If Rafe locked up everyone on Blacktip with mental issues, most of the island'd be in jail. End of the day, Jerrod's never seriously hurt anyone. He's one of us. One of the family."

"Never *seriously*. . . so another day in paradise?"

"Pretty much." Marina laughed. "There's worse on Blacktip than Jerrod."

"I have *got* to get off this rock. Before I go nutty, too."

"Not before we get you certified."

There was something odd in Marina's voice. Regret, maybe. Something not happy, at any rate.

"You hungry?" Marina said.

"I skipped breakfast," Cal said.

"I can help with that."

The garish, teal-and-pink-colored building came into view, 'The Last Ballyhoo' in neon orange cursive script over the door. Marina pulled in among a handful of island vehicles already there.

"You haven't lived until you've had a Ballyhoo conch burger," Marina said.

"Conch burger?"

"Ballyhoo specialty. Nothing else like it."

Inside, the Ballyhoo was dark, grimy, wood-paneled, with light filtering in through floor-to-ceiling windows across the back wall. Beyond the windows was a broad, covered patio overlooking the sea, with a wooden bar to one side. A few people sat at the half-dozen tables there. Marina cut through the bar and out to the patio, picking a table near the railing where they could look down on the water 150 feet below. Hugh and Jessie were at the next table. They nodded a greeting. Cal started to warn him about Jerrod. Marina elbowed him, gave him a faint shake of her head.

"Rafe's on it," she whispered.

The server wandered up.

"I'd like . . ." Cal looked at Marina. She nodded, face solemn, as if this were Cal's most important decision of the day, ". . . the conch burger, please."

The server raised an eyebrow, but said nothing.

"Caesar salad," Marina said. She whispered something to the server. Then, louder: "On my tab."

"Not a conch burger?" Cal said.

"Watching calories."

Hugh and Jessie grinned at the exchange.

"You work quick. Already out caving?" Hugh motioned to Cal's scraped legs.

"Just getting lost on the bluff, actually," Cal said.

"Uh huh. I know cave scrapes," Hugh said. "Find anything good?"

"Ironshore scrapes. No caves I'd crawl into. And the only thing I found were mosquitoes, heat stroke, and a random metal marker."

Marina, Hugh, and Jessie all looked at each other, then back to Cal.

"This is the first you've said about a marker, Cal." Marina lowered her voice, leaned closer.

Hugh and Jessie leaned in, too.

"It wasn't anything special. Flat disc about this big . . ." Cal made a circle with his thumb and forefinger ". . . with a right-angle plus-sign or cross or something."

"Little letters and numbers around the outer edge?" Hugh kept his voice low, as well, so no one overheard him.

"I think so." How much should he tell? No way he would show them the photo. He shouldn't be saying anything at all, but they seemed to know what the marker was. And it sounded like he needed to know, too.

"You found an old Royal Survey marker," Hugh said. "Predates the modern lot lines."

"Meaning?"

"When the English first discovered Blacktip, they surveyed it, marked off a grid to use in case this little rock was ever populated, then left. Then the papers with the coordinates got lost. When people came here in modern times, they drew new lot lines. Still a hot topic. Lots of old-timers who'd held land for generations based on that survey lost it if they had nothing to back up their claims."

"That's how the Skerritts and Bottoms ended up with all that beach-front property," Marina said. "One family member would subdivide the new map, then another would snap it up. They root up any of the old markers they find, in case a copy of the original survey ever turns up and supersedes the modern plot lines."

"Well, I don't think I could find this one again," Cal said. "Even if I wanted to."

He kept his tone light, but his mind was racing. Had Rhodes found old markers? Was that what the map and its intersecting lines showed? Had he found more than one? He had been plotting out the original lots around his house? Did that mean he had a copy of the original survey hidden in the house somewhere? On a computer or thumb drive? Was that what people kept tearing up Batten's Down to find?

"A salad and a conch burger!"

The server slid plates of food onto the table. Cal's burger was a grainy, pale gray patty glistening with grease and smelling of fish, garnished with lime wedges. He poked at it with a finger, not liking the look of it.

"It supposed to smell like this?"

"It's a giant sea snail. What'd you expect?" Marina said. "Trust me. It's like nothing you've ever had."

Cal covered the patty with the bun top and bit into the burger. It was as greasy, as grainy as it had looked, and bounced back into shape as Cal chewed, as if he were chewing ground pencil erasers. Pencil erasers that tasted like day-old fish fried in rancid grease. Marina smiled at him. At the next table, Hugh and Jessie were grinning. Cal tried to swallow the mouthful whole. His throat tightened. He didn't want to be rude, gagging the first time the tried the local delicacy. He tried to swallow again. His throat tightened again. His stomach clenched. He opened his mouth, let the half-chewed bite fall to the plate.

"What the hell did I just put in my mouth?" Cal rubbed his tongue with his napkin. It didn't help.

"It's an acquired taste." Marina laughed. "Squeeze some lime juice on it."

"That helps?"

"It's what people do."

Cal opened the burger. The ground snail meat looked slicker, grayer than before. His throat clenched again. He pushed the plate away.

"You really eat these things?"

"God, no. Conch burgers are disgusting!"

Hugh and Jessie howled.

"You said they were good!" Cal said.

"I said it was like nothing you'd ever had."

"I fell for the same thing when I first got here," Hugh said.

The server was there then, taking Cal's plate away and replacing it with another, this one with a hamburger and a pile of fries.

Marina chatted, laughed with Hugh and Jessie, reminding Cal again of the girl he had been friends with. Cal chewed slowly, processing everything he had learned. When they finished eating, Cal and Marina made their way back through the Ballyhoo.

"Be careful in those caves," Hugh called after them.

Cal waved without turning or slowing, his mind already on the house, wondering where Rhodes might have hidden important documents besides his will. He would check the tops of all the inside doors. If there were other documents hidden, could he trust Rosie? She was a Bottoms, after all. Was that her angle? Make sure Cal got the house, like she had promised Rhodes, then let Cousin Sandy snatch everything away? Or should he be more worried about Sandy Bottoms and Rich Skerritt wanting him gone, arranging for an accident?

Marina said nothing on the drive back, though she glanced at him every few minutes, as if trying to guess what he was thinking. Soon the Spider Bight houses appeared.

"Hey, don't put too much stock in that Royal Survey talk," she finally said. "It's more a local legend than anything else. Just don't let anyone know you found a marker. They'll tear up half the island to find it."

"You saw the inside of the house, right?"

Marina pulled up to Cal's front door. Rosie looked out to see who was there, then ducked back inside. Cal grabbed his scuba gear from the back.

"Thanks for the dive. And the lunch," he said. "I'll keep an eye out for Rafe."

"Any time." She smiled. "And watch out for sharks and duppies and howling mersquatches."

Cal stared, surprised by the mersquatch mention.

"Dude, you're asking about big animals and howling."

"Someone, something's been shuffling around at night."

"And you should know better than to take anything 'Tonio says seriously. I'll let you know when your last dive'll be."

14

Rafe, short tempered, took Cal's statement, inspected the computer bag, and gave Cal the number for the U.S. consul on Tiperon.

"Tourists lose their passports time to time." He gave Cal a suspicious look. "Have to fly over, apply in person with what I.D. you have. Usually get you a new one in a few days. You need to get on that immediately."

Cal drove the nine miles back to the airstrip. The first off-island seat available was in three days. Cal paid with cash, then, ticket in hand, rushed back to the house and spent the rest of the day hauling broken housewares to the roadside.

That night he barricaded himself in, couch wedged against the door. He slept fitfully in the armchair, golf club across his chest, dreaming of the bluff-top jungle, of shadowy animals circling the shuddering house. Of long brown legs kicking slow through gin-clear water. He woke several times to footsteps outside, but no one tried to come in. Boat engines roared offshore, but Cal tuned them out.

The eastern sky, was beginning to pale when he gave up trying to sleep. He rose and pulled out Rhodes' scribbled bluff map. If the intersecting lines showed Royal Survey markers, he should be able to find the next closest marker down the coast: an intersection south of the one he had found, near the bluff edge above the Maples' house. He needed to climb up there, see what he could find. If the markers were the key to what was going on at

Batten's Down, he would turn the tables on whoever was sneaking around, breaking in, and put an end to all this nonsense.

Cal filled one of Rhodes' military surplus knapsacks with water bottles, bug spray, and a couple of apples, then changed into jeans, a long-sleeved shirt, boots and gloves. He turned off the lights, waited for his eyes to adjust to the darkness, then peeked outside. No sign of anyone watching, though it was still ink-black by the bluff. No one would break in this morning if people thought he was still inside. He eased the sea-side bedroom window open, slipped out and made his way to the road, keeping to the shadows as much as possible, listening for people sounds, animal sounds.

Daylight was growing when he reached the bluff's base. Cal felt his way up the route he had climbed down before. Atop the bluff he glanced down at the house. An odd fondness washed through him again. The house was family, of sorts. A crazy uncle, maybe, but family. He gave it a final look and scrambled into the jungle. With luck, he could finish exploring before the day grew too hot.

To his left, southeast, nearly on the cliff's edge, the nearest lines crossed. Cal picked his way along the cliff until he was even with the Maples' place, following what could have been a rough path of semi-clear rock screened from the road below by thick brush. He pulled out the hand-drawn map, guesstimated the correct angle and pushed inland where the brush thinned. The air was stuffy here, the brightening sky all but blocked by a dome of branches. Mosquitoes buzzed around him, but the bug spray kept most of them off.

The underbrush cleared. Sure enough, another metal marker was set into the rock there. Beside it a four-foot wide hole led down, angling back toward the sea. Bits of rock around the cave's lip were crumbled, as if something had passed over them. The sound of waves drifted up faint from below, along with a fishy smell. The cave opened onto the sea. And someone or something had been in it. Marker forgotten, Cal eased himself in feet first, squatted and half-crawled, half-duckwalked down the shaft. Light appeared dim ahead. Two-thirds of the way to sea level the floor jutted up, wall-like, to within a foot of the roof. Beyond was clear sky and roof tiles on the Maples place. The vague stench of rotting fish came stronger. Cal clicked on his flashlight, stepped back. At his feet were the picked-clean bones of a dozen or more whole, mackerel-sized fish, jumbled one on top of the other. Had a wave washed the fish in here, then receded? No, that would have flooded the Maples' house. Someone, something had put them here. Not for storage. To rot, purposely? That made no sense, but neither did anything else on this island.

Cal scrambled back up and out. He sat, dug out a water bottle, and took a long drink. The sea breeze wafted the fish stink faint up the shaft. The brush thinned to the south, as well. He stood, picked his way that direction, pulled at a pile of dried branches, and uncovered a hollow big enough to curl up in. In it rested an outdoor speaker tilted up and toward the sea at a 45-degree angle. From its back a power cord snaked through the pocked ironshore, running north at the same angle as the line leading inland on the map. Where the wire ran above ground, it was covered by leaves and rubble and other debris. Cal followed it through the upland jungle.

The terrain roughened as he went, with trees crowding closer and the ground jutting up in ragged fangs. Larger cracks opened, forming deep pits. He had to pick his way around several, then re-establish his line of travel on the other side. He slowed, making sure he had a tight grip on branches and tree trunks before each step. A fall here could be fatal. Whirring, fluttery sounds of birds flitting through the treetops. Rustle of small animals in the dry leaves and underbrush. Land crabs or iguanas, probably.

He rested against a massive gumbo-limbo trunk, the red-paper bark chuffing off on his shoulder, and checked the map again. He had to be close to the next intersection, but ten feet was as good as a mile in the thick brush. He worked his way through the bushes, scanning for signs of another clearing, of cut branches, a survey marker.

Rustlings of some larger animal sounded ahead of him. Then again. Different than the earlier rustlings, louder, as if a dog or pig were pushing its way through the brush. Looking ahead, Cal misplaced his next step. The spike of rock beneath his boot crumbled, and only his grip on the nearest tree kept him from falling to the jagged ground. The rustlings stopped. Cal pulled himself up, continued on.

More rustling, but slow and quiet, as if whatever it was were moving carefully. A shape moved among the trees in front of him. Not low on the ground, but upright, as high as Cal's chest. Then it was gone. What kind of animal that big, that walked upright, lived out here? Adrenaline surged through him. He pushed thoughts of the mersquatch aside. It had to be a person. But who would be out at first light, risking life and limb on the bluff? Maybe it *was* a 'what,' not a 'who.' Cal crouched, barely daring to breathe, straining for another glimpse of whatever it was. Nothing moved. Even the birds overhead were silent. A low, faint moan drifted up from the caves.

Cal crept forward, following the power cord, quiet as he could. It had to be a person. The thought rang hollow, but he clung to it. It had to be a person. Looking for the same markers as Cal. The brush crowded more densely here. Cal crouched on his hands and knees, inched sideways through the shrubbery quiet as he could.

He popped out into another clearing six feet across. In the center, set in weathered cement, was a ten-foot wooden post, power cord running up its side to a solar panel on top. Cal barely had time to register all that when the bushes across the clearing exploded and something charged.

Rosie stopped a foot from him, cheeks flushed and eyes blazing, three-foot branch held high, angrier than Cal had ever seen her.

"What the *hell* you doing out here?" There was no lilt, or humor, in her voice.

"I . . . looking for that." Cal shot a look at the post. "Why're *you* here?"

"Same. And about to knock you senseless. You sound like a buffalo coming through that brush."

"Yeah, well, they threw me out of Boy Scouts." A suspicion came over Cal then. "How'd you know to look here?"

"Your daddy liked to poke around up in here a lot." Her lilt was back. "Never knew why. Now, with your story . . . two and two."

"So . . . Rhodes wasn't hunting survey markers. He was . . . playing a joke? On the Maples?"

"*Mister* Rhodes acted the island bogey legend to make sure folks didn't come poking around. Dropped fish in that hole, let the northeast wind carry the smell down." Rosie looked at the sky overhead. "Remote speaker for the howling, solar powered so he didn't have to come out here, draw attention."

Watching her speak, Cal could have been seeing Rosie for the first time, as if she were someone different than the person he thought he knew.

"Rosie, why are you so interested in all this? In Rhodes and the house and everything?"

"I owe your daddy on multiple counts," she said. "He's not here, but I pay my debts. If I can help his family, I will. But I can't do that properly without knowing what all's going on."

"What do you *think's* going on?" Cal didn't buy her explanation, but at least she was talking.

"Don't know all of it. Yet. Only bits and pieces," she said. "Some not-good folks involved, though. Safest thing for you is to be ignorant. And not get caught sneaking around up here."

"No. I need answers about this. *All* of it."

Rosie shook her head.

"Once I get things sorted, I'll tell you everything. Promise." Rosie held his gaze. Her voice lost some of its lilt again. "Until then, you be the dumb expat fixing up his daddy's house."

"I need . . ."

"You need to get back to your house with nobody seeing you. If somebody ain't going through that house right now, it's only 'cause they think you're sleeping in. *No one* can know we was up here."

Rosie pinned the post on her phone's map, photographed it.

"How'd you know where to find this place?" She gave him a suspicious look. "Or the fish cave?"

"When things get sorted, I'll tell you everything." Cal smiled. Two could play that game.

Rosie scowled. Waved him on. Cal traced the power cord back to the cave. At the bluff's edge, Rosie took the lead, taking them past Batten's Down, back to near where Cal had climbed up the first time. The Spider Bight flats glistened in the morning sun.

They watched the road for several minutes, making sure no one was in sight before they stepped from the trees. He and Rosie climbed down quick as they could. At the bottom, Rosie pulled her bike from behind a sea grape thicket.

"I'm biking to the house, like normal," she said. "Gimme those boots, roll up your sleeves and pants, and go down the beach, like you're out for a before-breakfast walk. Won't do for nobody to see you walking down from here dressed in hiking clothes."

Cal unlaced his boots, dropped them in his backpack, and gave the pack to Rosie. Seeing her deviousness first hand, he was glad the island busybody was on his side. Or seemed to be. She was putting together things he couldn't even imagine, and he had to hope he could take her at face value. For now.

Rosie rode away. Cal picked his way toward the water, angling for the long green strands of grass at the top of the beach. They would be soft, cool on his aching feet. He set one bare foot in the grass, howled when 100 tiny needles jabbed into his sole. He hopped onto the other foot. Needles lanced into it, too. He spun, launched himself as far as he could toward the beach and landed butt-first in the sand. The soles of his feet were covered in pea-sized, sand-colored burrs. He plucked one out, yelped when it bit into his finger and thumb. Cal grabbed a stick, scraped at the burrs, grimacing at the pain.

Minutes later he stood, the warm sand easing the sting in his feet. He walked to the water, let the sea wash over them, cool them. Cal took his time now, truly out for a morning stroll. He laughed to himself, thinking of Rhodes taking an island tall tale and making otherwise rational people like the Maples worry about an aquatic bigfoot lurking on the bluff, vandalizing their property. And now someone was copying Rhodes, howling and throwing branches and scuffling around the house, trying to scare Cal away. Had that person been part of Rhodes' scam, or was someone simply using the same island legend to try to spook Cal?

The familiar booming of the surf grew louder nearer the house. The place was still growing on him, despite everything. He walked up the slope, smiling at Rosie's bike leaning against the wall. Yes, she was tricky, that one.

Cal rounded the lean-to. Frank Maples was stomping across the broken ground between their houses.

"You certainly know how to stir the pot!" Maples said when he was within hailing distance.

"I have so many pots stirring." Cal half-laughed. "Could you be more specific?"

"You finding a Royal Survey marker." Maples glared at Cal. "You have tongues wagging, and not a few people concerned."

"How could you know about that?"

"It's Blacktip Island." Maples snapped. "You sneeze at the Ballyhoo, someone says, 'Bless you' at the north-end lighthouse. And Sandy Bottoms' bar is halfway in between. Sandy's one of the concerned ones. So am I."

"I stumbled across it by accident. No big deal."

"It is to some of us," Maples said. "I could potentially lose my property. Rich and Sandy will dig that thing out of the ground, *tout de suite.*"

"They're welcome to get scraped up looking for it. I couldn't find it again, even if I wanted to."

Cal motioned north along the bluff, away from Rhodes' mersquatch cave. If Frank and the others wanted to go on a wild goose chase, Cal would steer them that way, away from Rhodes' mersquatch ruse.

"Intentionally or not, you've complicated my life." Maples face reddened. "But that's a Batten tradition, it appears. If this negatively impacts my property or its value, you'll answer to me."

"With no original survey, there's no way one marker could do that."

"Unless Rhodes has a copy of the survey stashed in that house. That would be just like him."

"He has everything but that. I promise you. I've pretty much cleaned the place out. Everyone's property's safe."

Cal waved Maples off and went inside.

Rosie had moved Cal's diving gear aside, by the underwater scooter, and was sweeping up debris in the workshop.

"Uh huh." A smile played at the corners of her mouth. "You and M'rina have fun yesterday?"

"We survived a dive and had lunch after, if that's what you mean. One more dive and I never have to do it again."

189

"Oh, you do make sacrifices." Rosie grinned.

Cal had barely started straightening furniture when a vehicle pulled up outside. A moment later Rafe stepped through the open doorway.

"Heard you been doing some exploring, day before yesterday," Rafe said.

"Word travels."

"Didn't think to mention it yesterday?"

In the workshop, Rosie had stopped sweeping and was standing in the doorway behind Rafe, arms crossed, eyes narrowed.

"I didn't know it was important. Frank Maples already chewed my ass about it. In a fairly threatening manner, I might add."

Cal focused on Maples, relieved Rafe wasn't here because of his lunch with Marina.

"Don't doubt it. But Frank's not one you need to worry about." Rafe paused, glanced at Rosie, choosing his words carefully. "More than ever, you need to leave Blacktip. Can't protect you 'round the clock out here. Or up on the bluff. Rhodes was mixed up in all kinds of things. Only thing kept him healthy—and out of jail—were friends having his back."

"But if you know who . . ."

"You, Cal Batten, don't have any friends on Blacktip." Rafe stepped closer. Too close for Cal's comfort. "And you're turning up things that's got people . . . agitated. Best for all concerned if you were out of harm's way."

"I'm not leaving until I know why someone's so determined to tear up this house." Cal's anger was rising. Cop or no, he wouldn't be pushed around. Not in his own home.

"Then you might be leaving on a stretcher."

Rosie coughed behind Cal. Rafe turned, faced her, face as hard as ironshore.

"You know who's behind all this, don't you?" Cal said.

"Things'll get worse." Rafe stepped back from Cal. "You'll get hurt if you stay."

The constable stalked out the door and drove away.

"He's trying to scare me off, right?" Cal said. He needed verification. Validation.

"Rafe Marquette's always been a hard one to read," Rosie said. "Usually plays things close to his chest. That's why he's been constable so long."

"Are there really people who'd hurt me?" Cal thought of the hidden pistol. Of other people on the island maybe having pistols. He was rattled, despite his defiant front.

"Funny island," Rosie said. "Most of times what people *think* is more important than what *is*."

"So, would the Skerritts or Bottoms send someone out to make sure . . ."

Rosie bounded from the workshop, eyes blazing.

"Don't you believe everything you hear!" She shook her finger up at his face. "Only folks fool enough to be threatened by an old marker are the ones living close by, not people on the other side of the island!"

Cal took a step back. Rosie wasn't finished.

"You think I'm here to spy or steal, we gonna have it out right now."

She stepped closer. Close enough to hit him. For a moment Cal thought she would. And was sure she could drop him.

"Rosie, I can't trust anyone right now. Especially Rich Skerritt and your cousin Sandy. But I'm not leaving this house until I understand what's going on. You want to rifle through stuff, knock yourself out. I don't think you're a spy *or* a thief, but something about you doesn't add up, so where's that leave us?"

She stared him down. Then, saying nothing, she went back to sweeping the workshop again, inspecting the floor as she went. Something she had said jumped out at Cal.

"Might some of the Spider Bight gentry want to hurt me?" He couldn't imagine Frank Maples getting violent. But sergeant-major what's-his-name?

Rosie stopped her shuffling, studied him.

"People do strange things. When they're scared."

"Why would Rho . . . my dad have been looking into these old lot lines?"

"You *really* think your daddy was mapping property?"

"Well, people jumped to that conclusion . . ."

"Uh huh. And found you already there. You're smarter than that, Cal. What you think was going on? And what you got up *your* sleeve?" She stalked back into the main room, eyes on his. "How'd you know just where two markers were? And that cave and power pole? Damn sure wasn't blind luck."

He had given away too much. But Rosie seemed to know everything anyway. It was time to play another gambit, hope it panned out. He pulled Rhodes' map from his pocket, spread it on the coffee table.

"I found this a few days ago. I didn't know what it marked, so I climbed up to see if I could find anything. The time I found the first marker, I got lost and barely made it back to the road."

Rosie leaned over the paper, turned it sideways, then upside down. She took it to the doorway to look at up close in the sunlight. Tilted it counter-clockwise to a 45-degree angle. Pulled out her phone, photographed the map.

"Maps things out, all right." She looked back at Cal, eyebrows raised. "Shows where other stuff might be, too. Way in on the bluff. Where no one's ever gonna build anything."

"Meaning what?"

"Cal, you found a unicorn out there. A unicorn your daddy found, too. Something he wanted secret for who-knows-why. Don't mean a thing, more than likely. But now other people'll come looking for it. Maybe want you to show it to them. People who'll make this house-messing business look like a walk on the beach."

"I need to tell Rafe."

"How's that worked so far? No, you and me'll sort this out."

"What's your angle?" Did she know about the gun? About other people on the island who might be armed? As tied in to island doings as she was, she probably did. On both counts.

"My angle's keeping your *daddy's* name clean as possible. And keeping you healthy, and this house in one piece."

"With Rhodes gone and no one knowing about his speaker system, who might be howling on the bluff to make people . . . me . . . think there's a mersquatch?"

Rosie gave him an appraising look.

"Somebody wants folks spooked. And you not thinking straight. I'll look into that, too."

"Rosie, who *are* you?"

"Your daddy's friend. And the one who's got your back."

Rafe had said Cal had no friends on Blacktip. Maybe not, but, for reasons he didn't completely understand, he had an ally, however temporary.

Rosie went back to her workshop sweeping. Cal gathered up debris, his brain racing. If this wasn't about land, then what? Something bad enough for Rhodes to keep a hidden gun. And Rosie to want things kept quiet.

He spent the rest of the morning hauling out junk. He stacked twenty years of *National Geographics* neatly on the roadside in case anyone wanted them. Then went back inside and straightened the couch and table so they sat square with the floor tiles.

By midday he had given the place some semblance of order. Cal sat, relaxed.

Sound of a car outside. His shoulders slumped. The first chance he had had all day to sit and now someone was disturbing him. He stepped outside, expecting Skerritt or Bottoms. Instead, it was Marina, stepping from her borrowed Jeep, waving to him.

"Hey! No p.m. dives at The Cove today, so I thought I'd get an update."

"You drove all the way out here for an update?" Cal blocked the doorway. Marina was going out of her way to find out what was happening at the house. But he still needed to be polite. "Can I get you something to drink?"

"No, thanks. Just a quick stop to see how you're doing. And to make sure we're on to dive tomorrow."

The wind swirled around her, sending the smell of salt and a floral something washing over him. She was standing close. Closer than usual. And still smiling, dark eyes on his.

"Yeah. Sure," he heard himself say. "When and where?"

"I'll meet you here after work. A semi-dusk dive. Not many skills left to do, so it'll mostly be fun, with you navigating."

Rosie gave Cal a knowing smirk after Marina drove away. Had she guessed his suspicions? It didn't matter. She thought he was interested in Marina, and there was nothing he could do to change that. He would ignore her comments, her smirks. And hope word of he and Marina still spending time together didn't get back to Rafe.

15

The sun was well up when a tapping at the window woke Cal. Jack Cobia peered in, grinning, shading his face against the glass, cigar clenched in his teeth and a sheaf of papers in his hand. Cal slid the couch aside and swung the door open.

Cobia made a show of scanning the house's exterior—the graffitied door, the lean-to, the junk piled at the road.

"I see what you mean by it needing renovation," he said. He stepped inside. "Wanted to give you the good news as soon as I could. The will cleared uncontested. Never seen anything zip through so fast, though I *may* have helped that along. This thing's meant to be. You ready to list?"

"Thanks for driving out so early," Cal said. Cobia had probably fast-tracked the process to speed up his commission.

"I need a first-hand look if I'm gonna sell it. And there's no shortage of interest. It doesn't get any better in there, does it? Heart still set on the full $2.5?"

"Let's . . . hold off on listing it. For a bit." Cal still needed to know why so many people were so interested in the place. And with no passport, he wasn't heading back to Naperville anytime soon.

Cobia looked surprised.

"Gauging interest. Bumping up the price. Smart." Then a worried look crept over his face. "You *are* selling. Right?"

"I just need to finish going through all Rhodes' things," Cal stifled a smile. The old pirate was seeing his commission disappear. "No telling how long that'll take."

Cobia smiled then, as if in on some conspiracy.

"More time to pal around with Marina, you mean?"

"She's just teaching me to dive."

"That what they're calling it these days?"

"I know it's a small island, but how do rumors like that get started?" The man had been off island and still knew about Cal and Marina's lunch.

"The Ballyhoo may be off the beaten track, but it's about the most public place on the island. Even when it's empty."

"Oh. We dived at Duppy Cove. I needed a drink after." Marina had to have known word would get out. Did she not care, or was that why she had stopped?

"Good to see you fitting in on Blacktip." Cobia slapped Cal on the back, winked. "A week ago I'd have laughed at that idea."

Someone cleared their throat behind them. Cobia's leer faded. Rosie had come up without them hearing her, scowled at Cobia. She slipped back to her usual non-expression, but Cal had seen the look for an instant.

"You walk quiet as a cat, don't you?" Cobia said.

"You two gabbing loud enough to wake the dead."

Cobia studied Rosie, as if appraising her value. Rosie brushed past him on her way inside. The sound of clattering dishes sounded a moment later.

"What's she still doing out here?" Cobia said.

"She won't leave. Rhodes paid her through the end of the year." Cal tried to sound as nonchalant as he could. Rosie didn't like Cobia, and it seemed the feeling was mutual. "I fired her twice and she's still here. I've made peace with it."

"Well, *when* the place sells, she has to go."

"That's between her and the new owner."

"Right. Hey, I'll keep you posted about any offers. But don't take too long. You have questions, you know where to find me."

Cal watched Cobia drive away. Something had happened while the man was here, something subtle. A shift in Cobia's body language, maybe, not related to the commission. The hairs on the back of Cal's neck stood on end, but he couldn't put his finger on any specific reason why. Cobia was pressing. Why would his attitude change, now the house was free and clear?

Cal walked back inside. With buyers lining up, more than ever he needed to know what made the property so valuable. Before the house was destroyed or he was physically assaulted. The night before had been too quiet. And Cobia was antsy. Something was brewing.

Marina was coming to dive that afternoon. Or to see what Cal was doing in the house. That gave him most of the day to explore. With any luck, she would forget. A twinge of regret at that. He enjoyed her company. There was no way she would forget, though. Or cancel. She was intent on finishing Cal's class. In making sure he wasn't doing whatever it was Rhodes had done. He would search everywhere he could, before Marina got there.

"Rosie, is there any chance Marina's mixed up in any of these break ins? Or with my passport going missing?"

Rosie gave him an odd look.

"You really worried M'rina'd steal from you?"

"Well, she wants me not to sell the house, she's been asking questions about the place since Day One. And with no passport I'm stuck here."

"M'rina's playing her own game, but she's not the type to break and enter." Rosie skewered him with a withering look. "You ought to know that by now."

Cal turned his attention to the house's interior, not sure what, exactly, to make of Rosie's comment. He checked every door, every door frame, every window sill for hidden compartments. He stomped on the floors when he crossed a room, listening for hollow sounds. Rosie was doing the same as she sorted through Rhodes' things, hauling to the roadside more than she had before. Cal racked his brain for what Rhodes might have hidden, hoping for an indication of where to search. He tried not to think about the pistol, about other people with pistols. The afternoon wore on, and still there was no sign of Marina. Just as well. His search of the house, the grounds, was more important than some silly scuba dive.

Rosie left, and Cal had moved on to the lean-to when Marina arrived an hour before sundown. He walked out to greet her, glad to see her, but relieved she had arrived too late to dive.

"So much for that last dive, huh?" he said. "Tomorrow, maybe?"

"Dude, we're dusk diving, remember?" She gave him an annoyed look. "Can't say you're a diver without diving in the dark."

"Right. Nice try." At least she wasn't trying to get into the house.

Marina's expression didn't change. Behind her, scuba fins and cylinders stood upright in the blue Jeep's back seat.

"You're serious?" Cal remembered reading something about big fish being more active at night. "Why would anyone dive at night?"

"Different fish are out. The coral's awake and feeding."

"That's what I'm saying. After dark *I* should be feeding. And drinking."

"It'll make your navigation more challenging." Marina ignored his protest. "You have a dive light? No? No worries. I brought two."

Defeated, Cal fetched his dive gear from inside. When he came back out, he was surprised to see Marina already suiting up.

"We're diving here?" This had to be a joke.

"The waves have laid down, and there's some nice shallow coral right out there. It's usually too rough, so no one dives here. That and everyone was terrified of your dad."

Cal slid into his scuba gear and followed Marina down the flattened strip of ironshore by the trebuchet. He hesitated at the water's edge, dark as spilled oil in the failing light. There was no telling what was lurking underneath the surface.

"There likely to be any sharks out there?" Cal tried to keep his voice calm.

"You and your sharks." Marina rolled her eyes. "Sure. Rosalita Flats is a sharky section of the coast, for whatever reason. That's what makes it such a good dive. And, as you've seen, they don't give a damn about divers. If we're lucky we'll see another one."

Cal was more worried about a shark seeing him than of him seeing a shark, but he said nothing. He followed Marina into the dark water, so close he could touch her. He stayed close after they submerged, too.

Once underwater, Marina signaled for him to lead. Cal wound his way around the shallow coral heads, glancing back at Marina every minute or so to make sure he wasn't getting them lost. The water darkened and they switched on their lights. Soon Cal's attention was locked on the ovals of their milky beams. After ten minutes he realized he wasn't sure which direction the shore was. He glanced at Marina.

Behind him, Marina motioned, excited, shone her light next to a stringy-looking bit of purple soft coral sticking up from the sand. There, at the edge of her light's glow, something yellow was wrapped around the purple strand. The something shifted, revealing a long snout and a small orange eye. A seahorse, tail curled tight around the base of the coral. She handed Cal a magnifying glass, motioned for him to take a closer look.

A buzz sounded somewhere, as if a giant mosquito were circling nearby. Cal studied the seahorse. Its eye pivoted as Cal moved, studying Cal. The buzzing grew louder. Metallic. Cal looked to Marina. She made the cupped-hands sign for 'boat,' then waved her finger toward the surface. A fisherman, maybe. The buzz must be a propeller. Cal looked back at the seahorse.

The buzz grew louder, as if the boat were on top of them. Marina looked concerned. She motioned Cal to lie flat on the sand bottom, then shined her light in a fast, broad circle at the surface to get the boater's attention. The sound of the prop steadied to a constant grind, seemingly from all around them. Circling them. Someone was looking for them? Trying to get their attention? Whoever it was had to see their dive lights in the dark water. Cal pointed a thumb at the surface in a silent question: go up? Marina shook her head, signaled 'no,' motioned for him to stay flat in the sand.

Something drifted down, settled on the sand in front of them. A severed fish head. Other fish parts followed: guts, tails, then a split-open snapper still twitching. Reef fish swarmed in on the chum. Silvery snappers. Brown-striped groupers. Bigger shapes circled at the edge of their lights. Why would someone throw chopped-up fish where people were obviously diving? Marina's eyes looked worried. She signaled 'shore,' turned off her light, then Cal's, and took his hand. Foot by foot, they dragged themselves toward shallower water in the near-darkness.

The prop revved higher, louder. Cal glanced up, saw a skiff's hull cut six feet in front of them, propeller spewing a gash of white water behind it. Whoever was in the boat knew they were there. If this was a prank, it wasn't funny. And Marina wasn't in on it. Someone was trying to scare them? Or him. More fish guts rained down.

Marina gripped his hand tight. A dark shape shot past so close the water in front of Cal vibrated. Longer than Cal, sharp dorsal fin jutting up, then a high thrash of tail. Another came from the opposite direction, snapped up a chuck of dismembered fish from the bottom without slowing, and shot off into the darkness. Cal froze. Marina dragged him forward. Other dark shapes blurred past at the edge of his sight. Cal pushed off the bottom, headed for the surface. Better to risk a lunatic fisherman than to stay down here in a feeding frenzy. Marina pulled him down, dragged him forward again. The water was shallower now. Shore had to be close.

The propeller sound was fainter, as if the skiff driver had lost their bubbles in the darkness and the white water of its own wake. Or didn't dare venturing into the shallows.

Cal pulled himself forward, digging his light into the sand like an ice ax. He kicked as much as he dared, tried to strike a balance between propelling himself forward, but not so hard his thrashing attracted more sharks. Bulky silhouettes flashed all around Cal and Marina now, zipping past so fast they were gone almost before Cal registered them in the dusky water. The surface rippled nearer now. The bottom changed from sand to rock. The boat circled behind them, it's prop idling, faint enough now to be drowned out by Cal's labored breathing.

A glob of fish guts drifted down directly in front of them. Marina held Cal back. A gray shape, mouth wide with ragged teeth snatched the guts mid-water. Marina pulled Cal forward again. Something bumped Cal's fin. Cal kicked as hard as he could, shooting ahead so quick he dragged Marina behind him for a moment. Marina kicked hard, too. Something bumped Cal's side. He swung his light at it as hard as he could, felt it glance off something fleshy.

A black wall loomed in the semi-dark ahead of them. The submerged portion of the rock shoreline. There seemed to be fewer sharks, too, though every shark in the Caribbean could have been behind him and Cal wouldn't have known it. The boat prop sounded fainter, as if the driver were staying well out. A darker patch of wall stood out to their right. Marina angled toward it. Rocks, jagged as any bluff-top cave, crowded above and beside them in a submerged arch three feet wide. Marina put her right fin tip in Cal's left hand, pulled herself forward with her hands, dragging him behind her.

Utter darkness. Cal's free hand gripped rough rock inches below him. He looked back, could see the lighter open water through the rough arch they had swum through, looking for all the world like the maw of a giant sea monster. Cal shuddered. A cave, then. Like the ones on the bluff, but completely submerged. The skiff driver wouldn't be able to see the entrance.

Something pressed down on Cal's back. Cal rolled, fists balled to fight off a shark. Cool air wafted across his face. They were in water so shallow his tank had broken the surface. He stood. The sound of splashing beside him told him Marina was standing, too.

"I'm gonna chance a light," she whispered.

Her dive light snapped on, aimed at her chest to keep it from showing outside the cave. Her hands shook. The roof was lost in darkness.

"Didn't know this cave was here." Marina's whisper came ragged. Her voice cracked. "Good thing it is."

"Someone was purposely chumming around us!" It was part question, part outraged statement.

"Yep. And I'm going to find out who as soon as we get out of here. If that was a joke, it was *not* funny."

"Someone's trying to scare me off." Cal shuddered as the adrenaline drained.

"Maybe. By now, whoever it was thinks we're on shore. Or worse." She dipped one side of her head in the water for several seconds. "I don't hear the motor. Let's risk a little more light."

She cupped her hand over part of the light's lens to dim it and swung the beam away from the sea, into the cave. The cave's roof rose twice as high as Cal's head, crusted over with sea algae and chiton shells. Thirty feet ahead was a natural shelf at Cal's eye level, and more darkness. They waded to the smooth shelf. Cal took off his scuba gear and climbed up. He shone his light toward the back of the cave. It ended ten feet beyond. At the base, where it joined the wall, were a half-dozen black, squarish blocks.

"Anything worth seeing?" Marina's voice came sharp from behind him.

"You should probably climb up and take a look."

He lifted his gear out of the water, then hers, and helped Marina up. He shined his light on the shapes. Waterproof storage cases. The smallest was the size of a small toolbox. The largest was as big as a footlocker.

Marina gave him a quizzical look, then knelt by the closest one.

"Been here a while, with all the salt crust on it," she said.

"But opened recently." Cal played his light's beam along the breaks in the salt on all the cases and on the crust-free latches. "Rhodes must've been in this one not so long ago."

"Nothing for it." Marina snapped open the latches and raised the lid.

Inside were stacks of U.S. currency, divided into piles of $20, $50 and $100 bills. Cal lifted a handful. The money filled the case, with no spacer in the bottom. Marina stared at the money, mouth open. Cal thumbed through a bundle of $100s, counted how many stacks were on the top layer, then mentally multiplied by how tall the stacks were.

"There's several hundred thousand in here." His voice sounded faint, as if someone else had spoken.

"Guess we found what Rhodes did for money," Marina said.

"And what people are looking for in the house." Cal put the money back. "And why they want me out of the way." Cal's mind raced. Where would Rhodes get this much cash? Why would he hide it here? And who knew about this stash? Or suspected it existed? Marina was still staring at the money.

"No one has any idea this place exists, or none of that cash would still be here," he said.

Cal bent over the next case, snapped it open. Inside were spare clothes. The next contained water, dried food, candles, and a small stove. A small velvet bag, like the one in the hidden kitchen nook, but bigger. with a palm-full of bright-colored gemstones. Palm-sized gold bars lay beneath the bag.

"We just found that 'gold en la boca,' Cal whispered.

Marina knelt, put her hand on his back.

The next held modern scuba gear, including dive lights and spare batteries. Behind that case was an underwater scooter.

"He had himself a short-term hide out," Cal said.

"Or set up for a quick getaway," Marina said. "What now?"

"We tell *no one* about this," Cal said. Whatever Marina's interest in Rhodes' affairs, in Batten's Down, if anyone learned of this cave, he and she would both be in danger. He would figure out her angle soon enough. "This is why whoever's been breaking in the house. And chumming around us. Even though they don't know exactly where it is," Cal said. Stating the obvious helped him get his head around what had happened, made it less surreal. "Someone wants me gone so they can tear the house apart looking for all this." He waved a hand at the bins.

"Makes sense." Marina was staring at him now, eyes still wide. Reappraising.

Cal paused, waiting for the words to come.

"Someone tried to kill us."

"And we're gonna find out who."

"Jerrod trying to smite us?"

"No. He goes for the face-to-face approach. And I've never seen him in a boat." She paused, thinking. "Unless someone ran a skiff all the way around the island, they had to come from Mango Sound. Below the Ballyhoo. No place else is close." Marina's voice was steady now. And angry.

"So let's go."

Cal snapped the storage bins closed, then started back toward the shelf's edge and their scuba gear. Marina held back.

"You okay getting in the water again?" she said. "They won't be feeding, or as aggressive, but there'll be sharks."

"Don't have a choice." Cal gritted his teeth, told his heart to slow. "There's bigger sharks on land, and we have to find out who they are."

Marina joined him, lowered her BC into the water.

"We'll hug the coast. It's only fifty yards or so to our entry point. We'll be out quick."

Cal paused, stepped back to the bin with the cash. He stuffed a bundle of $50s into his wetsuit, slipped into the dark water behind a grinning Marina and donned his scuba gear. He paused, thinking, then took off his gear, climbed out, and put the wet cash back by the box where it could dry.

"Why'd you do that?" Marina's puzzled face looked comic in the low, reflected light.

"It might not be Rhodes' money," Cal said. "It might belong to . . . people . . . who are . . . desperate . . . to find it."

"And who'd do anything to get it back . . ." Marina's voice trailed off.

"Bingo."

Marina's eyes held his for a long, appraising moment.

"Okay. You ready?"

Cal nodded.

"Hold hands so we don't get separated," she said. "We'll be on shore in no time. In one . . . two . . . three."

Cal lowered his gear and slipped into the dark water. He clenched his teeth on his regulator mouthpiece, Marina's hand tight in his. At the cave's mouth they submerged, crawled out into the open water, not daring to turn on their lights. They swam up the shoreline quick as they could, hugging the dark ironshore wall on their right, trying to ignore any shapes, real or imagined, in the water around them.

16

M inutes later they dragged themselves onto the ironshore. Shaking, Cal squatted, letting the tank pull him backwards so he sat on the rock. Marina stood, looking out to sea. She was shaking, too.

"Whoever that was will regret they ever even *thought* about chumming around us!" She shone her light out across the waves, looking for the boat, but it was gone. There was not even the sound of its outboard.

"There's only so many skiffs on this island. Someone'll know who was out here tonight." She put her hand on Cal's shoulder. "You Okay? No cuts? No bites?"

Cal shook his head, not daring to talk. Trying to get his heart to slow, to not crack his ribs. Trying to get his mind off the dark, streaking shapes. He clenched his jaws to keep his teeth from chattering. There was a ragged sound, like wind roaring through the trees. His breathing, he realized. Marina's hand helped, warm despite having been in the water.

"Let's go find this joker before he gets away."

She took Cal's hand, pulled him up and across the broken ground to the house. They dropped their scuba gear by the borrowed Jeep.

"Here." She tossed Cal a towel. "Dry off while I drive."

Marina slipped on a pair of shorts, wrapped her hair in a towel and jumped behind the wheel. Cal climbed in beside her, still wet, shirt in one hand and towel in the other. Marina spun the Jeep's wheels in the gravel. She pulled onto the road and raced south, face livid in the dashboard lights.

"Any idea who it was?" Cal said.

"No, but we're going to Mango Sound to find out."

Cal nodded, watching her eyes, her lips moving in the dash's glow. Her thighs tensing when she shifted gears. They roared down Mahogany Row, houses passing in a blur.

"Who would do that?" Cal tried to get his mind off Marina's legs and lips. Tried to get his head around what had happened, make it less surreal. And if she threw out some names, one might be familiar.

"There's three, four people not named 'Jerrod' who take regular breaks from reality," Marina said. "But none of them would do anything like this."

Marina shot Cal a thin smile, squeezed his knee for an instant. An electric jolt shot through him.

"We're calling Rafe, right?" he said.

"Signal should be good at the Sound."

They sped past the Ballyhoo and its flashing neon lights, then down the bluff-face road. A hard, skidding left, then past Duppy Cove. The road narrowed to two ruts, wide enough for one car. Then the roadside vegetation fell away, and Marina stomped on the brakes. In the headlights' beams lay a calm expanse of water, a sheltered cove. Three rough wooden piers extended over the water, small fishing skiffs resting motionless next to each. There was no sign of people.

Marina jumped from the Jeep, stalked down to the first dock. Cal followed, dive light in hand, as angry as Marina now the shock of the dive had worn off. The reality of what had happened was setting in. Someone had tried to kill him. Them. Marina was right—if they found the chummer, they would take care of him themselves before they called Rafe.

The Jeep's headlights flood-lit the cove. Marina jumped into the closest skiff, pressed a hand to its raised outboard. Cal swung his light's beam across the other piers, alert for any sign of movement, of anyone hiding in the open boats or the surrounding bushes.

"This one's cold," she called back to Cal.

Cal kept close to her, ready to tackle anyone who might be lurking, waiting to attack them. Both skiffs on the first dock had cold engines, as did the lone skiff on the second dock. On the third dock was a beat-up skiff reeking of fish. Cal played his light's beam across buckets, two hand lines, blood and fish guts strewn across the bilge's fiberglass. Marina stepped in carefully, picked her way back to the outboard.

"Gotcha!" she yelled.

"Whose boat is this?" Cal said.

"Not a clue. But it won't be hard to find out. We need to . . ."

The Jeep headlights snapped off, leaving Cal's flashlight the only light in the cove. Car tires spun on loose gravel, sped away. Cal and Marina ran up the dock. The Jeep was still there, but the keys were gone.

"Whoever that was didn't want us to follow them," Marina said. "And didn't want a confrontation."

"But knows we're on to them," Cal said. "And now we're stuck here."

"Dude. Seriously?" Marina pulled the ashtray free of the dash, reached into the slot and pulled out an ignition key. "Always carry a spare."

She started the car, left the door open so the dome light would stay on, and dug through the car to see if whoever had left her keys inside. Cal searched the ground around the car. Both came up empty handed.

"Let's see what cell service we have." Marina tapped at her cell phone, smiled when her call went through.

"Rafe? Marina. Your night just got complicated."

She spewed out the story of their evening, from the dive to the missing keys. Marquette let her finish before asking questions.

"Just diving," she said. "No. We were underwater. "Didn't see who here, either . . . Well, it's the only boat with a warm engine. Green, with a beat-up Evinrude. Where *else* would a boat go down this way . . . You *know* it's not pulled up on a beach somewhere . . . That doesn't justify someone damn-near killing us. How about you look at this boat, find the owner and ask them?"

She hung up.

"We have his attention," she said. "He's not happy about it, but he's on it. No choice, with an assault on two people."

"So we wait for him?" Cal dreaded facing off with Rafe. "The sharks didn't finish me off, but he will."

"Rafe'll be fine. He barks a lot but rarely bites. And he'll take his time getting here. We'll take photos of the skiff in case it wanders off, then go from there."

Marina pocketed the Jeep key but left the headlights on and walked back down the dock. With her phone she photographed the skiff's hull, its engine, the fish guts and blood in the bilge, then stepped into the skiff and took a close-up shot of a small spot on the boat's stern.

"Hull I.D. number," she said. "They can paint over or gussy up this puppy anyway they want, but the hull number won't change."

Marina put a foot on the dock to climb out. Her other foot, slick with fish blood, slipped when she pushed off. Cal grabbed her shoulders, caught her before she hit the dock face first. Marina clutched his arms, pulled herself up again and steadied herself against him on the dock.

"Thanks." She smiled, still holding his arms, so close he could smell her breath, her sweat. "I got ahead of myself there. About lost some teeth."

Like he was a third person watching, Cal saw himself lean in, kiss Marina. Her lips were warm, soft, salty. Unresponsive. Cal pulled away, let go of her shoulders.

"OhcrapI'msorry!" Cal went cold, as if the blood had drained from his face and hands.

Marina looked surprised. Then a faint smile crept in.

"Don't worry about it."

"It just . . . happened, like I was watching myself . . ." Cal choked down vomit.

"It's fine." She paused. "Let's get you home, okay?"

"Things have been going great," he said. I don't want this to screw up anything between us."

"Cal. Stop talking."

They rode back to Batten's Down in silence. Marina drove slow, eyes on the road, lost in thought. Cal stared out the window, replaying the night's events in his head to keep his mind off kissing Marina. Off her lack of reaction.

Why did it have to be sharks? Where had Rhodes come up with the amount of cash in the cave? And gems and gold? He must have used the underwater scooter from the house to shuttle the stuff into the cave without anyone knowing. And had the second scooter in the cave as a backup.

Someone knew Rhodes had a hidden stash. With so much cash, that explained the repeated break ins. But why threaten Cal's life? And why now?

Had Cobia told people Cal wasn't planning to sell right away? And whoever was responsible wanted Batten's Down as soon as possible so they could search at their leisure? That narrowed the possible culprits, though he couldn't imagine Rich Skerritt or Sandy Bottoms going through the house themselves. He, Cal, simply happened to be in the way. He was still missing something, some critical piece of information for all this to make sense. Cal didn't notice the passing trees, the houses, was surprised when Marina stopped the Jeep and gasped.

Batten's Down was in the headlights, but it was barely recognizable. Holes had been gouged in both ends with picks or sledgehammers, leaving bare plaster and plywood strewn across the ground and splintered beams exposed. Cal's stomach tightened. Someone had realized the ends of the house were hollow. Had torn them apart to see what was inside, though they hadn't finished the job. The Jeep's arrival must have interrupted them.

"Why would someone destroy your house?" Marina's voice was faint beside him.

"For what's in that cave. It couldn't have been the person in the skiff . . . Unless the chumming was an excuse to get us away from the house."

Near-panic gripped Cal. What if Rhodes' hidey holes had been discovered?

"Stay here while I look inside . . . to make sure no one's still here."

Cal slipped from the car and jogged through the open front door. He flipped on the lights, exhaled slowly. Someone had been through the place, but both hidden compartments were untouched. It wouldn't take whoever long to find them, though, now they knew to look in the house's ends. He would have to empty them, now, to keep the contents safe.

Cal crossed to the reading nook, knelt, pulled off the fake vent. He emptied the strongbox into a plastic grocery bag and snapped the vent back in place. He straightened, glanced behind him to make sure the house was truly empty. Marina stood in the doorway, eyebrows raised.

"That why we got chummed tonight?"

"No. Well, I don't know. Someone's after the stuff we found in the cave, not this little bit of cash and Rhodes' passports." He caught himself before he mentioned the missing laptop and drives.

"That you knew was hidden there."

"I found it a few days ago. Figured leaving it there was the safest option. Was."

"What else you got hidden?"

"Me? Nothing." Cal didn't dare tell her about the pistol or the fake passports. Or retrieve them with her there. "Rhodes stashed stuff all over."

"Like in a secret underwater cave."

"There's probably more hiding places, too."

"Anything in the other end?" Marina eyed the kitchen wall by the stove.

"Not that I could find." Cal hoped his voice didn't give him away. "At least I know the mystery ransacker's not interested in the house as a going concern."

"And now I'm in the middle of whatever's going on." Marina scrunched her mouth to one side. The lips Cal had kissed twenty minutes ago.

He went to the kitchen, pulled down a bottle of single malt scotch from the back of the cabinet, poured two glasses.

"Here." He handed a glass to Marina. "I was saving it for something special, but we deserve it after tonight."

Cal settled on the couch. Marina sat in the chair facing him.

"I'm sorry," he said. "About . . . earlier."

"I'm more concerned about all this." She waved a hand at the disarray around them.

Marina's dark eyes were locked on his. She was in danger now. Because of him. She deserved some sort of explanation. Cal took a long drink of his whisky.

"Okay, whoever that was trying make us shark bait, that had to be because of whatever my old man was mixed up in."

"I picked up on that."

"That marker I showed you the photo of has something to do with Rhodes, too." He paused. He shouldn't share this with anyone, but after the sharks, she needed to know. "He also dumped fish in a cave on the bluff and rigged up a speaker to make people think there's actually a mersquatch up there, to keep them from poking around."

Marina stifled a laugh.

"Hey, people bought it," Cal said. "Several warned me off. And someone's been scuffling around the house at night."

"And what's that have to do with tonight?"

"This morning Jack Cobia drove out to tell me the will cleared and the place is mine. And pressed hard for a fast sale. I put the brakes on that. Then the sharks happened. Oh, and Rhodes has fake passports."

He winced. The passports were hidden with the pistol. He had said too much. Marina didn't seem to notice.

She scanned Cal's face.

"Someone wants you out of here yesterday so they can search the place."

"Which isn't gonna happen. Not until I find out what's going on. And I can't leave anyway. Not without a passport. And it's not like I have anything to go home to. Except creditors and a boxed-up apartment."

It would be rough re-opening his clock shop, making a go of it. He would need every cent from the house sale.

Marina looked worried.

"Rafe's right. You're in harm's way."

"I'm not gonna be pushed around."

"Let's see what Rafe turns up," Marina said.

An odd thought struck Cal.

"You know, I'm more pissed off you're in danger than I am about being attacked. I put you in danger. This is my problem. You're a bystander. You shouldn't get hurt."

"This place is growing on you." Marina stood, leaned in and kissed him soft on the mouth, then sat back down. "We just need to keep you alive and healthy."

Cal sat frozen, electricity surging through him again. A friendly, thank-you kiss? But on the lips. More than friendly? But earlier that evening . . .

"I'm really confused." He didn't dare move. "Antonio said you were interested, but on the dock . . ."

"And Jerrod said *you* were interested . . ." Marina's face eyes narrowed. "And all but begged me to use that Jeep. Those rats. They set us up. For a laugh."

"So, what now?"

"Nothing. I like you, but you're leaving. I don't do hook-ups." She smiled. "But thanks for the concern."

"So, we just hang out, knowing that there's . . . stuff . . . churning beneath the surface?"

"It's called 'being an adult.'"

"I've . . . never been good at that."

"Well, then, this'll be good practice, won't it?"

Marina tossed back her drink.

"Thanks for everything . . ." Cal paused. "Look, I'm sorry I freaked back there. In the water."

"You were fine. We got out safe." Marina gave him a weak smile. "And this time, I was as nervous about the sharks as you were."

"Yeah, well, sorry to drag you into whatever this is."

"I can take care of myself."

A knock on the door. Before Cal could move, Rafe Marquette lurched in.

"Scared for your lives, so you come back here to celebrate?" Rafe glared at Cal.

"We found the house like this and had a drink to calm our nerves," Cal said.

"Uh huh. Creating drama to impress M'rina." Rafe loomed over Cal. "Then getting her liquored up?"

"Hey!" Marina stepped between Rafe and Cal, pushed Rafe back with one hand. "There's nothing going on between us!"

"Saw you kissing. Through the window. You two together now?"

"I was saying 'thanks,'" Marina shoved Rafe in the chest again. "To a friend I just went through hell with. He's selling this place and'll be gone any day."

"Friends don't kiss on the mouth." Rafe glared past Marina.

"Rafe, we weren't . . ." Cal started.

"You need to shut up." Rafe tried to step toward Cal. Marina held her ground.

"Back off, Rafe. Someone tried to kill us both tonight, and you're focused on a meaningless kiss."

"It meant . . ." Cal said.

"Shut up!" Rafe and Marina said together.

"Cal and I are friends. Period." Marina's voice was calmer now. "Someone tried to kill him, then tore up his house. The same day Rhodes' will cleared. Can you please find out who's behind that?"

"Wasn't you did this to the house? Looking for hidden valuables?" Rafe's voice was calmer now, too. Worry, or something like it, played across his face.

"When I'm trying to sell it?" Cal chose his words carefully, making sure he said nothing that would get Rafe angry again.

"How'd the will prove so quick?" Rafe looked suspicious.

"Jack Cobia hand-held it through the process," Cal said. "Probably pulled strings, called in favors."

Rafe nodded, thinking. He turned to Marina.

"You were diving right here?"

"Within shouting distance."

"Couldn't have been someone just out fishing? Who didn't see your bubbles?"

"Rafe, we had our lights shining up at the surface. It was *raining* fish guts, buckets of them, all around us," Marina said. "The boat circled our bubbles until we got up next to the shore."

She pulled out her phone, let him flip through the photos she had taken of the skiff.

"I'll go take a look at that boat," Rafe said.

"Last finger pier on the right. Green paint. White Evinrude. Follow your nose. The bilge's full of fish guts."

Rafe paused at the door, glared at Cal again.

"For safety, you need to stay somewhere else." Rafe glanced at Marina, then back. "A hotel."

"I'll be okay here tonight," Cal said. "By *myself.*"

Rafe slammed the door behind him.

"I'll follow him to Mango Sound, walk him through everything," Marina said. "You sure you don't want a hotel room?"

"No one's chasing me out of my house. Whoever's behind the chumming'll probably lie low, see if they scared me enough to sell and run. I'll be fine tonight."

Cal crossed to the door, hefted his pitching wedge. Marina laughed.

"Well, you'll be safe from golf balls anyway."

She grinned at him and was gone, easing the door closed behind her.

Cal jammed the couch back against the door. No one would try to get in tonight. Whoever had chummed around him didn't necessarily want him dead, they just wanted him gone. They would wait, see how Cal responded before they tried again. And when they did, would try to make things look like an accident again, not break down doors and attack him directly.

Cal needed to get rid of the pistol and ammunition before anyone found it, but he had to assume the house was being watched. He was being watched. There was no way to take it out, toss it all into the sea unnoticed. And he wasn't about to drive around with stuff, looking for a place to dump it. It would have to stay where it was, at least for the night. He would tell Rafe the next day, show him both hidden compartments and hope for the best.

Cal scowled at the shark books stacked beside the book case. He poured more scotch, then turned off all but the kitchen lights and propped himself up in the armchair, arms wrapped around the golf club. If anyone did come, he would be up and at them in a flash.

17

In the morning, Cal pulled the couch aside and walked the house's perimeter. There were no signs of fresh scrapings around the house's foundation. Chickens clucked at him from the sea grapes and the lean-to, as if nothing had happened the night before. Cal ignored the torn-up walls and walked to the sea, sat by the trebuchet and watched the sunrise. This had become his favorite part of the day on the island. He turned at the sound of a motorcycle. Marina. She pulled off her helmet and joined him.

"I wanted to talk to you before I went to work." Her eyes scanned the damaged house, then Cal's face, concerned. "Rafe went all over that skiff last night. The more he inspected, the more pissed he looked."

"He knows who it was?"

"Didn't say, but yeah." She put a hand on Cal's arm. "How'd last night go for you?"

Before Cal could answer, Rosie pedaled up. She paused at the end of the house, staring open-mouthed at the damage, then made her way down to Cal and Marina.

"Hey, Rosie." Marina slid her hand off Cal's arm.

"M'rina." Rosie half-smiled at Marina. "Wondered how long it'd take, two of you getting back together."

"We weren't 'together' before," Cal said. "And we're not now. Marina stopped by on her way to work."

"Uh huh."

"Rosie, I just got here. My bike's engine's still pinging," Marina said.

"Heart wants what the heart wants." A smile danced across Rosie's face.

Marina looked at Cal.

"*This* is how rumors get started on this island."

"Who tore king hell out of this house?" Rosie said.

"You know whose boat this is?" Marina showed Rosie the photo of the skiff from the night before.

Rosie studied the photo for a moment, her face expressionless.

"That's a rough boat, there," she said. "It belong to who did this?"

"You know whose it is?"

Rosie said nothing.

"Rosie, someone in that boat nearly killed us last night," Cal said. "On purpose. They chummed the water around us to draw sharks, then drove between us and the shore to keep us . . . me . . . there. The house damage happened when we were looking for the boat."

Rosie's gaze locked on Cal, anger building behind her carefully-managed features.

"Cal, you need to not be scuba diving anyplace right now. And you need to find somewhere else to stay, just for a little bit. In town. Around people."

Rosie glanced at Marina, eyebrows raised.

"Not a chance . . ." Marina started.

"What the hell's going on, Rosie?" Cal said. "Once and for all. I need to know what's happening."

"Old island business's coming to a head," Rosie said. "The less either of you knows, the better. Now, where'd you dive?"

"Seriously? That's your first question?"

"Just out there. The Flats." Marina interrupted. "We'd like to know who to thank for our adventure."

"Lots of people do use that boat." Rosie turned to Cal. "Those flats are bad news, and plenty sharky. Anywhere near here is. What time?"

"Seven thirty, seven forty-five."

"And you were just pleasure diving?" Suspicion crept back into Rosie's voice.

"Certification diving," Cal said. "Until the sharks showed up. You're asking more questions than Rafe did."

Rosie gave him a withering look.

"I'm gonna get to the bottom of this. Before Rafe. Meantime, Cal, you grab anything you value and get into town for a few days."

"Just on your say-so."

"That, and Rafe's. And those sharks."

Rosie grabbed her bike, pedaled hard up the coast road.

"*Rosie's* going to sort everything out before the police do?" Cal said. "What is she, the island Godfather?"

"The Bottoms *are* Blacktip," Marina said. "Sure, Rosie was gone for a while, but she came back a year or so ago. She *does* seem to know everything that goes on."

Cal ground his teeth. He didn't want to leave the house. His house. This was the only home he had, however temporary.

"Her cousin Sandy threatened me yesterday. Any chance both are in this together?"

"I doubt it. She and Sandy couldn't be more different, and they don't mix much. But who knows."

"So I camp in town for a few days. Someplace not owned by anyone named Bottoms. Or Skerritt."

"No Eagle Ray Cove, then." Marina glanced at her watch. "Oo! I'm late. I'll check back this evening." She ran to her motorcycle and roared away.

Cal went inside, sorted through what he would need for a few days away from the house. Clothes. Toiletries. His copy of the will. All the cash from the battery backup. Rhodes' knapsack to put it all in. He would leave the gun, for now, and hope no one found it while he was gone. Knocking interrupted him. Cal opened the door and Rafe Marquette stepped in.

"I looked at that skiff," Rafe said. "Saw no evidence of foul play."

"What about the buckets and fish guts?"

"It's a fishing skiff, y'know."

"And the owner?"

"Linford admitted he was out fishing . . ."

"There you go!"

". . . but was blind drunk and doesn't remember much of anything. Was drinking white rum at the Sand Spit all afternoon, in front of lots of people."

"It's okay to assault people if you're drunk?"

"Linford'd never do a thing like that." Marquette's voice took on a menacing tone. "Not on purpose. He allowed he was drunk, seen lights in the water, circled them, overcorrected his skiff and some fish fell overboard. But not purposeful chumming."

Cal stared at Marquette in disbelief.

"So that's the end of it? Two people report an attack, hand you the weapon, and you do nothing?" Any thought of telling Rafe about the pistol was gone. In this mood, Rafe would arrest him simply for owning the house it was kept in.

"Cited Linford with public drunkenness and operating a vessel under the influence. That's all I have evidence of. And I'll keep an eye on him. You need to be more careful diving. And about who you dive with."

"I'm done with diving. The only way someone's going to get me with a skiff is if they launch it fifty feet up the ironshore!"

Marquette scanned the room, as if memorizing everything, cataloguing it all and where everything sat. Jaw muscles working.

"Rafe, where would I find Linford?"

"*You* don't. You do, you and me have trouble." Rafe paused. "I'm finished with asking. Now I'm *telling* you to clear out of this house."

"I'm packing right now." Cal patted the knapsack.

Rafe held Cal's gaze several seconds, then left.

Cal stuffed clothes, cash, toiletries, and everything from the strongbox into the knapsack. There were other valuables in the house, but there was no time to sort through them now. He slung the pack in the Thing's back seat, then worked the ignition switch and gas pedal until it started. He would see if Club Scuba Doo had a spare room. The resort's bungalows were next to the Sand Spit. He could check in there and walk across for breakfast. And if he happened to run into Linford, that would be a chance meeting, not something Rafe could fault Cal for.

The sun was well up when Cal pulled into the Club Scuba Doo lot. The Sand Spit's outdoor bar, shaded by palm trees, beckoned as a welcome refuge after the drive in the topless Thing. Breakfast would be good. With luck, Linford would be there, and sober enough to make sense. Cal had visions of punching the man, pushed those thoughts aside. He needed information: why the man had tried to get sharks to eat him, how he had known where Cal and Marina would be. Then Cal could hit him.

He neared the bar. A stocky figure detached itself from the half-dozen people there, blocked Cal's way.

"What you doing here?" Rosie said.

"Breakfast." Cal kept his voice neutral. "And I need to talk to someone."

"Already talked to him. You talking'd just mess things up."

"I need answers."

Cal stepped to the side to go around Rosie. She stepped with him, still blocking his way.

"Linford's not the one you want."

"I'll see about that."

Cal stepped to the side again, put a hand on Rosie's shoulder to keep her from blocking him again. Rosie grabbed his hand, twisted it, spun Cal around. Holding Cal's arm high between his shoulder blades, she steered him to the nearest deck chair, sat him down hard.

"This's done with, Cal. Rich Skerritt made a random remark, Linford put two and two together and got twenty-two, then got stupid. And by now, he's high-tailing it somewhere no one's gonna find him. If he got any sense."

Shouting came from across the bar. Running feet. Clattering bar stools. Linford staggered across the deck, wild eyed, running into chairs, tables in his rush to get away from something. Behind him came Jerrod, eyes equally wild, an empty plastic pitcher in hand.

"You attacked a stranger living among us!" Jerrod roared. "You committed violence against thy neighbor! I will stretch out my hand and smite you with all my wonders . . ."

Linford glanced over his shoulder, tangled his feet in the legs of an overturned chair, hopped along the pool's edge trying to free himself. Jerrod tackled him. The momentum launched both men and the chair into the shallow end of the pool. Linford stood, coughed up water. Jerrod held him by the collar with one hand.

"Behold! I will smite with the rod that is in my hand upon the waters . . ." Jerrod whacked Linford on the head with the pitcher in time with his words.

The bartender and two servers jumped into the pool, tried to pry the men apart, were smitten for their efforts.

"Jerrod got to him before you," Rosie said. "His next stop'll be the clinic. Leave him be for now. She pointed at Club Scuba Doo. "You get yourself a room. Stay there."

Rosie guided Cal off the bar deck and to the Thing parked by the road. He rubbed his arm where Rosie had twisted it.

222

Cal drove to the store for a breakfast of bottled water and a meat pie.

"That'll be $10.75." Peachy smiled at him, as if she had wished him all the happiness in the world.

"For water and a patty?"

"I *did* give you the ten percent locals discount." Peachy was still beaming.

"Ten percent off robbery is still robbery!"

"You want the water and patty or not?" Peachy's smile disappeared.

Cal slammed a ten- and a one-dollar bill on the counter and stomped out the door. He coaxed the Thing into starting again, then headed back south for Club Scuba Doo. A siren wailed somewhere. The police truck. Rafe must be on the way to deal with Linford and Jerrod. The wail grew louder. Red and blue lights flashed in Cal's rear-view mirror. Rafe racing up the road behind him. Cal pulled to the edge of the road to let him pass. Instead, the police truck skidded to a stop in front of the Thing at a forty-five-degree angle, blocking Cal from driving forward. A stone-faced Rafe climbed out. Cal got out to meet him.

"Cal, I need to see the registration for this car," Rafe said.

"It'd be back at the house. There's nothing in the glove box." Cal pointed to the door-less compartment. "Lights and siren for registration?"

"I been letting it slide, one time, maybe two, but with you driving every day, and you giving rides to other people . . . You need registration and insurance. And a Tiperon driver's license."

"With everything else going on the last twenty-four hours?"

"Anybody else driving illegally like this, they'd already be in jail." Rafe's face stayed expressionless. "I been lenient."

"Fine. I'm sure I have the papers, just not with me."

Cal's mind raced. He thought he remembered a folder marked 'auto,' but he hadn't paid any attention to it.

"Then you can't drive."

"Even back to the house to get the registration?"

"And have an accident, uninsured, between here and there? Uh-uh."

"An accident? It's only four miles. And there's no traffic."

"You can walk; I can drive you or you can go to jail. Your choice."

Cal ground his teeth, trying to stay silent.

"You're the one who told me to move to town . . . This isn't about registration and you know it!" It was out before Cal realized it.

Rafe moved so fast Cal wasn't sure what happened. One moment he was facing the constable, the next he was sprawled face down across the Thing's hood. His arms were pulled behind him, then metal bands tightened around his wrists.

"What the hell?"

"Driving with no license, registration, or insurance," Rafe said. "Failure to obey a peace officer. Disorderly conduct. And chasing down Linford when I told you not to. You win a trip to the Blacktip jail."

Rafe stuffed Cal into the back seat of the police truck, tossed the knapsack in the front seat, and drove back north. Past the airstrip he turned right onto a thin track leading inland, then stopped at a low, square cinder block building. Inside was a small foyer, with an office to one side and a single, jail cell to the other, a small window set high in the solid door. Rafe undid the handcuffs, took Cal's watch and wallet, pushed him into the cell and shut the door behind him.

"Don't I get a phone call?" Cal said.

"Nope." Rafe crossed the foyer and into the office.

"How's anyone supposed to know I'm here?"

"I'll tell them once I've sorted out the charges," Rafe said from the office. "Until then, no need for anyone to know you're here."

"This isn't legal!"

Rafe walked away.

"Hey! This is illegal!"

The sound of fingers tapping a keyboard came from the next room, then. After several minutes Rafe came back out.

"I'll be back," he said and left the building.

Cal sat on the bunk bolted to the wall. He was certainly in a fix now. When Rosie had told him to find someplace else to stay, she hadn't meant this. He leaned back against the wall, stared at the ceiling. At least no one could attack him in here. They could ransack the house at will, but he was safe.

Time passed slowly. With no clock, no watch, no reference, Cal had no idea how long he had been in the cell. How long it had been since Rafe left. It was well past lunchtime, if his grumbling stomach was an accurate gauge. He lay back on the bunk, closed his eyes, let his brain work through everything he knew about Rhodes and the house.

Rhodes had been solitary, secretive, and belligerent. Had lived comfortably on a large piece of valuable property without any obvious means of income. That meant some sort of criminal activity. Activities. And he had been good with numbers, with finances. What Cal had seen on the thumb drives before they disappeared showed Rhodes had been involved a host of nondescript banks and property companies, probably on-disc-only shell companies. And fake passports. So . . . organized crime. Cal shuddered at that. He was probably in the safest place on the island. Unless Rafe was on the take.

But were the people tearing through Batten's Down Rhodes' partners wanting to get their files and money back, or competitors hoping to take advantage of Rhodes' death? Both? Whoever had taken the drives thought they were more valuable than the cash stored with them. Someone looking for a bigger stash. The cases Cal and Marina had found in the cave.

Rosie had known most, if not all this from Day One, he was sure. Except for the submerged cave. That was why she had stuck so close, refused to leave the house. And hadn't been surprised when Cal found the hidden laptop and drives. She probably knew about the pistol, too. Rosie was guarding whatever it was, from whoever it was . . . until the right person arrived? She wasn't necessarily on Cal's side, but she didn't seem to be on the bad guys' side, either.

He needed to unload Batten's Down as soon as he could, get that target off his back. Kat was gone. His shop was gone. He needed to get back to Naperville, put all this behind him, start over. Or he could sell the house, be done with it and use money from the sale to rent someplace here while he figured out what to do next.

His stomach grumbled. It had to be getting late in the day. Was Rafe going to leave him locked in here, unattended, forever?

As if in answer, the sound of a door opening came from outside the cell, then voices.

"... safe in here where he can't cause any more trouble," Rafe's voice said.

"Come on, Rafe." Marina's voice. "All your fake jealousy and mersquatch scare tactics were bad enough. Locking him in jail crosses a line!"

"He failed to obey a constable's orders."

"Don't be an ass!" Marina's face appeared in the cell door window, then disappeared. "Let him out! Have you even started any paperwork?"

"It's been a busy day . . ."

"I didn't think so. Open this door." Her face popped up in the window again. Her eyes met Cal's. "You okay?"

"A little hungry," Cal said.

Marina rounded on Rafe.

"You left him in there all day with no food?"

"It got busy."

"Now, Rafe!"

Not meeting Cal's eyes, Rafe fumbled with keys, opened the door. He stepped to the office, came back with Cal's watch, wallet, and pack.

"Still not safe for you to be out," he said.

"That's it?" Cal tried to keep his voice down. "You lock me up all day, never charge me with anything, then act like it didn't happen? No apology? No 'my mistake?'"

"Charges were dropped." Rafe was back to his angry-looking self. "You're free to go."

"Oh, no! You have a supervisor somewhere. I'm gonna—"

"Come on, Cal." Marina cut him off, pulled him out the door. "Let's get some food in you."

She pulled him out the door. It was dark outside, the sun sinking below the tree line casting the sky in shades of orange and red. Cal stared, stunned. He had been in the cell all day. Marina shut the door behind them and dragged him across the parking area. They climbed in the borrowed Jeep, the back overflowing with thick yellow mooring lines for a dive boat.

"Don't press your luck with Rafe right now," Marina said once they were on the main road. "He's super edgy today. And you pissed him off good,"

"We did, anyway."

"No, this is all about you. You rubbed him the wrong way about something." She paused, thinking. "Or he really *did* want you out of play for a while."

"Out of play of what?" Was Rafe making sure Cal was away from the house so someone could search it?

"Of you getting hurt. Of whoever put chumming in Linford's head. He's been concerned. That's why he was trying to spook you with his mersquatch act. I thought he was being overly worried until last night."

"You were in on the mersquatch crap?"

"I knew about it." She half-laughed. "It was kind of funny. Hey, you're hungry. Where do you want to eat?"

"There's stuff at the house. I'm worried about leaving it empty all day. Rosie's been out sleuthing since this morning."

"Rosie's been on a mission." Marina laughed. "Dealing with her and Jerrod the Avenging Angel took up most of Rafe's day."

She drove across the cut-over road, then turned south. Cal stared at the leaves blurring past, thinking of Rafe in the bushes pretending to be a bigfoot. He didn't know whether to curse or laugh. The island was definitely getting to him. His stomach rumbled. Food would be good, even if it was cold leftovers.

The sunset glowed brighter ahead of them. In the wrong part of the sky. An optical illusion. Something in the atmosphere making the sunset skip across low clouds, maybe.

"We're headed south, right?" Cal's stomach tightened, but not from hunger.

"The jail cell mess you up that bad?"

"That's not the sunset," he whispered.

"Beach bonfire, maybe." Marina sounded doubtful.

She sped up, catching Cal's growing apprehension. Whatever it was, it was near Batten's Down. They rounded the last curve.

Flames engulfed the house, shooting high into the twilight sky. Marina stomped on the brakes, and she and Cal jumped from the car.

Even at the roadside the heat was nearly unbearable. There was no way to get closer to the house, and there was nothing they could have done even if they did.

Rosie hadn't been there all day. How would an empty house catch fire? Faulty wiring? A trespasser had started it by accident? Or arson—another warning for him to leave. Or someone destroying evidence?

Movement to their right. Frank and Helen Maples running out to them.

"Rafe Marquette's on his way, but there's no way to stop that," Frank Maples said. "Any idea how it started?"

"I was going to ask you that," Cal said. "I've been away all day."

A section of the roof over the kitchen collapsed, sending embers swirling and flames climbing. A crackle of small explosions, as if a string of firecrackers were going off. The pistol ammunition. The others didn't seem to notice. Cal wouldn't have to tell Rafe about the gun now—Rafe would find what was left of it in the debris.

The flames jumped to the lean-to then, charring the wooden posts and beams, flashing bright when they hit the oily rags. Someone had driven the Thing back during the day. The car glowed, beautiful for a moment with flames visible through all its rusted-out panels. Then the gas tank exploded, sending flames and burning debris flying. Cal, Marina, and the Maples ducked behind Marina's Jeep.

"At least Rhodes kept the brush trimmed way back from the house," Helen Maples said. "Otherwise the entire island would be burning."

Cal sat, leaned back against the Jeep's tire, watched the flames. He hadn't wanted the house, but it had grown on him. Whatever secrets it had hidden were gone now. He couldn't bear to watch. But he couldn't look away, either. A hand on his shoulder.

"Why don't you come back to our house," Helen Maples said.

Cal shook his head. He would watch to the end. Batten's Down collapsed in on itself as it burned, as if the burning roof and walls were evaporating with the rising smoke and ash instead of piling up like in photos he had seen of burned buildings.

The Maples left, began hosing down the sparse grass between their house and the fire. Marina sat beside Cal. The police truck arrived. She left him then, talked with Rafe for a while before he drove away. She came back to Cal, sat, put her arms around him.

The fire slowed, dimmed. Sometime during the night Cal fell asleep, head against the Jeep and Marina's arm around him, offshore wind blowing the burning stench away from them.

18

C al woke to a choking, acrid reek. He coughed, spat. Morning. Red sun halfway above the horizon. The wind had shifted, sending the smoke from the house over him. Marina, asleep, leaned against him, hair, face, and clothes covered in gray ash. Cal's clothes were coated, too. He eased Marina up against the Jeep so he could stand. She woke, blinked up at him, then at what was left of Batten's Down. Cal walked up the road to get out of the smoke, get a better view of the house remains. Marina joined him, wiping soot from her face.

The cement slab and smoldering debris were all that was left of the house. The ground around it was scorched black. Cal walked to the pad to see if anything was salvageable. All was charred beyond recognition. He tried to image the house as it had been. A pang at that. As much as he had cursed at the ugly thing, as much aggravation as it had brought, it was as if a family member was gone. As if the pain, the grief he should have felt at Rhodes' passing, was hitting him now.

He stepped onto the pad, imagining the house as it had been. His stomach tightened with each step. The central room had been here. The kitchen to his right, the reading nook to his left. He pushed smoldering debris aside with his feet as he stepped through where the kitchen had been, past the scorched hulks of the stove and fridge. The lab had been across the pad, Rhodes' bedroom here. Cal stopped, stunned. In the floor where the bedroom had been was a ragged hole the size of an overturned refrigerator, jagged ironshore ringing its edges, as if it were the jaws of a giant sea creature. The pad's cement had been poured up to the hole's edge. A pair of scorched hinges were bolted into the cement on the far side. Between Cal and the hole lay the charred shape of the pistol, flung across the slab when the wall had collapsed. He stepped toward the hole without looking down, dragged his right foot, and scooted the pistol into the hole. A second later a splash came from below. Cal squatted, peered down into the darkness.

Gray light filtered up. Sunlight, faint on undulating water twelve feet below. A faint breeze wafted past, bringing the smell of sea wrack and charred wood. A house-sized cavern, with a rocky ledge at water level on the inland side. Bulky, square-ish shapes crowded the ledge, coated in burned debris. Something bobbed in the water at the cave's far end.

Cal shivered, chilled despite the rising sun and the still-smoldering wreckage. Long-forgotten memories rushed back. He sat, scooted back from the hole, clenching his hands to keep them from shaking.

"What is it?" Marina knelt beside him, hands on his shoulders. "What's down there?"

"Sharks," Cal said. "Lots of sharks."

"Enough with the shark thing," Marina said. "It's not funny anymore."

Water sloshed in the cave below, waves slapping against stone in counterpoint to the waves crashing against the headland. Marina stared at Cal. A scorched dinner plate lay next to the hole. She nudged it in with her toes. A splat as the plate hit the water, then the sound of thrashing on the water's surface.

"How did you possibly know that?" Marina's face went pale.

"I was down there. When I was little. In the water. I fell. My . . . dad hauled me out." His whole body was shaking now, remembering the dark water, the shapes bumping him, Rhodes' face a mixture of rage and terror as he snatched a twelve-year-old

Cal from the water. "Beat my ass for it. My mom took me away the next day. I . . . just remembered that."

Marina's arms were around him. His shaking slowed. Cal stood.

"You still have that mooring line in the Jeep?" he said.

"Sure. Why?"

"I need to see what's down there."

Marina backed the Jeep to the cement pad. Cal tied one end of the rope to the bumper and dropped the rest into the cave. He knelt, peered in, visualizing how to shinny down without falling into the water. Cal gripped the rope tight as he could, swung his legs into the hole. Something inside him tightened thinking about the sharks.

"Don't even *think* about going down there!" The voice was familiar and unfamiliar at the same time, as if a friend were acting in a play.

Rosie stalked past the Jeep, body language subtly changed, more commanding now than belligerent. Details from the past week snapped into place in Cal's mind.

"This cave, what's in it, that's what everything's been about." Cal said.

"Mostly," Rosie said. "And you going down there will contaminate evidence and land you in jail."

Cal studied Rosie, as if seeing her for the first time. Her island lilt had been replaced by a flatter North American accent, as if she were a neighbor from Naperville. An authoritarian neighbor barking words he had never imaged Rosie using. To the side, Marina was looking at Rosie with the same reappraising look.

Rosie pulled a neck wallet from inside her shirt. Something flashed gold in the sun. A badge?

"Federal Police," Rosie said. "Your father, this house, was a waypoint for drugs and money. Among other things. Rhodes played up the mad scientist routine to keep people distracted.

And made deliveries to boats with that catapult." She pointed south. "Columbia. Venezuela." She pointed west. "Honduras. Nicaragua." She pointed north. "The U.S."

"I knew nothing about that!" Cal scrambled to his feet.

"I know. I reckon your father left you those haikus as a clue to how to find all this. His way of leaving you everything."

"I want nothing to do with this."

"I know that, too. That's why I said stay out of the cavern until my people get here to catalogue everything."

"You knew this was here?"

"Something like it had to be somewhere nearby. He muffled that trap door damned good. I stomped on every inch of floor in that house and it all sounded solid."

"Below the teeth and sea cave thunder," Marina said. She looked to Cal. "But *you* knew it was there. You just said so."

"I remembered it just now, when I saw it," Cal said. "I had no clue before . . . when I was little . . . Rhodes left the trap door open when he thought he was alone. I . . . went down to explore. He came down, I tried to hide, but fell in the water. There were lots of sharks. There was a bucket of fish he'd been feeding them."

Cal fetched a dive light from the Jeep and shined it into the cavern. Rosie crouched beside him, grabbed his hand and played the light across the scene below. On the ledge were footlocker-sized bins. Farther in, the wall was lined with head-high cabinets. The bins and cabinets were secured with heavy padlocks.

At the far end of the ledge a boat bobbed on its dock lines—dark blue, long, slender, built for speed with two big, black outboards on the stern.

Near the boat's bow was a slim opening, barely wider than the boat, angling out to the open sea. Sunlight filtered obliquely through the slot.

"Just big enough to get the boat in and out," Rosie said. "And opening at that angle, you wouldn't notice it from outside unless you were right on it. And looking for it. I scanned that rock face from a skiff a couple of times and missed it."

Cal shuddered at the memory of sharks bumping him, of bracing for one to bite and powerless to stop it.

"What is it?" Rosie had noticed the shudder, was watching him with narrowed eyes.

"Rhodes. He fed sharks. He wanted them here. And around here."

"Good way to keep people out," Rosie said. "Or scare off anyone who tried to get in on scuba."

"He could have killed me. What he did."

"You seem to have bounced back okay." Rosie thought for a moment. "Dollars to doughnuts that ring of keys to nothing'll open all those cases down there. If we can find it in all this."

"It's in my backpack," Cal said.

Rosie gave him an impressed look.

"We need to get off this slab," she said. "The whole place is a crime scene."

Cal backed away, scuffling his feet over the pistol's skidded track through the ashes. The three of them walked back to the road. Cal dug the key ring from his bag, handed it to Rosie. So much still didn't make sense, though. And Rosie was talkative.

"So . . . how's the cave related to the laptop and thumb drives?"

Marina looked puzzled. Rosie shook her head.

"It's not. Not directly. Rhodes was also shuffling cash around for some unpleasant people. Keeping his cut."

"Who stole them?"

"Oh, that was me." Rosie waved a hand, dismissive. "I sent them to Tiperon. FinCEN cracked those days ago. And a team's in the air for here now. Couple of big island names would've loved to get their hands on those drives."

"Who?"

"Two people trying hard to get ahold of this house, like a pair of circling sharks."

"So who kept tearing up the place?"

"Pilot fish helping one of those sharks. Or getting conned, like Linford."

"I need to know who, exactly."

"No, you don't. We may never make anything stick. If we don't, you know nothing."

"So, you need me to stay here while you chase down . . . the sharks?"

"I'm not budging 'til my team arrives," Rosie said. "Nothing and no one goes in 'til then."

"Rafe Marquette could help," Cal said. "He's probably on his way now."

Rosie gave Cal a stern look.

"No one," she said. "Especially Mr. Mersquatch."

Marina laughed.

"You don't trust Rafe?" she said.

"On Blacktip, I trust myself," Rosie said. "I take nothing he does at face value."

"He was mixed up in what Rhodes was doing?"

"The sole constable looking after the island has no oversight. The policeman's been watching you? I've been watching the policeman. And he's way too tight with Rich Skerritt."

"Do I stay until your people show up, or can I go get cleaned up?" There were rinse-down showers by the Eagle Ray Cove pool. It would be good to wash the soot off, get some water to drink.

"You don't leave. You're the property owner," Rosie said. "Someone burned your house down. Constable Marquette will definitely need to talk to you. Both of you. Oh, yeah. This is yours, too."

Rosie handed Cal his passport. Cal stared, confused.

"I took that, too. Needed you to stay on-island while all this played out. Then things . . . escalated. That wasn't supposed to happen."

Something still puzzled Cal.

"Why would anyone burn the house?"

"Someone got spooked, wanted to destroy anything incriminating," Rosie said. "Or was desperate to find that." She pointed to the hole. "Your nighttime visitor kept poking around the foundations. Mr. Mersquatch about had it figured out. If he did, so did others."

"No one would've found this place if someone hadn't burned the house," Cal said.

Rosie surveyed the burned frame.

"Probably not. And we'll never recover everything," she said. "Or even know what we're missing."

Cal shot Marina a quick glance, mind on the cash, the gemstones, and the gold bars in the submerged cave. Would she keep quiet about that?

Cal took a deep breath, searching for the right phrasing.

"So, you . . . got together . . . with Rhodes to get information out of him?"

Rosie's glare lanced into him.

"*That* wasn't supposed to happen, either," she snapped. "Your father caught me poking around his room. I covered by acting flirty, hoping for an awkward getaway. Rhodes . . . called my bluff. And died. I feel awful, but he wasn't young, and he'd lived hard. His heart gave out."

Tires sounded up the road then, a car speeding toward them. The white police truck shot from the trees lining the roadway, skidded to a stop. Rafe sprang out, face a mixture of anger and worry. He nodded greetings, eyed the thick yellow rope running from the Jeep's bumper down into the cavern. He stared at the rope and the cave mouth for several seconds.

"Any of you been down in there?"

"We're waiting for the authorities," Cal said.

"All right, then. I'll take a look."

"No one's climbing down there." Rosie blocked his way.

"Rosie, what the hell you talking about? I'm the police."

Rafe sidestepped. Rosie shifted, blocked him again

"So am I."

Rosie pulled out her badge. Rafe's eyes widened. He bent down, scrutinized the badge and I.D. card.

"*Federal* Police? This's local."

"The house fire is. That cave under it isn't."

"You're playing games, Rosie. You got no jurisdiction in a Blacktip Island crime." Rafe loomed over her, but didn't crowd her like he did Cal.

"I have a letter expressly granting me jurisdiction in ongoing international criminal activities. This is bigger than you, Rafe, and you know it. Odd you're not surprised the cave's there. And are more interested in that than in a possible arson."

"I could arrest you and seize everything myself," Rafe said.

"Last thing you'd do as constable. No one touches anything in or around that cave but me and my people. Who're on their way."

"I got a right to inspect . . ."

"Rafe, you're not getting anywhere near that hole." Rosie stepped toe-to-toe with Rafe, hands on her hips, lowered her voice so Cal had to strain to hear. "Whatever your game is, you're out of luck."

"I'm the government representative on Blacktip. The government has a right to know what's down there."

"And there'll be a detailed, itemized list of everything we catalogue and take with us as evidence. As soon as we're done, and not before. Why don't you get a statement from Cal about his house so he can go get cleaned up."

Jaws clenching the entire time, Rafe took statements from Cal, then from Marina.

"This wouldn't have happened if you hadn't arrested him." Marina's voice was full of reproach. "The fire started when he was in jail."

"He hadn't been in jail, the fire may have started while he was in the house. Sleeping or knocked out." Rafe's voice was cold. "I been doing everything I can to keep him alive and healthy and safe. Whether you *or* him believe that. He's been in way over his head since he got here."

Helen Maples was there then, eyes wide at the sight of the charred timbers. She saw Cal. Her jaw dropped. Then she had her arm around his shoulders, guiding him and Marina back to her house.

"We have three bathrooms, so you'll each have a private shower," she said. "I'll get some spare clothes for both of you, too, though they might be a bit baggy."

A half hour later Marina and Cal were driving north, Cal wearing one of Frank Maples' Hawaiian shirts and an oversized pair of cargo shorts, Marina in a flowered, sleeveless sundress.

"Hey. I'm sorry I gave you such a hard time about sharks," she said. "I had no idea it was a *thing*, not just you being squeamish."

"Neither did I."

Cal shuddered at the mention of sharks. He stared out the window at the booby pond blurring past, let his mind go blank. They rode in silence the rest of the way across the island. Marina turned left on the west coast road.

"I'll drop you at Club Scuba Doo, then go change into my own clothes," Marina said. "Lovely as this dress is."

"At least you have something else to wear," Cal said.

"The CSD gift shop'll have stuff. Shorts and t-shirts anyway."

Cal clutched his knapsack tighter to his chest. His cash was still safe inside it. At least that hadn't burned with the house. He could camp at the resort a few days while he figured out his options.

At the resort gift shop, he bought three Club Scuba Doo shirts and two pairs of shorts—enough to get him through a few days—and collapsed in his room, luxuriating in the air conditioning. With the house's mystery solved, there was no reason not to sell the land and head home. With a hefty cashier's check in his pocket.

A tapping on the door. Cal opened it, stood face to face with Jack Cobia.

"Cal! Stopped by to make sure you're all right!" The man already reeked of rum and cigars. "Damn shame about your house. Anything left worth keeping?"

"Nothing recognizable." Something in Cobia's voice made Cal think he should say as little as possible.

"Well, that's too bad." Cobia didn't sound upset. "And the police are all over it, like somebody kicked an anthill. The Feds. Who would've guessed little Rosie Bottoms . . ."

He let his voice trail off, waiting for Cal to respond.

"It was news to me," Cal said.

"You get a look at what they were finding?" Cobia said it nonchalantly, but his eyes were bright, locked on Cal's.

"I gave Rafe a statement, showered at the Maples and came here." He lifted the Club Scuba Doo bag from the bed. "Had to buy new clothes. Whatever they find, it's going to Tiperon with them."

Cobia nodded, eyes going from Cal's Hawaiian shirt to the gift shop bag.

"Well, with the house burned, you gonna level the place, or leave it as is?"

"Whatever it takes for a quick sale."

"Yeah, well, about that. The . . . ah . . . house didn't add much value to the property, per se, but I think the offers we had are probably off the table. I'll check, but there's not much interest in the place, houseless."

"But Sandy and Rich were going to tear the house down anyway."

"What can I tell you? Interest dried up. There's a pall on the place now. I'll let you know if anything comes up."

He slapped Cal on the shoulder and left. Cal lay back on the bed, mind going back to Rosie's comment about 'big names on the island.' Skerritt and Bottoms had wanted the house, not the property. To hunt for Rhodes' computer, files, and everything in the cavern beneath the house. They both had known what was hidden somewhere around the house, and everything Rhodes had been involved in. Now, with the police seizing everything, they had no use for the place. Cobia had known, too. Had dangled a huge selling price in front of Cal to get him to sell. Quick. To Bottoms. His buddy. His accomplice? Rosie had been right to mistrust Cobia, but Cal had misjudged the reason.

And Rafe, acting like the mersquatch to scare Cal away, was 'way too close to Rich Skerritt.' Sandy Bottoms had used Cobia to try to buy the house outright. Had Skerritt's angle been to frighten Cal off so he could search the place before Bottoms bought it? Either way, Cal was stuck.

His visions of flying back to Naperville flush with money, of starting over there, evaporated. Instead, here he was stuck with a piece of property no one wanted, and the cash in his pack would dry up eventually. Cal flipped through his passport, barely seeing the stamps. He could go home, put his life back together as best he could. Have Cobia, or someone, get whatever they could for the land and wire him the money. The alternative was to stay on Blacktip, start over here, as depressing that seemed. And do what for income? With Batten's Down gone, Marina was the only bright spot for him on this little rock. Cal stretched, realized he was on a proper bed for the first time in more than a week. And was exhausted. Mind on the clock shop, on what was left of Batten's Down, on Rhodes feeding sharks, he fell asleep.

The midday sun streaming through the window woke him. His stomach grumbled. He hadn't eaten since the day before. Cal changed Frank Maples' Hawaiian shirt for a t-shirt and crossed to the Sand Spit. Lunch would be great while he pondered his next move.

He was thumbing through his passport, and on his second beer, when Marina plopped into the chair beside him.

"You cleaned up all right." She grinned at him. "How you holding up?"

"Still getting my head around Rhodes not being a crazy beach bum."

"Dude, your dad was a pivot guy for the mob. Your mom didn't snatch you away because of sharks. She found out what Rhodes was mixed up in and bolted. That's why you never heard from him. And why he never crossed U.S. Immigration to visit."

"Sandy Bottoms and Rich Skerritt were part of that." Cal lowered his voice. "Jack Cobia was, too. Is."

Marina studied him for a long moment.

"So, the sale's off," she said. "Now what?"

"Back to Naperville."

"Makes sense." Something, disappointment maybe, filled her voice.

"I have to be there to sell off my inventory, collect my jewelry-making stuff, and close up shop," Cal said. "I'll need every cent to rebuild."

"Your shop?"

"The house."

"Batten's Down?"

"Well, not over that hole. And not shaped like a sat-on loaf of bread. But yeah."

"To live in?"

"There's nothing for me in the U.S. anymore." Cal took a long swallow of his beer. "Bad memories and ghosts."

"What'll you do?" Doubt crept into her voice. "There's not many island jobs you're qualified for."

"I'm thinking maybe a fix-it shop for, well, whatever. Frank Maples' pocket watch, for starters." He lowered his voice again, so only she could hear him. "With the . . . rocks and metal . . . we found in that sea cave, I could make some pretty upscale jewelry. If I can get it back onshore without being eaten alive."

Her eyebrows went up at that. Then she smiled, eyes on his.

"The stuff no one but us knows about. Or thinks the Feds seized. Getting that won't be a problem."

Cal smiled back.

"First thing I need, though, is a place to live while I rebuild. I'm homeless."

"Something'll turn up." Marina's smile was broader now.

"I also thought . . . .. we could see how things go. With us. If you're okay with that . . ."

"No lingering feelings for your ex?"

"She's well quit of me. And vice versa."

"I'll let you know." Marina gave him a crooked smile that reached to her eyes.

"What about Rafe?"

"His jealous act was to get you off the island. Rafe's always been . . . an opportunist. Knowing him, he wanted you out so 'the government'—him—could search through the place for evidence, wangle a promotion out of it. And snag whatever untraceable cash or . . . rocks and metal . . . he might find."

At the bar, Antonio waved, stepped to join them without either of them inviting him.

"Told you, young Cal. Belly of the beast." He slapped his own bulging stomach for emphasis. "Now here you set, looking happy, and little Rosie Bottoms and her worker bees crawling all over that labyrinth of yours."

"You're saying the house burning was a good thing?" The man could turn any chance occurrence into a self-fulfilled prophecy. "And you saw all this coming?"

"Got you to look down in there, face what happened to get you all shook up. Face what got you 'stranged from your daddy." Antonio grinned at Marina. "Got you and M'rina grinning with your heads together, too. All your problems're solved."

"Except I don't have a place to live."

"Oh, I got a great place for you. Seen you there before, but didn't understand it, you with your daddy house and all." Antonio's grin widened. "You already know the neighbors— Jerrod, Dermott, Hugo . . ."

I hope you enjoyed reading *The Secret of Rosalita Flats* as much as I enjoyed writing it. It's hard for books to get noticed these days, and reviews on Amazon, Goodreads, iBooks and Smashwords can be the difference in whether a book succeeds or fails. If you liked *SRF* (or even if you didn't) I'd love to hear your honest feedback, even if it's just a single sentence. I read every one, and they help others decide whether to read the book.

For more info about Blacktip Island, visit: https://blacktipisland.com/

To cyber stalk me, visit: www.timwjackson.com

To sign for email alerts, go to: www.timwjackson.com/contact

And if you haven't yet, check out *SRF's* prequel, *Blacktip Island.*

Cheers,

Tim

ABOUT TIM W. JACKSON

Tim W. Jackson's first taste of scuba diving came at the age of six when he sneaked breaths off his dad's double-hose regulator in the deep end of the pool. Later, as an ex-journalist armed with a newly-minted master's degree in English, he discovered he was qualified to be a bartender, a waiter or a PhD student. Instead he chose Secret Option D: run off to the Cayman Islands to work as a scuba instructor and boat captain by day and write fiction at night. Two decades later, he still wishes that was half as interesting as it sounds. Or even a quarter . . .

Jackson is the award-winning author of the comic Caribbean novels *Blacktip Island* and *The Secret of Rosalita Flats*, as well as *The Blacktip Times* humor blog. His "Tales from Blacktip Island" short stories have been published in literary journals worldwide. He is currently concocting his next Blacktip Island novel and still enjoys scuba diving with his dad's old double-hose reg.

CPSIA information can be obtained
at www.ICGtesting.com
Printed in the USA
LVHW010255071121
702612LV00001BA/6